Praise For

CiTy Of RoSe

"Well executed...rough without being sadistic, gritty without being sordid...An engaging read...characterized by Hart's quick and witty turns of phrase." —*Kirkus Reviews*

"CITY OF ROSE has my favorite kind of hero, a tough guy romantic with a smart mouth and a dark past. Terrifically written, and populated with rich characters, this book had me by the throat from page one."

—**Chelsea Cain**, *New York Times* **bestselling author of ONE KICK**

"Brilliant...CITY OF ROSE, Rob Hart's latest Ash McKenna novel, is as sharp as the devil himself. Hart is a master storyteller who can turn a city into just as vital as any flesh and blood character."

—**Brian Panowich, author of BULL MOUNTAIN**

Praise for

NeW YoRkEᴅ

the first Ash McKenna novel:

"The New York of NEW YORKED is a place of heartbreak and murder that I highly recommend you visit."

—**Josh Bazell, author of BEAT THE REAPER**

"Outstanding...I loved this novel. It may be the most quixotic hard-boiled I've read in ages. With clever nods to Chandler and lots of muscular metaphors, Hart has written an achingly lovely farewell to one man's past."

—Milwaukee Journal-Sentinel

"Hart's debut is a terse, grim, gritty, quickly moving noir that deftly explores post-9/11 New York...Ash is a wrecking ball of an investigator, a direct descendant of Mickey Spillane's Mike Hammer."

—Mystery Scene

"Edgy... relentless pacing and strong sense of place."

—Publishers Weekly

"There are good action scenes, nice offbeat characters, but what lingers is the swoony dialogue... Noir with a tingle of doomed but sweet romance."

—Booklist

"A bloody valentine to a New York fast disappearing, this debut is an urban noir populated with memorable characters."

—Library Journal

"A hard-boiled crime novelist in the vein of greats like Dashiell Hammett and James M. Cain, not to mention modern masters like Lawrence Block and Dennis Lehane."

—Staten Island Advance

"The literary version of THE WARRIORS."

—Lyndsay Faye, author of THE GODS OF GOTHAM

"One part Dennis Lehane, one part Lee Child, and one part pure Rob Hart."

—Jenny Milchman, author of COVER OF SNOW and RUIN FALLS

CITY OF ROSE

CITY OF ROSE

ROB HART

Copyright © 2016 by Rob Hart
Cover and jacket design by 2Faced Design
Interior designed and formatted by E.M. Tippetts Book Designs

ISBN 978-1-940610-51-1
eISBN 978-1-940610-56-6
Library of Congress Control Number: 2015951361

First trade paperback edition February 2016 by Polis Books, LLC
1201 Hudson Street, #211S
Hoboken, NJ 07030

POLIS BOOKS

ALSO BY
ROB HART

New Yorked

The Last Safe Place: A Zombie Novella

To my parents. Despite what reading this book might lead you to believe, they did an excellent job raising me.

"Now you run on home to your mother and tell her... tell her everything's alright. And there aren't any more guns in the valley."

—*Shane*

ONE

IT'S A SLOPPY punch, thrown from the shoulder and not the
hip, in an arc broadcast so widely it may as well be lit in neon.
It catches me on the side of my face, below my ear, and to anyone
watching it looks like a good land, but truth is, I barely feel it.

The vintage-T-shirt-wearing asshole who threw it shakes open
his fingers, eyes on fire at his newfound ability to be a tough guy.
Jumping and hollering in his too-tight jeans, a goofy smile warping
his patchy facial hair.

His garage band friends, thoroughly satisfied that he's
dominated me, grab him by the arms and make a big show of
pulling him away. Like they're doing me a favor, holding back the
beast.

It's almost enough to make me laugh.

"That's what you get," he says, slurring his words. "Fucking faggot with your faggy fucking hat." He yanks his arms free, points at me, and puffs out his tiny bird chest. "Next time I come back here I won't go so easy on you."

They wait for me to say something but I just shrug at them. There's not really an appropriate response to that kind of thing that doesn't involve taking his teeth. And there was a time I would have seriously considered that. Instead I watch them saunter down the block, the three of them laughing at the navy-blue night sky.

Control your anger before it controls you.

Inhale, exhale.

There are a few people outside now, pretending to smoke cigarettes but really watching what happened, probably bummed there isn't blood on the ground. I tip the brim of my straw cowboy hat at the spectators and head back into Naturals.

Now that those three idiots have been cleared out and people are finishing their smokes, it's fairly empty inside. Three men and two women nurse drinks at the bar running the length of the right wall. To the left, two young couples hover at the foot of the elevated stage, a fight not enough to draw them away from the view. The high-top tables surrounding the stage are empty, a few of them scattered with temporarily abandoned drinks.

Calypso is up on the stage, dancing to "Under Pressure" by Queen and Bowie. The couples around the stage toss dollar bills as she sweeps around and sticks her ass into the air, wraps her hand around the shiny brass pole, and dips, whipping her curly brown hair off her face. Her dark skin is nearly black in the dimness, the thin fabric between her legs glowing in the black light.

Tommi is behind the bar staring at me, pretending like she

wasn't just peeking out the window. I sit at the bar and she sets a glass of ice water down in front of me, picks up another glass to clean.

"Want some extra ice for that face, *Ashley*?" she asks, leaning into my full name like it's supposed to make me feel inadequate.

"Did that guy hit me? I hadn't noticed."

She puts the now-clean glass along the back wall, in front of the glittering rainbow of liquor bottles, and places her hands on the bar, her thick arms laced by worn tattoos. She leans toward me so I can hear her over the music.

"I'm a pacifist," she says. "And you know I don't want trouble in my place of business. But you're allowed to defend yourself. Especially with some asshole trying to stir shit up and act big. Everyone here is going to vouch for you and say it was self-defense."

Pacifist. Right.

Tommi keeps a gun loaded with blanks duct taped to the underside of the bar, to the left of the slop sink. The Condom, she calls it. Better to have it and not need it. Strange sort of pacifism.

The thing I want to tell her is that if I hit the guy, best-case scenario is I hurt him enough that he sics a lawyer on me or on the bar, because he seems like the type to do that.

Worst-case scenario is I start hitting him and can't stop. She doesn't need that kind of weight. Neither of us do.

"They're gone," I tell her. "No one's hurt."

"You could have gotten hurt."

"Doubtful."

The song ends. Next up is "Wasted Life" by Stiff Little Fingers. Calypso has good taste in music. With the mirrors behind the bar and the mirrors running along the back of the stage, it looks like there's an army of naked women twirling around us.

Tommi shakes her head. "Funny."

"What's funny?"

"Word was you were a tough motherfucker. The guy who recommended you called you dangerous. I figured, maybe a guy like that could be useful. Instead I get a guy who lets people punch him in the face and says twenty words a night."

I take a sip of my ice water, so cold it makes my teeth hurt. "Disappointed?"

She laughs, a sound that rumbles like it's coming from the bottom of a cave. "Maybe. I don't know. You're not what I expected."

I shrug, take another sip. Feel a slight swell of warmth on the side of my face.

The song ends and Calypso goes about picking up clothes and crumpled singles while Carnage waits in the back by the door to the kitchen and dressing room, wearing her patchwork schoolgirl outfit, red Mohawk spiked up into the air nearly a foot off her head, pointy like a buzz saw.

The trick is Elmer's Glue, she told me once.

It'll be quiet in the bar until Carnage gets on stage. This is a low-budget operation. Rather than paying a DJ, which Tommi can't do, the girl coming off the stage goes to the dusty iPod hooked into the speaker system and queues up the next few songs for the girl going up on stage. Not exactly elegant, and there's something very awkward about silence in a strip club, but it works for now.

"So, when are you going to tell us more about yourself than your name, cowboy?" Tommi asks.

I hold up my hands and count on my fingers.

She asks, "What's that?"

"Think I hit my twenty words for the night. What needs getting done?"

She shakes her head, this time like she really is disappointed in me. She says, "Check the bathrooms and straighten up downstairs. Got more beer coming in tomorrow."

Another thing Tommi can't afford yet is a janitor.

I begin to push away from the bar and Tommi leans close to me again, says, "Also, talk to Crystal before you leave tonight. She needs a hand with something, thought it might be in your wheelhouse." She arches an eyebrow. "Though after tonight, I'm wondering if she might be wrong."

Rather than ask for an explanation—because, truly, I don't care—I tip my hat at her and head off.

Carnage's song starts up, some metal thing I don't know, and she proceeds to hurl herself around the stage. Launching herself off the pole and catching herself on the thick-gauge chains that extend from the corners of the stage into the ceiling. Stopping herself just before she topples into the crowd.

She winks at me as I walk past. The asshole I kindly asked to leave had been making a grab at her, which sparked our little showdown. I give her a nod and knock loudly on the door for the ladies' room. No answer, so I duck in and it's mostly clean. I'll give it a once-over when the place is locked up.

The men's room destroys any hope I might get off easy. Someone missed the toilet by a wide margin, forming a puddle on the wide gray tiles in the back corner. The room smells sharply of ammonia. I head back into the restroom alcove, open the small service closet, and roll the mop and bucket in.

Get to work cleaning up some drunken asshole's piss.

YOU WANT TO get the true measure of a town? The strip clubs are a good place to start.

Back home, six months and a million years ago, I'd only been to one strip club, out in some industrial section of Queens. It was an anonymous building that disappeared into the night sky, the red brick painted black.

There was a big line out front. The line didn't seem to move. I was there for a friend's bachelor party and someone in our group knew the owner, so we got to skip the line. Then we got "bottle service," which meant two bottles of middle-shelf vodka and some containers of orange juice and cranberry juice, like you'd buy in a supermarket. I went and sat at the bar and ordered a whiskey, spent the rest of the night brushing off the women who were insisting on separating me from my money through the mechanism of lap dances.

It was like a plague of tanned and glittery flies buzzing about, and when you thought the swarm was gone, it would loop back. The night took a bad turn when the bachelor passed out, and a handful of girls proceeded to dance all over him in some private corner, then insist to us they were owed several thousand dollars for their trouble.

But that's New York, and fuck you if you can't cope.

Portland's polarity is completely reversed. The strip clubs

here aren't hidden behind black paint, tucked away in otherwise-abandoned neighborhoods. They look like bars. Sometimes you don't even know what it is until you walk inside, where you find an equal mix of men and women. Sure, you get the weirdos who are attracted to places where naked women congregate, but going to a strip club in Portland is like going to a bowling alley most other places.

There are no lap dances. The strippers aren't even allowed to touch you, by law. There's a difference between a guy who thinks he can cop a feel and a guy who knows it's against the rules right off the bat.

Lowered expectations keep the temperature down.

My absolute favorite part about the strip clubs here, though, is that any place in Portland that serves alcohol also has to serve food. And this is a town where they take their food pretty seriously. I have yet to eat a bad meal I didn't cook myself. Every menu in this town includes at least one instance of the word "artisanal." Like if you aren't making your own pickles you may as well give up.

There's one club where the guy who owns it also owns a cattle farm, and you get a solid steak for a few bucks and eat it while women take their clothes off for you. There's an observation about the American psyche in there somewhere, for someone smarter than me to make.

I don't work in that club.

Naturals is all vegan. This isn't even a new concept—Tommi was the third person to think animal-free products and boobs would make a good combination.

Most of the furniture is secondhand and the stage creaks when the music is low. The carpet very badly needs to be replaced. I try not to think too much about the carpet. People seem to like the food, which is mostly hummus plates and black bean tacos and cumin-dusted popcorn. Tommi is trying to crack the code on stuff like vegan cheesy nachos, but it isn't going so well.

She also has designs on the vacant storefront next to the club. Once the money comes pumping in she'll knock down the wall and expand. Any day now. Until then it's a low-key endeavor.

But Tommi is dedicated. She takes the name of the place so seriously she won't even hire dancers with bolt-on tits. Again, probably an observation there worth making.

This is not the job I dreamed about when I was a kid—archeologist—but as a layover, it's not so bad. It's enough money to keep me alive long enough to figure out where I'm headed next.

Which is hopefully: Someplace else, soon.

THE STAINLESS STEEL surfaces of the closet-sized kitchen are gleaming by the time I'm done with them. This is the one thing that's not supposed to be my job, but Sergio had to cut out and I offered to do it, because what the hell else am I going to do with myself besides sit alone in my apartment and stare at the wall?

It's been nearly two hours of cleaning and fixing stuff and everyone is gone and the only thing left to do is lock up, and I figure I've successfully avoided Crystal, but as I step out of the kitchen she's sitting at the bar, like she materialized out of thin air. I'm not even sure where she's been this whole time I was working.

She's in street clothes, which means a black T-shirt and tight gray jeans, the two of them not meeting, so there's a thin strip of cream-white skin around the middle of her. Black-and-white canvas sneakers on her feet and a small red purse sitting on the bar next to a bottle of beer. Her black hair is shaved down to stubble on the side of her head that's facing me, and on the other side it's draped like a curtain, reaching down to the middle of her back. Her face is flush and pink, freshly scrubbed free of makeup.

The way she sits, her back is arched a little, like she's posing for someone across the room. But she always seems to sit like that.

She gets up as I approach, and her voice and posture are normal, but her eyes, blue-green like tempered glass, are concentrating real hard, like she's carrying something that might shatter if she drops it.

"Hey, Ash. How's your face?" she asks.

As I get close I'm flooded with the smell of her. Something citrus.

"I'd say the guy hit like a girl, but you could probably hit harder," I tell her.

She doesn't laugh at that, asks, "Can we go outside?"

We step out and I pull down the front gate and clasp the thick padlock. The street is deserted, streetlights glaring yellow in the misty air. It smells like the ocean.

Crystal pulls out a slim cigarette and places it between her lips. She looks up at me as she fumbles with a small white plastic lighter. "I know these are a little girly, but would you like one?"

The truth is, yes, seeing a cigarette and I can feel the handjob tug of nicotine at my brain. But I resolved to stop pumping my body full of poison. Because in the not-too-distant past, my blood was mostly a mix of whiskey, nicotine, and whatever drug I had most recently gotten my hands on.

I shake my head, lean my shoulder up against the gate. "You wanted to talk to me?"

"I've heard things about you. Like you used to work as a private eye when you lived in New York?"

Ah, fuck. Tommi must have told her.

How I got the job at Naturals is, when I made a mess of my life in New York and decided it best to see the world—or flee, depending on how you look at it—I found it's hard to get a job in a place when you don't know anyone. It's even harder when you don't have any marketable skills. So I called around at the bars back home, figured someone might know someone and I could get myself a gig bartending or dishwashing.

So my friend Dave says he knows somebody who's opening a strip club and is looking for a bouncer. I don't want to take a job as a bouncer, my attempt at pacifism running counter to that. But I hear that Portland is a pretty chill town and my bank account is full of dust and dashed hopes.

Not that I'm called a bouncer, officially. I don't have an unarmed bodyguard permit, because who cares. I've got enough work to busy myself with that if anyone asks, I can say I'm a custodian. Tommi likes to keep things simple. I tend to agree.

So I go in for the job, and Dave wanted me to sound like an asset, so he told Tommi more about what I used to do than I would have liked.

And here we are.

"I wasn't like a licensed private eye or anything," I tell Crystal.

"I didn't do it professionally. I was more like a blunt instrument. People asked me to do things and I got them done and sometimes they paid me or gave me stuff in return. But I don't do that kind of work anymore."

Crystal takes a long drag and blows out the smoke hard. "I need some help. I know I don't really know you, but I don't know who else to go to."

"I'm sorry, but…"

"It's my daughter. She's missing."

The words vibrate in the yellow mist between us.

Before I can stop myself, I ask, "What happened?"

"My ex-boyfriend, her father, took her from day care. He's not supposed to have her."

"This sounds like a custody issue."

"Dirk and I were never married. No divorce. There's no custody or visitation or anything. Just, he's not supposed to have her."

Shrug. "Go to the cops."

She looks into my eyes like she's trying to burn a hole through them. Like she wants me to know the thing she's about to say is something she's not ashamed of. I know this look well, even though I've never been able to replicate it.

"I used to use," she says. "I stopped soon as I got pregnant and promised that I would never touch it again. But the cops see an ex-junkie stripper, they're going to take my daughter away. Do you know what kind of terrible shit can happen to kids in foster care?"

I nod. "No offense, but are you sure you're not overreacting?"

"This isn't an idle fear," she says, like I'm an asshole, which, probably. "I know a girl, same situation as me, single mom who dances and she doesn't have any family. Some shit went down and some holier-than-thou caseworker decided she wasn't a fit mom. So the caseworker made her get a legit job as a waitress, which she had to take a huge pay cut for. Then the caseworker said she wasn't making enough money. She has supervised visits with her son until this shit gets worked out. That's horrible. I'm not going to risk that."

"Okay. That's not an unfair point."

"All I need is someone to find him and get her. I'm not saying my ex is dangerous, just that he's more apt to listen to someone his own size. If I go... it's not going to end well."

"What does that mean?"

"He's hit me before. I'm going to hit him back. I don't want my daughter to see that. And I'm not even totally sure where he is."

Something sparks in my chest. As a rule I really don't like guys who hit women. Still. "I don't do that work anymore. And if he was hitting you this is something worth solving soon. If she's not safe..."

"He wasn't good to me, but he was good to her. If he wasn't such a fuck-up he might even make a good dad. I'm sure he wouldn't hurt her, but that doesn't mean he should have her. He's not someone you have to be afraid of."

The way she says it is like she's trying to reassure a frightened child.

The thing I want to say is: If you only knew.

Instead I tell her, "Talk to Hood. Call another friend. I'm sorry. I'm not the kind of person you want to put your trust in. Best of luck. Truly."

Her face contorts into something sharp so I turn to leave and walk in the direction of my apartment. Don't give her the chance to say anything.

I TURN ONTO WEST Burnside, past the long line of homeless people camping out on the sidewalk. I don't know why they're always here. Maybe there's a shelter nearby. Maybe it's where they gravitate. A few bug me for change, but most of them know me as a person who never hands any over, so they ignore me.

That's not a moral stand. I just don't have money to spare.

It's a nice night, teetering on the edge of summer, so I can wear a T-shirt this late at night and not feel like I should have dressed smarter.

The air gets a little chillier as I approach the Burnside Bridge. There's no one on the pedestrian pathway, with only the occasional car interrupting silence so deep I can hear the lapping of the Willamette down below me.

Halfway over, even though the wind is whipping and raising goose bumps on my skin, I stop and lean on the rail and look out over the river. At the gentle sprawl of the city, the lights dim and the buildings not tall enough.

This is the junior-varsity version of a city.

Truth is, more than anything, it reminds me of home home. The West Brighton neighborhood on Staten Island where I grew up. A mix of suburban and urban that came down too hard on the suburbia side for my taste. You could still walk to things, it just took a while. The streets eerie quiet after dark.

In fairness, that familiarity breeds a bit of contempt.

A big part of me still feels like a tourist. Six months now and any moment I'll have to pack my bags and catch a flight, go back to the things I know as normal.

Everything outside my East Village apartment was always moving, always alive, always flashing. So big it blotted out the sky, so bright at night you'd swear it was day. Here, though, it's just silence and damp, and everything is green and shadow. Quiet houses and people who seem to always be half asleep.

My rhythm and the rhythm of this place don't match up yet. Maybe with time it will, if I stay, which, probably not. This isn't the place for me but I don't know where to go next. Maybe Europe. I've never been to Europe. Though to pull that off I'd need to stow away on a freighter or something.

Until then I jump every time I hear a creak, because there aren't sirens or roaring trains or people screaming to drown those sounds out anymore.

I get back to walking and the smell of citrus lingers after me. I'm sorry for Crystal and her daughter. But I don't want to feel that feeling anymore, of flesh pulping under my skin and my fingers slick with blood, slipping on each other as I clench them into a fist.

It's pretty nice living a life without that feeling.

Tonight is the first night I've gotten hit in a long time, and even now it takes me a second to remember exactly which side of the face that dummy clipped me on.

Going headfirst into a situation where I might very well have to start swinging again? No. That's not me. Not anymore. The path of the righteous man, et cetera, et cetera.

I hang a right on SE 7th Avenue, a few blocks from my apartment now, and a car jets past me and coasts to the curb a half-block ahead. The driver gets out and darts across the street, into the cover of some trees.

I keep walking. Not wanting to think about Crystal and the kid, doing it anyway.

That's the thing tugging at me: There's a kid involved. And Crystal is right. I don't trust the cops either.

My dad's words come back to me, the thing he worked so hard to hammer into my head. *There are good guys and there are bad guys, and the good guys need to stand up for each other. The bad guys only win if you let them.* They're words that have gotten me into trouble, but that doesn't make them untrue.

As I come alongside the car that pulled to a stop, the trunk pops open with a soft thunk, gaping at me like a yawning mouth. I stop to look at it, because there doesn't seem to be anyone around, and for a moment I wonder if I did something to make the trunk open.

Behind me there's the crunch of footsteps, and before I can turn there's an arm wrapped around my neck, pressure on my throat, something hard poking into my back. Good money on it being a gun. Given the height and location I hope it's a gun. I feel spittle in my ear as a raspy voice whispers into it. "Hand over your phone. Reach for it slow. And don't look at my face."

It's a man. Strong. About my height. Can't tell much more than that. A few scenarios run through my head. They all end with me being shot. I am more than happy to give up my phone if it means this guy will fuck off, but the open trunk indicates this is more than a mugging. Still, I reach down to my pocket, slow as I can, pull it out, and hold it up.

The arm wrapped around my neck comes loose and snatches it away. The hard thing in my back presses harder.

"Now climb in," the man says. "We're going for a ride. I detect the slightest bit of tomfuckery and I will shoot you fucking dead."

I take off my hat, toss it into the corner of the trunk, and climb in, face down. The lid slams closed on top of me.

TwO

HERE'S SOMETHING I find a little funny, even though I probably shouldn't: This is not the first time I have been forced into a trunk. So I'm way less nervous than this asshole probably thinks I am.

Not that I'm excited about it.

I try to memorize the turns we're making, but I don't even really understand how to get around this town, so I give up and feel around for a weapon. The trunk is completely empty. I even manage to prop myself up and reach underneath the mat and into the wheel well, and nothing. Not even a spare.

Wish I had seen the plate before he pushed me in. Something so I'd feel less useless. Oh well. I stretch out and get comfortable.

Who this could be, I have no idea. I haven't fucked with anyone in this town yet. Everyone I pissed off in recent memory is three

17

thousand miles away, and enough of that got settled I didn't feel the need to look over my shoulder.

Maybe this is karma come to collect.

I've done a lot of bad things in my short life, and those things don't get wiped clean because you want them to. Eventually there's a toll that's got to get paid to the universe. Maybe this is mine.

Time comes untethered in the dark. I really have no sense of how long has passed when the engine cuts off. I listen to the sound of the hot car making *ping* noises and the crunch of footsteps crossing around to the back.

The trunk comes up and I swear I am hallucinating, that the guy pointing a gun at my face is not wearing a grotesque, poorly painted rubber chicken mask.

But he is. Red and yellow and white with dead, black eyes, staring at me.

He's wearing a charcoal sweat suit. An expensive one, too, from the cut and quality of the fabric. I can't see anything but the tanned skin of his hands. One of which is holding tight to a small, silver revolver. He grabs me and hauls me out of the car, strong for his size, and says, "On your knees."

I get down on the asphalt. He has me turned away from the car so I can't see the plates. That would have been nice.

We're behind a warehouse. The sun is beginning to lick at the bottom of the sky, but it's overcast, so it's cycling shades of gray. Raining now, too, but light enough to be pleasant, that you wouldn't be so upset if you got caught outside without an umbrella.

The world is so beautiful when it's like this. Seeing it filled with sunlight, every detail in sharp relief, no place to hide, it's too much.

The rain makes the world feel manageable.

I tilt my head back, let the raindrops peck my cheeks, taste the clean water on my lips. If this is the universe come to collect, if this is my last moment on earth, I want to be thinking about the rain when a bullet snatches my life away.

The man taps me on the side of the head with the gun. I look at him, annoyed at being snapped out of my happy place, and he says, "Pay attention. You are not to help the girl. Do you get me?"

Athletic. White guy. No visible scars or tattoos, though I can only see his hands up to the wrist. Can't place his accent, but it doesn't help that the mask is muffling his voice. And he moves on intel quick, considering I only blew off Crystal twenty minutes before he grabbed me.

"Take that thing off and threaten me like a man," I tell him.

I can't see his face so I can't get a read off him, but he seems to freeze a little at that. He shakes his head. "Shut up. Just listen. Stay away from the fucking girl. You get mixed up in that, I'm going to put a bullet in your face. I can find you anytime, anywhere. The cops can't help you. We own the cops. Do you get me?"

I ask, "Is the mask a matter of convenience, or a commentary on the nature of your personality?"

Am I goading him into shooting me?

Maybe.

The man steps forward, into me, and he smells like aftershave. Antiseptic. He presses the muzzle of the gun against my forehead, indenting my skin. The metal is cold and hard and indifferent.

It's stupid of him to get this close. I could dive for his legs and be under the barrel before he has time to fire. He might not even get a chance to pull the trigger. My hands aren't tied. All I have to do is knock him down. Then it's a party.

But I don't.

Instead I focus on the rain. It's picking up. Cool, but not too cool, and the air smells green, and there's no sound but my own ragged breath and the water striking the pavement. Gravel is biting into my knees and the chain-link fence surrounding us is rusty, but the clearing behind the warehouse is bordered by lush trees, their leaves heavy with water and hanging down, swaying as if to get our attention.

There's a sharp inhale of breath, like a sniffle.

Asphalt crunches as he sets his feet.

My life doesn't flash before my eyes, and for that I am thankful.

A dynamite blast explodes across my face, no sound, maybe it was too loud and it blew out my hearing, and I'm not happy, because my death is by no means swift.

As I fall to the pavement I wonder when the world will go black.

But the pain keeps on going, throbbing away at high volume.

My cheek collides with the pavement. Not shot. The bastard pistol-whipped me. My face is half-submerged in a puddle and I try to breathe in, end up with dirty water burning my sinuses. Over the sound of my coughing and choking, Chicken Man says, "Here's your phone back."

Sharp crack.

A car door opens. The engine roars. The car blows exhaust in my face as it peels out of the lot. I twist around to try and see the license plate, something specific about the make of it, but it's already turning onto the street.

It gets real quiet.

At this point I'm soaked, and my face hurts, so I roll onto my back and lie there for a bit. Listen to the rain. It's suddenly a lot less calming.

Well. I've got one thing going for me, at least: A solid blow to the head and I'm still conscious. I'd be pretty happy to get out of this without a concussion.

Not that I can do much more than lie here. I'm dizzy, and I want to vomit, and my brain feels like there's a small goat on the inside trying to kick its way out.

The rain stops, or stopped. The sun is really getting up there now, but not too high, high enough that the sky is a lighter shade of gray, like filthy snow. Did the rain stop now, or when the car left, and I'm only just noticing? My thoughts drift like tufts of smoke. Impossible to get a grip on.

It takes a bit but I manage to get to my feet, steady myself. Still feels a little like I'm falling. Okay, so actually, concussion, maybe. Which would not be great, because while I know what health insurance is, in theory, I can't say with any confidence how to engage with that sort of thing.

I run through the things I know.

My name: Ashley McKenna.

Where I am: Somewhere in Portland still, probably.

I close my eyes and try to recall the lyrics to "Thunder Road" by Bruce Springsteen. The first song I ever memorized the words to, so I know it's in there deep. I get through the first couple of lines and figure that since my brain is working, I'll be okay, at least for a little while.

Next, I look for my phone. It's a little hard to find because it's roughly the same color as the asphalt, but after a little while walking in a circle I find it lying in a puddle. I check the face and it's shattered, spider webs spun across the glass.

Son of a bitch.

At least the motherfucker left my cowboy hat. It's been sitting in the rain awhile, but it's rugged for a straw hat. It is a little lopsided, so I bend it back into shape and stick it back onto my head.

My legs are fine, but I limp anyway, not even realizing that I'm doing it, pain having taken up a big residence in my body. Like at any moment something might rip. I try to guess at where I am, but I don't know anything other than that I'm in a parking lot behind a warehouse that looks abandoned.

Empty wallet, dead phone, and I have no idea where I am.

Man, fuck today.

BETWEEN THE COLD that seeps into my skin from the rain and generally walking around, the bad feelings fade. The dizziness does, at least. I'm still a little nauseous. And my face hurts.

This neighborhood is mostly garages and warehouses and I don't recognize any of the street names. I watch the flow of traffic, where the stray cars that pass me are headed, and I follow them until I find NW Yeon, which I think puts me somewhere in the Northwest District. That's about two or so miles northwest of the club. I call that walking distance.

I point myself south and get going. I've got to pass the club on the way home anyway, so I figure on heading there. If it still feels like something has rattled loose, I'll grab some cash from the drawer, call a cab, and take that the rest of the way home.

Though I'm sure I'll end up walking the whole way there. Even when I'm tired, even when my face is throbbing, it's nice to walk.

There are a lot of things I miss about home. Big things, like my friends. Little things, like the shawarma at Mamoun's. One of the little things I miss that turned out to be a big thing is, I used to walk everywhere. It was the only reliable kind of exercise I got.

Here, you can't do that so easy. The neighborhoods don't link up. Sidewalks disappear. Expressways spring up suddenly and without warning, cutting you off from where you're going. There are so many goddamn bridges.

The public transit isn't so bad, but New York spoiled me. I could step outside the door and find six ways to get anywhere. Here there are bus routes to learn. There are trolleys, which are weird. The public transit does not run constantly and everywhere, so I deem it subpar and not worthy of my patronage.

You want a cab? You can't step to the curb and raise your hand. You have to call ahead and *then* you have to wait an hour. It's barbaric.

I haven't bothered to do much besides walk. I don't spend a lot of time outside the mile between home and work. Maybe one day I'll get a car. Until then, I walk. Walking is good. It gives me time to think.

I've got a lot to think about.

Someone shoving a gun in your face does a lot to change your perspective on things.

NATURALS ISN'T EVEN supposed to be open yet, but Hood is standing on the sidewalk outside, having a smoke, dressed in dirty jeans and a paint-streaked sweatshirt. I nod at him and he pats me on the shoulder. He drags on his cigarette and exhales as he gets a good look at my face. "The fuck happened, yo?"

I stop, think hard about asking for a smoke. But no, I'm not going to slip, and anyway, he's smoking Newports. That makes the decision not to bum from him a little easier.

"You look like you got knocked around pretty good," Hood says.

I press my fingers to my face and wince. It feels bad. Probably looks worse.

"Motherfucker, say something," Hood says.

I laugh at that. "I'm okay."

Hood is a nice guy. People think he gets called Hood because he's black. That's racist. The truth is he gets called that because he's the size of Mount Hood, the snow-capped mountain floating off the horizon line. His neck is bigger than my thigh and spreads out from there. If I had to take him down, I wouldn't even know where to start. He reminds me a bit of someone I knew from back home. The main difference being that Hood is nice, whereas Samson always seemed to be considering whether he should break my nose.

Hood also speaks with the kind of affectation goofy white people would call "ghetto." Truth is, he's a giant nerd. Dare to bring up *Doctor Who* around him and you will get a twenty-minute rant about why the revival series isn't as good as the original. I saw a guy get sucked into that once. He had a look on his face like he was about to die for some unperceived slight. Hood is also the closest thing I have to a friend in this town. I say that while acknowledging I don't even know his last name. Or his real first name. Unless it actually is Hood.

He asks, "The guy last night do that to you?"

"Different guy."

"How many people want to fuck you up, son?"

"Too many, it seems. What are you doing here so early?"

"Crystal wanted to talk to me about something. She's on her way over. I got some repair stuff to do anyway."

I scratch at my face, wince again when it stings. "Listen… this is going to sound weird, but why don't you let me talk to her first? I think I know what it's about."

"Whatever, man, I asked her to meet me here because the electrical in the dressing room is fritzy and shit. I want to get that done before tonight."

"I'll get things sorted with Crystal."

He shrugs, tosses his cigarette to the curb, and we head inside. There's some science fiction show I don't know on the television over the bar. Robots and spaceships. "What's this?"

"*Battlestar Galactica*. How do you not know that?"

"Easily."

"Shit, man, it just came off Netflix. You can borrow the box set."

"No thanks."

"Dude, fucking *Battlestar*, man. You don't even know."

"I'm good. Don't watch much TV lately."

"Whatever. I'm bringing it in for you. You'll watch it and you'll like it."

It sounds like a threat. Maybe he means it like a threat. That accomplished, he disappears to the back. I go behind the bar to make some coffee, hunting for Tommi's secret stash of good grounds, when the phone rings. I grab it off the cradle. The tiny orange LED screen says BLOCKED NUMBER.

"Naturals," I say.

Silence on the other end of the line.

Then a high-pitched male voice says, "I thought I was going to get the voicemail."

"It's your lucky day."

"Well... just... listen, I've got a message for your owner. Tell her to get her dyke ass out of town before something bad happens."

"I can relay that message. Though I'd prefer if you could come here and say it to her face. It would be fun to watch her choke you dead with your own intestines, you fucking coward."

Click.

Huh.

The front door scrapes. Crystal comes in through the velvet curtain that blocks the light and the view from the outside world. She sees me, and her face drops. "Where's Hood?"

"Can we talk?" I ask.

There's some noise from the back and Crystal heads toward the kitchen, ignoring me. I come around the bar and get in front of her and she gets a look at my face. She stops short and furrows her brow, asks, "What happened to you?"

"After we talked last night someone threw me in a trunk, threatened to kill me if I helped you, and pistol-whipped me. That's what happened to me."

She freezes.

"Ashley…" she says.

"Ash," I tell her.

"What?"

"Ash. Call me Ash."

She nods, not sure how to take it.

The thing I don't want to explain to her is the only person who can call me Ashley—besides my Ma—is dead. And Chell only got the privilege because I made the mistake of telling her that everyone always called me Ash.

"I have no idea who that could have been," Crystal says. "Dirk is an idiot but I think he would piss his pants if he saw a gun."

"The guy who grabbed me was only half an idiot," I tell her.

"So what does that mean?"

"It means I'm going to find your daughter. Let's go someplace and get a cup of coffee to hash out the particulars."

Crystal narrows her blue-green tempered glass eyes at me. "What's changed?"

Shrug. "Motherfucker broke my cell phone. He owes me a new one."

CRYSTAL SLIDES HER empty ceramic coffee mug around the table, having finished her story, letting it settle.

Pretty simple. The kid was in day care. Dirk showed up and

there was a new girl working who didn't know not to hand the kid over to anyone besides Crystal. Crystal's daughter, being four, didn't know better and was excited to see her dad. And here we are.

The coffee shop is quiet, just us and a couple of kids tapping away on laptops, three out of four of them wearing headphones. I take Crystal's cup along with mine up to the self-serve urns and pour some more coffees, bring them back to the table. She goes at hers with the cream and sugar. I keep mine black and let it cool.

"Tell me more about Dirk," I say. "So he's an idiot."

"I was young, and I was stupid…"

I put up my hand. "You don't need to defend yourself. I want to know if this guy is someone who could be a problem."

She shakes her head. "I don't think so. He's mostly talk. You're bigger than him, so he wouldn't raise his hands to you."

"Any idea why someone would be warning me off this?"

"None."

I take a sip of my coffee. Too hot.

"I have money," she says. "Not a lot. How much would it cost to hire you?"

"Don't worry about it."

Crystal shakes her head. "That doesn't sound right."

"I'm not licensed. This isn't a job. Call it a favor. I'll find him, look angry, chances are he'll hand the kid back."

"What about the guy with the gun? What if he's there?"

"I know what his car looks like. That's a start. And he probably thinks I'm smart enough to fuck off after he threatened me."

"But you're not smart enough?"

"Nope."

Crystal picks up a discarded sugar packet and folds it once, twice, and lets it drop to the table. "This is a little heavy. Maybe we should call the cops."

"Chicken Man said not to," I tell her. "He said he had hooks in with the cops. He could have been full of shit, but better to err on the side of caution."

"He threatened you with a gun. That doesn't bother you?"

"Nope."

"Why?"

"I'm cool under pressure."

She takes a long sip of coffee and puts the mug down. She brings her eyes up to mine, a smile pulling across her lips. "The girls were right."

"What girls?"

"The girls at the club. We wonder about you. You sit around all night in your cowboy hat and make a couple of smart comments, but no one knows anything about you. Everyone gets a good feel off you. Like you're a nice guy."

"I'm not a nice guy."

She squints. "Don't sell yourself short."

"Nothing to sell. If you want the truth, the reason I don't want you to pay me is because I'm hoping I'll earn a little karma. I'm in debt. Some might call that selfish."

I take a sip of my coffee, put the mug down. Crystal is still staring at me, like I'm a painting she's trying to understand.

"Got a pen?" I ask.

As she pulls one out of her purse, I get up and grab a napkin from another table, put it in front of her. "I'm assuming you don't know exactly where he is. How about someone who does know? A place I can start."

Crystal scribbles on the napkin and slides it to me. I don't know the name of the street. She says, "He hangs out at this house a lot. Northeast side of town. He crashes there sometimes. Someone there should have a better idea. It's off Martin Luther King. Need directions?"

"I get the gist."

"They're drug people."

"What does that mean?"

"I don't know," she says. "I don't know if they're dealers or what, but there's something about that house that's tied up in drugs."

"Got it." I fold up the napkin and stick it into my pocket.

"I would offer to come but there's a lot of… emotion there. I don't trust myself for what I'm going to say to Dirk and I don't want my daughter to hear that."

"There is also a dude with a gun. Better that you're far away."

Crystal balls up her fist and presses her thumb into the space under her lip. "Are you sure about this?"

"Gun is a coward's weapon. And he hides behind a mask. He got the jump on me. The trick is to not let that happen again."

Crystal exhales, stares off into the distance. The look in her eyes like she's short-circuited. Her thumb comes up again and she chews on the nail. Her eyes get a little softer when she does this.

Her other hand is on the table. That thumbnail is white and jagged around the edges.

"I don't have a car, so I'm going to call a cab," I tell her. "I'll go up there, scope it out."

"Do you want to take my car?"

"That sounds better. Sure."

She takes out a heavy fistful of keys and drops them on the table, then shakes her head. "I hate this. I just… I love my daughter. And I try so hard to keep her separated from this."

"It'll be fine."

We get up from the table, walk to the door. I hold it open for her. "You know, I should have asked," I tell her. "I can't believe I didn't ask. What's your daughter's name?"

"Rose," Crystal says. "Her name is Rose."

THE CAR IS a beat-up white sedan with stuffed animals lining the rear window, the passenger side full of discarded coffee cups and receipts and fliers. I climb into the driver's seat and can barely fit, fumble underneath for the lever to push the seat back.

I look into the rearview mirror as I'm adjusting it. There's a car seat behind the front passenger seat, fabric navy blue with white flowers, holding a pink teddy bear, like the bear is waiting to be buckled in.

So, this should be fun. Despite being a born and raised New Yorker, I do have a license, and I do know how to drive—but I haven't done it a long time. Everything goes smooth when I pull away from the curb. The brakes are a little loose and the steering column a little tight. But the feel of it comes back easy.

Two blocks later and I nearly get into an accident, swerving to the right because the guy in the oncoming lane drifts over the double-yellows. I brush a row of parked cars and fantasize about ramming this car into his.

At the next green light the person in front of me comes to nearly a complete stop in order to make a right turn, which inspired more fantasies of death and destruction.

I'm not used to this. I'm used to speed limits and traffic rules being polite suggestions, and other than that it's a melee. This is like everyone else on the road keeps forgetting where they are.

Maybe I don't have the right temperament for driving.

Control your anger before it controls you.

Inhale, exhale.

It takes me a little while to get where I think I'm supposed to be. A couple of wrong turns, and for a while I think I'm going in the complete wrong direction, but once I find MLK it's cake. The town is starting to imprint itself on me. Still, I'm sure if I knew where I was going, it wouldn't have taken half as long.

I stop the car when I find the street I'm looking for. Better to not turn onto it. If Dirk is in there he might recognize Crystal's car. I park and get out, flooded with relief to be off the road, and walk to the corner. Chicken Man was driving a dark sedan. Something close to an Impala. I don't really know cars. But nothing on the block matches.

I'm about to head for the house when I realize: What if Rose actually is there? She'll have no reason to trust me over her dad. I go back to Crystal's car and grab the pink teddy bear. Better than nothing. I probably should have insisted on Crystal coming. Even if she waited in the car.

The house is a rustic one-story ranch with some shrubbery out front and a bike sitting in the driveway, about the same as every other home in this town. As I get closer, the truth becomes a little more apparent.

This area is the Portland version of a bad neighborhood. The homes around here are generally unkempt but this is a mess. One of the windows is broken and has a board blocking it from the inside. The paint used to be purple, now faded to lilac. The yard is overgrown where it's not bare and brown.

No car in the driveway. No lights on. It's quiet. The whole block is quiet.

I open the chain-link gate and it creaks, make my way up the concrete walkway, and stand in front of the door, my boots echoing in the hollow under the porch. The pink teddy bear bounces against my leg. The whole walk I'm wondering how to handle this. I've never had to find a kid before. And truthfully, guys like me are in a poor position to pick up kids they don't know.

Sorry, officer, this kid belongs to someone I work with. No, I don't want to tell you who. No, I don't want to tell you where I got her or where we're going. Can't you trust a strange man with a kid who doesn't belong to him?

Dammit.

I press the doorbell and don't hear anything so I knock and wait. Silence from inside the house. Could be no one is home. Great. It's not like I can ring up Crystal and ask for another lead, because my phone is broken. Another thing I should have considered. I'm rusty. Making mistakes. I put my ear against the door, call out, "I'm here for Dirk."

Something thumps on the other side. There's definitely someone home.

"It'll take a minute," I say.

There's another sound.

Metal on metal. *Chunk.*

The sound makes me think of movie shotguns, like how when someone cocks it, using the hard metal clank of it to punctuate a sentence.

That's exactly what that sounds like.

Fucking fuck.

I dive to the side of the porch as a blast tears a hole the size of a basketball in the front door.

THREE

SOME AMOUNT OF time goes by. I can't measure it from my spot in the corner of the porch. The world has frozen in the echo of the blast. I'm on the left side of the door, Rose's pink teddy bear is on the right. There's a puff of white stuffing coming out of its flank. I think it got clipped. Poor little bear.

The noise didn't seem to rile the locals because the block is still empty. Nobody outside their homes, nobody peering out of their curtains. At least not that I can see from my vantage point all the way in the corner. I could get up and run, reevaluate this whole thing. I think shotguns aren't supposed to have an effective range past a certain distance, but that's not something I'm ready to gamble on.

And yet, no one has come outside. No one has said anything. Just silence. Shotguns tend to foretell bigger problems.

I crawl back toward the door, staying under the windows,

trying to keep quiet, every creak of the wooden porch echoing across the stillness like a shockwave. I come alongside the door and hold my breath.

There's mumbling from inside the house. Metal sliding against metal. Something heavy is dropped on the floor.

I move a little closer, and the mumbling sounds like someone who's frustrated by a task but also not particularly engaged with it.

Fuck it. I get on my knees and peek through the hole. See a shotgun, and a pair of hands picking a shell up off the floor. Trying to load it in, dropping it. The guy is right on the other side of the door and can't seem to get his gun loaded.

I twist the knob and throw the door open hard enough to hit him and knock him back. The shotgun slides across the floor. I burst into the house, shut the door behind me, and it's dark, the outside world streaming through the hole in the door, gray light dancing around motes of dust.

The guy on the ground is trying to say something, struggling to get up, on his hands and knees now. I kick him in the stomach hard enough to flip him on his back. I get a good look at him. He looks like a gay lumberjack. Big, carefully trimmed beard that reaches past his collarbone, rainbow plaid shirt with denim short-shorts, and work boots laced tightly to his feet. No socks. Can't be Chicken Man. This guy looks anorexic in comparison.

He holds onto his stomach and groans and says, "The universe is too small for the both of us. You could destroy everything by being here."

Seems he's also high as fuck.

He stays on the floor, not too interested in getting up, so I grab the shotgun and turn it over in my hands. It's heavier than I thought it would be and I have no idea how to work it, with the loading and the cocking and all that. Guns aren't my thing. I've never even seen a shotgun in real life. But I figure it's best to hold on to it. I take another peek out the hole in the front door. No cops, no sound of sirens, no one even outside. It's early in the day. Most people are probably at work. Might be nobody even heard the gun.

It's now I can smell something in the house, harsh and unfamiliar and chemical. The guy on the floor is still talking about relative size and dimension so I look around to make sure he's alone. The living room is tidy. Two couches and a cast iron stove and a bookshelf, and some old pizza boxes and beer bottles arranged carefully on the table. Kitchen looks like it came out of a catalogue from the 1980s and hasn't been touched since.

Toward the back there are two bedrooms. One has a couple of mattresses on the floor, with sheets poorly stretched over them. There's a gas mask lying on one of the makeshift beds.

That's not encouraging.

The second bedroom, the bigger one, looks like a lab. On one table there are rows of beakers and electric hot plates. Glass baking dishes, small metal containers of lighter fluid. There's a large pile of pills and a mini-fridge humming away, the only sound in the room. I lift the flap of a cardboard box with my boot. It's filled with bulk packages of empty gelatin capsules. The smell in here is like being downwind of New Jersey refineries in the summer.

At first I think: Meth. But my rudimentary understanding of how meth is made, based entirely on the first two seasons of *Breaking Bad*, seems to indicate this setup is too small, with not enough ventilation.

Then I find a pile of boxes of cough medicine discarded in the corner.

I pick one up. They're all the same. A generic store brand. I check the trash and it's full of small dark bottles, tendrils of red goo clinging to the white caps. I look at the box again, check the active ingredients.

Dextromethorphan.

It's a cough suppressant, and in high quantities it makes you trip. The technical term is "robo-tripping," which makes me think of Robocop tripping balls on acid, which is a very funny thing to think about.

I don't have a baseline of comparison here. Psychedelics and hallucinogens are not my thing. I once saw a kid who weighed a third of what I do get caught up in the throes of a bad trip. He tore through three cops like a windmill. It was the fourth cop—and a Taser—that brought him down. The thought of me out of control scares the shit out of me. Especially since I know what it looks like when I lose control.

No, pills and powders are my thing.

Or, were my thing, until I realized what a mess they were making me into.

So, robo-tripping. People guzzle a bottle of this shit and hope they don't puke it up before the trip starts. Given the setup here it looks like they're extracting it. Which makes sense. Who wants to drink a whole bottle of cough syrup?

Maybe the kid out front took too much. He seems more concerned about his own metaphysical state than me being here to rip him off.

I head back out to the living room and find him sitting on the couch with a Rubik's cube in his hand. He's not trying to solve it, just staring into the center of it. I stand in front of him, still holding the shotgun, which is making me uncomfortable, but I don't want to put it down in case he might grab it. Or, worse, someone more lucid walks in.

"I'm looking for a guy named Dirk and his daughter, Rose," I tell him. "Have you seen either of them?"

He shakes his head. "Perhaps the answer lies at the center of the cube?"

I snap my fingers in front of him. He won't look up at me. I consider hitting him in the side of the head with the shotgun but that's sort of unfair. I have no idea how to handle this.

The shotgun is still in my hands. Someone could come back. Maybe someone did call the cops. I don't like any of what's happening right now. I place the gun on the counter and pick up a dishtowel and go to work, wiping it down the best I can.

I go back to the lumberjack, get down at eye level with him. "What's your name?"

"I am the jester of infinity."

"When you aren't the jester of infinity, who are you?"

He stops looking into the cube and gazes up at me, his vision so out of whack he looks nearly cross-eyed. "They call me Thaddeus."

"Thaddeus, do you want to come for a ride?"

"Will we travel to the center of the cube?"

"Yes. Absolutely."

He smiles and tucks the Rubik's cube to his side. "Thank you.

Thank you so much."

Druggies. You have to know how to talk to them.

We step out of the front door and I find the teddy bear lying on the porch. There's a small gash on the side where one of the shotgun pellets nicked it. Better the bear than me.

The cut isn't so bad. I could probably sew it up myself.

That much is a relief.

THADDEUS IS SO intent on counting the threads in the maroon carpet on the floor in the back that I figure I could trust him alone for a little bit, so I pull into a small storefront for my cell phone carrier, making sure to leave the car in view of the window.

I know my priority should be Crystal and the kid, but this job is getting a bit more complicated than anticipated, and not having a cell phone isn't going to make it any easier.

There's a goofy-looking guy behind the counter. Beige polo shirt and beige face. He's the only person in the store. There's some peaceful music playing over the speakers and still I'm on edge because every time I walk into a store like this, all I can do is think about the ways the salespeople want to screw me out of money.

He pulls up my records and launches into some spiel about all the different shiny new smartphones I can buy and what they cost. He seems to fancy himself a cutthroat salesman and his face droops when I ask him if I'm eligible for a free phone and yes, seems I am.

I settle on something that makes calls and send texts and also has a whole bunch of other bells and whistles I don't give a shit about. I agree to re-up my contract for another two years, and rush through everything else, one eye on the car.

The salesman tries to talk me into a bunch of peripherals—case and car charger and whatnot, so I tell him to fuck himself, and after that he silently completes the transaction and hands me a white plastic bag with everything in it. Though the phone was technically free, there was a thirty-dollar "service charge" for activating it and re-upping my contract. I fold up the receipt and put it in my wallet so I can make sure to get Chicken Man to reimburse me after I'm done beating the shit out of him. I bring the bag with the phone to the car and of course, of course Thaddeus is gone.

Why wouldn't he be?

Why did I think this was a good idea?

I'm in a small strip mall across from a Plaid Pantry, the West Coast version of 7-Eleven. The sign is colorful, and it's the only thing around here that's colorful, so I figure that might be where he headed.

I head to the street, not paying attention, and I nearly walk into oncoming traffic. I look up and there's a Prius coming to a stop to let me cross, the bumper a few feet from my kneecaps. And yet the driver is smiling.

I can't believe the guy driving it stopped to let me cross and doesn't even look angry. I also can't believe how it snuck up on me like that, but as it pulls away, the engine barely makes a gentle hum, so that explains that.

If we were in New York that driver would have run me over to teach me a lesson about looking both ways.

And it wouldn't have been a Prius, probably.

This town is weird.

Inside the Plaid Pantry, tucked behind a fort of candy bars and high-fructose corn snacks, a pear-shaped woman with purple hair is looking toward the back, her face turned up like she smelled something bad.

Bingo.

I find Thaddeus staring into the swirling frozen drink machine, red and white twisting together in a spiral of sugar and slush. I get up alongside him and he taps it and screams into the machine, "Did you speak with the orb?"

Control your anger before it controls you.

Inhale, exhale.

Dammit. It's not working. I'm still angry.

I grab him by the scruff of his neck and pull him toward the front of the store. He pushes away from me and takes a swing. I duck, grab his arm, and wrap it behind his back. Not enough to pop out his shoulder, but enough it'll hurt and I can lead him around pretty easy.

Thaddeus yells nonsense obscenities and the woman at the counter dives for the phone.

"Everything's fine," I tell her, and she pauses. "Be out of your way in a minute. My friend had too much to drink."

She clearly doesn't believe me, but she also doesn't pick up the phone.

Thaddeus thrashes but doesn't have much of a choice but to let me push him out into the parking lot and across the street. His behavior is erratic. This is a stupid drug. Even stupider to take it if he was in charge of a makeshift lab.

Once we get to the car he's calmed a bit so I open the door and toss him across the back seat. He smacks his head on the car seat but I manage to get him all the way in. I hope the woman in the convenience store didn't call the cops. And even if she did, that she's not looking out the window, or at the car's license plate.

As I'm climbing into the front seat he asks, "Where are you taking me?"

"I swear if you say one more word I am going to knock the living shit out of you."

I pull my new phone out of the bag. A generic Android phone, and the battery is half full. I figure out the basics—phone calls and texts. I can't call Crystal because I don't know her number, but I do know the number for the club, so I call there. Tommi answers. Before I can say anything there's a shuffling sound and Crystal is on the line. Excitement spills out of her voice. "Was she there? Do you have Rose?"

"There's been a complication."

She doesn't say anything to that.

I'm about to say she should wait there, but figure it's probably best not to interrogate someone in the throes of a drug trip at a strip club, so I rattle off my address and tell her to meet me at my apartment.

From the back seat Thaddeus yells, "The carpet tastes like purple."

This is going to be a fun afternoon.

IT DOESN'T TAKE much convincing to get Thaddeus to follow me up to my apartment. I jingle my keys at him and that does it. I walk alongside him up the outdoor concrete staircase, past the smell of food I can't afford drifting out of the Korean barbecue joint on the ground level, past the serene music and incense fog of the yoga studio on the second level.

We get up to the third floor and I lead him through to the orange metal door of my apartment. I park him on the couch and set up my laptop, fire up some *SpongeBob Squarepants* on Netflix, and he stares at the screen in awe. He's so enraptured he doesn't even bother with the Rubik's cube.

This is the first time someone other than me is in the apartment. Plus, now I have a lady coming over. I walk the length of it. It's railroad style—bedroom at the far end, kitchen and bathroom at the other end, living area in the middle. The bright tangerine walls look horrifying to me but I figure most people would find the color kitschy. My favorite part: A window that leads out onto a roof, so I can sit outside and pretend real hard like I'm sitting on my old fire escape in the East Village.

This apartment isn't much, but it's also twice the size of my old place and a fraction of the price. Or, the price I would have been paying had I not scammed a rent control property from a dead woman.

Long story.

When I left home, I didn't bring much with me. Mostly clothes. When I rolled into Portland I scavenged some furniture, bought some books. The whole thing is pretty sparse. Which makes it look neat. It's easy to keep things neat when you don't own a whole lot of stuff.

There are two things on the wall I don't really want Crystal to see because I don't want to talk about them.

The small map of the United States with little x's scattered across it.

And the picture of my dad.

But I also don't want to tear things down.

Oh well.

I do move a few things around to make the place appear a little tidier. At the kitchen island, I put the three empty coffee mugs in the sink and take the community college brochures and put them into a neat pile. I put on another pot of coffee, figuring that might help snap Thaddeus out of his trance, and also I want some coffee. The pot is gurgling when there's a knock on the door.

Crystal is wearing black jeans and a green sweater so threadbare it gives off hints of a black bra through the weave. The look on her face is equal parts confused and terrified. I bring her inside and she looks toward the couch and says, "Thaddeus."

Thaddeus doesn't look up.

"You know him?" I ask.

"I know he's one of Dirk's dumb-ass friends."

I run her through what happened with the shotgun and the dextromethorphan lab. She shakes her head, says, "Has he said anything?"

"Nothing that makes any sense. He's on another planet. Have you ever dealt with this before?"

"I've never done it but I've seen it. It can hit some people pretty hard." She looks around. "It's too dark in here. Can you turn on the

45

lights? Bright light can help."

I flip the switch and the track lighting barely illuminates the room.

"Not enough," she says. "Does it get bright in the bathroom?"

I grab Thaddeus by the arm, pull him to his feet, and drag him over. He's looking back at the laptop and asks, "But what about the starfish?"

Crystal snaps on the light and I put Thaddeus on the toilet, and she leans down to him, trying to get him to look into her eyes. She snaps her fingers and says, "Thaddeus. It's Crystal. You know me."

Thaddeus finally focuses on her and says, "You aren't Crystal. You're a lizard in a skin suit."

Crystal puts her hand on his cheek. Says some nice things trying to soothe him. Says she needs to find her daughter. Begs and pleads. While she does that I turn the shower on to the coldest setting. I grab Thaddeus by the shirt and pull him to his feet. Crystal yelps as I pull him past her and he screams when the water hits him and he tries to struggle against me but I'm twice his size so it's not much of a fight.

Crystal yells for me to stop. I tell her, "I'm tired of playing."

I hold Thaddeus under the water and we're both getting soaked and it's freezing, so cold that my muscles tighten like rods of rebar, but it seems to be working, because the faraway look in Thaddeus's eyes is swimming into focus. Like someone came home and turned the lights on in a vacant house.

I get a bead on him, get him to look at me, and ask, "Where the fuck is Dirk?"

He sputters, water spilling into his mouth, says, "I don't know."

"Not good enough."

"Really, I don't," he says. "His Mexican... he was going to see his Mexican before he sold the girl. That's it."

A stone hand wraps around my heart and squeezes.

I push into Thaddeus to ask him what he means about selling Rose, when his eyes go blank and I know this look from how much time I spend in bars, but I don't have enough time to twist out of the way before he vomits about a gallon of foul liquid that collects where my hands are gripped onto his shirt.

The smell hits me, sea animals rotting on a beach, and the feeling starts as a scratch at the bottom of my esophagus. I turn to Crystal to tell her to get out, but before I can get the words out I'm puking on Thaddeus, screaming chunks onto his face, because unfortunately for Thaddeus, I'm taller than he is.

This makes Thaddeus puke more.

Which makes me puke more.

In my peripheral vision Crystal is stumbling out of the bathroom, her hand over her mouth, and I think we've saved ourselves from her blowing chunks too, but she retches in the kitchen.

I slam my eyes shut, hold my breath, and push both of us further into the freezing water to clean off. Try to think about anything but puking, which of course means I can't think of anything but puking. Thaddeus is still going, too.

Sense prevails and I turn him around to look at the white plastic wall of the shower stall, focus on my breathing, let him finish. Not having to look at it makes it a little easier. I turn the water up until it's a little bit warmer, because I feel like we're going to be in here for a little while.

This is not an auspicious start to the investigation.

FOUR

CRYSTAL APPARENTLY HAD a light breakfast, so cleaning her mess out of the sink was easy enough. The shower took a little longer, and I could only do that after Thaddeus and I had properly cleaned off and I could get him into a borrowed pair of dry clothes.

I figured him puking a bunch would clear some of the garbage from his system, make him a bit more useful. Instead he fell into a catatonic state, like he'd been awake for a few days straight and it finally caught up with him.

Crystal and I move around the apartment like ghosts. Thaddeus's words hang in the air.

Dirk selling Rose.

That dredges up all kinds of imagery that's almost too horrifying to acknowledge, and I think we need to steel ourselves before having that conversation.

Crystal's phone buzzes on the counter. She picks it up and nods. "Cab."

I take Thaddeus by the arm and bring him outside and down the stairs, shove him across the back seat of the cab, lean down and give the driver the address of the DXM lab and a couple of bills. Hopefully enough to get him home. It must be, because the cabbie takes it and slowly pulls away from the curb before I've even got my arm all the way out of the window.

I climb the stairs to my floor, where at the end of the hallway there's an alcove overlooking the sidewalk. There are two beaten office chairs and a bucket full of sand filled with drowned and crushed cigarette butts. Crystal is in the chair on the right so I sit in the one on the left. She holds the pack of smokes up without looking at me.

Stay strong. I wave her off. Take a deep breath. The world smells that way it does right around when it rains. Sweet and earthy and heavy and alive.

"Do you smell that?" I ask. "That rain smell. I love that."

Crystal snaps back into focus. "Petrichor," she says.

"Petri-what?"

"That smell. It's called petrichor. It's an aerosol mix of oils put out by plants to protect their seeds. It gets absorbed into the soil."

"I didn't realize you were such a nerd."

"It can't be true," she says, looking up at me. "Dirk wouldn't just… sell our daughter."

"Thaddeus is not a reliable source."

Crystal slides her finished cigarette into the bucket of sand and puts her head in her hands. "I know I should call the cops. I know

I should call the cops. I just..."

"What?"

She leans forward, eyes drifting away. "When Rose was a baby, there was this one night, she wouldn't stop crying, and Dirk got so mad because he couldn't sleep. At me, not at her. He didn't understand why I couldn't make her stop. He thought I wasn't trying. We got in a fight and he hit me. Split my lip." She presses her finger to her lower lip, tugging it down, showing her teeth. "The neighbors called the cops. So they show up and they hear the baby screaming and see the blood on my face and you can see they don't want to fucking deal with this. One cop goes in to talk to Dirk and the other takes me outside, and he gives me some empty spiel about my safety and shit. And he asks me if maybe I wasn't overreacting. Being a new parent can be stressful and my lip didn't look too bad. That's what he said. I was bleeding because Dirk hit me in the face but it didn't look too bad."

"What a dick," I tell her.

"They left." Her voice catches. "They left me there. Bleeding. Screaming baby. Like maybe it would work itself out."

"What did you do?"

"Dirk made some big fucking show in front of the cops about being sorry and apologizing," she says. "A little while later Rose started crying again and he started yelling so I pulled a kitchen knife on him. And the fucked-up thing is I felt safer with the knife than I did with the police at the door."

"I know that feeling."

"Do you?"

Deep breath. I don't want to play the sharing game, but I'm

in it now. "Maybe that was a fluke. Maybe the cops in this town are on the level. I don't know. All I can tell you is my experience. Six months ago I got dragged into a police station and nearly got my brains bashed in by some asshole detective who was trying to make an arrest quota. So between that and what Chicken Man said, I'm going to back your play on this. If you have a bad feeling, then it's a bad feeling for a reason."

"So what now?" she asks.

"We find Dirk."

"I don't know where he is. I called him on the way over. He's not answering his phone."

Crystal sticks her thumb into her mouth, contemplates chewing, then unfurls her fist and reaches down and pulls out another cigarette. Her sweater moves up and flashes a pink strap of underwear, peeking out from her jeans. I feel like a jerk for looking.

"When you call, is it going straight to voicemail or is it ringing?" I ask.

"Ringing."

"I have an idea."

I head back to the apartment, grab my laptop, place it on the counter, fire up Skype, and see that Bombay is logged on. I ring him up and his face appears on the screen, fish-eyed and from a low angle, blue from the glow of the computer screen, square reflections on his glasses.

Bombay is growing out his hair, which is a little jarring, seeing him like that, because he's been shaving his head for so long now. The second you look away, things start to change.

We started junior high together. On the second day of school

I came across a bunch of kids calling him a terrorist and shoving him into a locker. I made them stop. I've never liked bullies. We've been friends since.

His real name is Acaryatanaya. That's a vicious thing to put on a kid, so I took to calling him Bombay, because there's where his family is from.

Technically Mumbai, but Bombay sounded better.

He's my closest friend back home. The only person beside my mom who I truly miss on a profound level. Mostly because I lack the survival mechanism of a conscience, and he's good at pointing out when I am about to do something incredibly stupid.

He's also a computer technician, which is often helpful.

"Hey, brother," he says, a big smile stretched across his face. "Long time."

I'm not sure whether to look at him or the camera, distracted by the little picture of me in the bottom corner of the screen. "Everyone happy and healthy back home?" I ask.

"Yeah, why?"

"I hate to do this, but as long as everyone is good, I don't have time for pleasantries. I'm looking for a little girl…"

"That's sick, dude."

"Hey," I snap and he recoils. "Don't make jokes. There's a kid and she's missing and I have to find her. I need your help."

The smile disappears off Bombay's face. He's all business now. "Got it. What do you need?"

"Say we have a cell phone number. The phone is still on. Can you track it? Get a location?"

He tilts his head. "I'd have to call a guy. That's not even

53

something I can do myself."

"I thought you were a hacker."

"I'm a computer nerd with a deep yet narrow set of skills. Phishing isn't one of them. I can't magically conjure up information you need at a moment's notice. Dude, you should call the cops."

"No cops. Not yet." I look up at Crystal, ask her for the number to Dirk's cell. She rattles it off. Bombay picks up a pen and writes it down.

"No promises," he says. "I'll see what I can do. But really, please, don't trust I'm going to come back to you with an answer."

"Okay. Have you been by to see my mom?"

"She misses you. You should call her more often."

"I'll do that."

"You should actually do it instead of pretending like you will."

I close the lid of the laptop, cutting off the chat.

Crystal asks, "Your brother?"

"No. Why do you say that?"

"He called you 'brother.'"

"He meant it more like 'brethren.' He's a friend from back east. Figured it was worth a shot." The coffee maker is still on, the carafe radiating heat when I put my hand near it. I pull a mug out of the cupboard, open the freezer, drop an ice cube into it, and pour some coffee. The ice cube snaps and crackles. I hold the pot toward Crystal and she shakes her head. "So what's this about Dirk's Mexican? What does that mean?"

Crystal shakes her head, staring out the window. "I have no idea. Dirk was into some shit but he always kept me out of it."

"I fucking hate this," I tell her. "I don't know anything about this city. I feel so lost."

"One thing at a time," Crystal says. "We need information, about something of an unsavory type. Where do we get that?"

We both nod, not needing to say it.

Not to stereotype, but a strip club is a good place to start.

HOOD IS LOOMING outside the club. It's daytime, overcast, the street empty. Probably empty inside. He doesn't look like he's rushing through the cigarette. It's warm and even a little muggy but Hood is wearing a gray sweatshirt with the sleeves pushed up.

Crystal kisses Hood on the cheek and heads into the club to say hi to Tommi and I lean against the wall next to Hood and say, "I need some help. I'd appreciate it if this could stay between us."

Hood looks around to make sure that the street is clear. Whether he wants to be safe or he's mocking my cloak-and-dagger routine, I can't be sure.

"What do you need?" he asks.

"Crystal's ex, Dirk. Did you know him?"

"I know he was a fucking dummy."

"That seems safe to assume, yes. I don't know if this means anything but I'm trying to find information about a Mexican that Dirk might have had an affiliation with. Does that jingle any bells for you?"

Hood's eyes narrow. "Are you asking me this shit because I'm black?"

"I don't even know what Mexican means."

"You don't know what a Mexican is? How white are you,

exactly?"

"C'mon. Stop. This is serious."

Hood tosses his cigarette to the curb, looks around again. "Are you into drugs? Is that it? Because I don't touch that shit. And I'm not comfortable having this conversation. So maybe look for someone else to help you, okay?"

He turns to walk away and I step forward and put my hand on his shoulder. It's so big I can't get a grip on him.

"Fuck, man, I'm not looking for a hookup," I tell him. "Dirk took Crystal's daughter. Pulled her out of day care and disappeared. We're trying to find her. I'm coming up empty. I know he was going to see someone I only know as his Mexican. That's all I have."

Hood pauses. His face drops and he shakes his head, slowly. "Fuck. What about the cops?"

"A few reasons. The big one is the cops might not look kindly on Crystal and her employment situation, and they might assume she's caught up in whatever bullshit game Dirk is running. She doesn't want to get wrapped up with child services. The cops are last resort. I'm trying to find her first."

"Cops in this town aren't so bad," he says. "I would know. I was born on the law enforcement shit-list."

"No cops. Not yet."

He nods. "Fine. I don't really agree, but fine. So, years ago Portland made pseudoephedrine illegal. You know what that's used for?"

"Meth."

"Right. So when it became illegal, there was a void to fill, and the Mexican cartels moved up from the south. Most of the drug game here is run by the cartels. They've got weed and scrips, too."

"So if Dirk had a Mexican, it would be like his contact in the cartel?"

Hood nods. "They set up in legit businesses. Auto shops and food distributors and restaurants and shit, places where there's a lot going on and things moving around and chemicals and shit. Places they can hide what they're doing."

"Okay. That's something. I can work with that."

"I want you to understand the reason I know this shit is because I saw it in a documentary. Discovery Channel or some shit. So don't think I swim in these circles, okay?"

"I'm not accusing you of anything," I tell him.

"Good. Now, I don't have to tell you that cartels are bad fucking news, right? Chop you up into little pieces and mail them to your family bad news."

"I read the paper sometimes."

"Well, whatever you're playing at, you really should rethink your strategy of not calling the police."

"Can't."

"The fuck is wrong with you, then?"

"Just… can't. Got a thing. Need to do it."

Hood shakes his head.

BACK INSIDE THE bar I relay to Crystal what I learned from Hood. As soon as I mention auto shops those blue-green tempered glass eyes get a little brighter.

"Dirk had me drop him off at an auto shop sometimes, but

he would never tell me what for," she says. "He called it a business thing."

"Well then. I guess that's where we're going."

We head for the car, neither of us saying anything. Not really wanting to. There's a black cloud on the horizon now.

Sell the kid.

What does that even mean?

We climb into the car and Crystal tears away from the curb, whipping around someone going too slow in front of us. I tell her, "You aren't as bad as the other drivers around here."

"I'm from Chicago. I learned how to drive in a tougher place than this."

I laugh a little at that.

"What?" she asks.

"Chicago is the only city in America where if you say you're from there, then no one can tell anything about you."

"Really?" She says it like a challenge. "What exactly does that mean?"

"You're from New York, you're a type-A asshole with boundary issues. From Portland? You eat organic and everything you own is vintage. Seattle? You smoke too much pot and wish you were from Portland. Los Angeles? You are dead inside. Any city in Texas or Arizona? You're either trapped or right at home, and either way, I'm sorry. Philly? You live in an open-air frat and your only claim to fame is a sandwich I could assemble from food in a freezer case. Boston? Same thing except you have no signature dish, so you drink too much to compensate. Most cities in middle America and you carry a chip on your shoulder because you come from a long

ROB HART

line of people who lost their jobs to machines or Mexico. Any city in Florida, then you are guaranteed to have seen some really weird shit, and you're a sadist, living in heat like that.

"But Chicago? What the fuck is in Chicago besides shitty pizza? If you tell me you're from Chicago I don't know if you're going to hug me or jam a pen in my throat."

"Wow," Crystal says, laughing, not nicely. "Okay. A few things. First, that's the most you've talked since I met you. Which I guess isn't surprising, because isn't that a typical New Yorker thing to do, to shit on everything that's not their precious little city? And second, Chicago pizza isn't shitty. It's a meal. Two slices of New York pizza and you're hungry ten minutes later."

"No you're not. You're satisfied with the appropriate amount of food that you've eaten."

"You've never had good Chicago pizza."

"There's no such thing. Chicago pizza shouldn't even be called pizza. It takes everything beautiful and amazing about pizza and warps it into a mess of gluttony and bullshit."

"So you are passionate about something," Crystal says. "And you're right about one thing. New Yorkers are type-A assholes."

She stops at a light, pulls out a smoke, lights it, and takes a drag. She doesn't offer me one this time. She cracks the window so the smoke can get sucked out. When she ashes out the window, the two flat rings on her finger click against the glass.

"Have you even been to any of these places you're shitting on?" she asks.

"Some. Others, you meet people from around. Gets easy to see the patterns."

59

"So all this clever posturing is just assumptions."

"Well, that was the nice thing about living in New York. I didn't have to go far to see a lot."

"So why'd you leave if it was so fucking great?"

"Trying something new."

"Where are you headed next?"

"What do you mean?"

Crystal throws a quick glance my way. "I saw the map in your apartment. Are the x's places you've been?"

"No. Places I don't want to go."

"There were a lot of x's," she says.

"I don't want to go to a lot of places."

"What are you looking for?"

"What is anyone looking for?"

Crystal sighs. "How very existential of you."

Shrug.

She takes a deep breath, blows it out. Makes a hard left, cutting off the car that was already trying to make a left but was afraid of crossing in front of a car that's so far away, I can't even tell the color.

"Why are you helping me?" she asks.

"I need to get reimbursed for my cell phone," I tell her.

She shakes her head and sighs again.

WE LEAN AGAINST the hood of the car, Crystal smoking a cigarette, and already I can feel adrenaline pumping hard through my blood. I'd like a cigarette too, something to wash the adrenaline out, but I don't ask. Together the two of us stare at the auto shop down the block.

It's a blank industrial stretch. Quiet and out of the way. Concrete and graffiti. So anonymous you can barely make out where the buildings stop and start. We've been sitting here ten minutes and haven't seen a single person. I am not a drug dealer but this seems like a great place to be one.

Crystal finishes her cigarette, drops it to the curb, and crushes it with the toe of her sneaker. She asks, "So what's the plan?"

"You stay here. Maybe keep the car running. I go in and ask for Dirk."

"That's it?"

"That's it."

"Sounds like a really terrible plan."

"It's better formulated than other plans I've had."

"This is a Mexican cartel."

"And I'm a native New Yorker with a bad attitude. Anything else is bush league."

"You're not looking at me right now," Crystal says. "But you need to know I rolled my eyes so hard I pulled something. Do you have a death wish?"

I turn, toss my hat onto the passenger seat through the open window. "Don't worry. I'll use my words."

And I'm off.

It's a long walk to the auto shop. The occasional bit of gravel or broken glass crunches under my boots. The sky is gray because Jesus, the sky is always fucking gray. Nearly the same gray as the concrete on the exterior of the shop.

The long walk scares me.

Not because of what might be there.

Six months ago and a million miles away, I stood in a man's kitchen with a gun to his head. The gun wasn't loaded. I didn't actually want to shoot him, I wanted him to listen.

Which is a bit of a lie.

I did want to shoot him, but I chose not to.

The reason I was there was because the woman I loved was dead and he was responsible. She may not have loved me the way I loved her, but someone needed to restore balance to the universe. Make up for the fact that he was still breathing and she wasn't.

But the route I took to that kitchen was littered with destruction. I was so intent on getting revenge I didn't care who got hurt. Friends, people who weren't involved, people who were trying to help me. I was like a wrecking ball. Lying to myself the whole time, telling myself I was doing the right thing while I smashed everything that stood in my way.

Bone-deep anger, the kind that's imprinted onto your DNA by a catastrophic event, is like a bag of sand. It weighs you down, sometimes so much it takes your breath away, and you can't think of anything to do but beat someone to death with it. And also the sand is a slow-acting poison, because this metaphor isn't belabored enough.

That's all to say, I couldn't be that person, driven by nothing but hate. It would have burnt me up to cinder.

I still think about it sometimes, in dark moments. How it would have felt. What it would have looked like. Pulling the trigger. Ending his life the way he ended hers. But I didn't.

I chose a different route.

And yet, here I am, retracing my own footsteps in the snow.

The thing that's really scary about this walk to the auto shop is it feels so familiar. The lingering smell of the nicotine from Crystal's cigarettes, clinging to my clothes, placing me back in time to where I liked to chain-smoke and hit things.

I push that feeling down. Think about that righteous path. Of taking the bullets out of the gun and throwing them into the harbor before I stood in that kitchen. Letting that monster live so he could rot in a cell.

A better place for him, a better place for me.

I think about those things so hard I feel like I'm going to snap.

The auto shop seems empty, the dingy, rusted gate pulled down, and through the door at the front, the lights are off. I go over and bang on it with the flat of my balled-up fist.

A few seconds pass. I figure I can climb up on the roof or go around back, see if there's a way to break in. Maybe there's something useful inside.

Still stupid to sneak in, but slightly less stupid than confronting a Mexican cartel head on.

Turns out, someone is home. A light pops on somewhere inside, reflecting through the window on the front door, which is crisscrossed with security wire on the inside of the glass. A sleepy-eyed Hispanic guy in a sleeveless T-shirt with tribal tattoos up and down his upper arms appears at the window. He squints at me and mutters something in Spanish, which I understand better than I speak, but I figure I can get through something simple.

"*Pregunta*," I tell him. Question, I think.

He opens the door a crack. Not to let me in, but enough so he knows I can hear him.

"*Cerrado,*" he says. Closed, I think.

"*Habla inglés?*" I ask.

He shakes his head and closes the door, turns away.

"I'm looking for Dirk," I yell through the window.

The man freezes. Looks at me over his shoulder.

I put my face closer to the window. "Dirk. I need to find him. Find. Uh, *encontrar.*"

The man comes back to the door and opens it. I can see him full now, and he's a small guy, but tight, hammered out of iron. He smiles at me and puts his hand up, waves his fingers at me, beckoning me inside.

How could this possibly go wrong?

I follow him, and most of the lights inside the garage are off. We're in a large room with spots for three cars to be worked on, lined up in a row. It smells like grease and gasoline and something sweet, like burning sugar.

Two of the spots in the garage are empty, cluttered with trays of tools and hydraulic devices. At the far end there's a sedan that's stripped down to the gunmetal-gray bones, the panels leaning up against the wall.

The car is probably being used for smuggling product and the fact that I'm seeing this can't possibly be good, and that's confirmed when the tattooed man spins and body-checks me into a rolling cart loaded with tools that spill and scatter across the oil-stained floor.

Five

I FALL TO THE floor in a jumble, tools bouncing off me, the clatter of them echoing in the corners of the dark garage. I try to stand and the tattooed man grips my arms, digging fingers into my biceps from behind, and pulls me to my feet.

He pushes me forward and he has great leverage. I can't fight, can't get away. He slams me into a workbench, his body crushing mine, his hand pushing my face down so I can't see. There's something sharp and cold under my cheek.

There's another Hispanic guy standing off to the side now, watching us, like he's been standing there the whole time. Not even too far away, like if I had a free hand I could just about reach him. He's wearing greasy coveralls and a pair of safety goggles on top of his head. I stop struggling and the guy holding me stops pushing, but doesn't let up.

"What do you know about Dirk, homes?" asks the man in the coveralls, in heavily accented English.

"I don't know anything about him. I need to find him."

"Why do you need to find him?"

"He's got a kid with him. I need to find the kid."

The mechanic shrugs. "I don't know nothing about a kid. All I know is Dirk owes us money and now some motherfucker is here looking for him. Maybe you're here to see what you can score off us?"

"I knocked. What kind of asshole rips off dealers by knocking?"

He leans against the workbench, looking across the garage. "Who said what we do here?"

"Lucky guess?"

"You seem to know a lot about us."

"I don't know anything. I didn't see anything. I'm looking for a girl. A little girl, man. She got taken from her mom and I need to get her back."

The man in the coveralls pushes away from the bench and leans toward me, looking me in the eyes. They're like pieces of slate, heavy and unmoving. They crush me almost as hard as the guy holding me down. He says, "Do you know how much Dirk owes us?"

"I don't care what Dirk did."

The man in the coveralls says, "Ten grand."

"Tell me where you think he might be, I'll bring the money back. Fuck, man, I don't give a shit about Dirk. He sounds like an asshole. I just need to find him."

The man in the coveralls stands up and says, "I don't know

where he is."

"I guess we're at an impasse?"

"We are. I've got two problems." He disappears from my field of view. The place is filled with silence, the sound of my breath exploding across the table, the creak of the bench I'm being pressed into. My heart is slamming into my chest so hard I'm a little dizzy.

There's a clatter of a metal tool being picked up and dropped onto a hard surface.

CLANG.

And another.

CLANG.

Each one making me flinch, chipping away at my bravado.

The tattooed man laughs.

I think I got a little ahead of myself, thinking this would be a quick q-and-a.

"The problem," the man is the coveralls says, "is that you even know we're here, which you can imagine is bad for business. That, and I don't give a fuck about some little girl. Ten G's I do give a fuck about, so I would say my desire to find Dirk is greater than yours."

"I feel like we're not doing a great job of communicating here…"

There's a rumbling noise and a huge suck of air. It feels like a fan. Like the air in the garage is suddenly lighter. The man in the coveralls appears again. He's holding a long bronze nozzle attached to a hose.

"I want to know everything that you know, homes," he says. "We can do this easy or hard. Do we have to do it hard? Then it's balloon time." He squeezes the lever on the nozzle and a hard burst of air shoots out. So strong I can see the white gust of it. He looks over my shoulder and says, "*Baje sus pantalones.*"

Take down his pants.

I think I know where this is going.

Fuck.

Fucking fuck.

I kick out as hard as I can. There's resistance and a crunch, and the guy holding me screams from someplace primal. Figure I got him in the knee, and when his grip loosens on me I don't waste time looking back, just throw all my weight into him.

He falls off and I rush at the mechanic. There's a wrench as big as my forearm and thick as my wrist sitting on the workbench so I pick it up and it's so heavy I need two hands to swing it.

I smash it across his cheek. His head jerks around and his body begins to fall but I don't even see where he lands, because I drop the wrench and I'm out the door as soon as I'm at the end of the arc.

Outside there's a trace of sun and it stings my eyes before it disappears behind a veil of clouds. I run at the car. Crystal is sitting in the driver's seat. She sees me running and leans over to pop the passenger side door. I vault over the car, stumble on the sidewalk, throw myself into the seat, and yell at her to drive before I even get the door closed.

WE'RE A GOOD two miles away before my heart stops screaming. Before I feel comfortable that no one is following us and I can turn around in the seat.

Crystal asks, "What the fuck was that about?"

"Dirk owes them money. They wanted to pump me for information."

Oh, I didn't even mean it like that. I do a full-body cringe at the thought of what they were planning.

"So, did they try to beat you up or something?"

"They were going to shove an air compressor up my ass and turn it on."

Crystal doesn't say anything to that.

I've had guns and knives pulled on me. Been beaten on pretty hard. Even been shot once. I've seen some shit. Being turned into a human balloon is taking things to the next level.

Crystal asks, "Do you think they're following us?"

"Doesn't look like it. There were only two of them, I think. Busted one of their kneecaps. Brained the other with a wrench."

"Ash, are you fucking kidding?"

"They did try to tear a hole in my colon. When you're threatened with something like that, the rules of engagement go out the window."

Crystal jerks the wheel and pulls the car to the side of the road, nearly killing a biker, who shakes his fist before taking off, his reflective yellow vest disappearing into the distance.

She grips the steering wheel so tight her knuckles go white. For a few moments she's completely still. Then she slams her fist against the steering wheel. Three, four, five times.

"Ash," she says, fighting at holding something back. "What the fuck are we going to do?"

I stare out at the empty street, grinding the gears in my head.

69

What's the next step?

"He pissed off a cartel," I say, feeling it out. "He owes them money. So that means it's not safe to stay here, right? He's got to be leaving town. Does he have a car?"

"No. And his license is suspended."

"Then he's probably not driving. If he gets pulled over he's going to be in a shitload of trouble."

"And nobody is going to trust him with a car," Crystal says.

"Maybe the airport?"

Crystal takes a deep breath. "He has an inner-ear thing. It hurts to fly. If he was going to leave he would take a train or a bus."

"So if I wanted to take a train or a bus, where would I go?"

"Portland Union Station. Whenever he goes anywhere it's out of there. It's on the west side of the river."

"Let's go. We'll hang out for a bit. Ask around, see if anyone saw him. And if it doesn't pan out, maybe we revisit going to the cops, take our chances. Because other than that, I've got nothing. I can't think of anything else."

Crystal nods slowly. There's a very brief moment when I think she's going to cry. The muscles in her face pulling tight. But she puts the car in drive and slowly pulls away from the curb, her face blank.

I hold my hands in my lap, clasp them together to keep them from shaking. Close my eyes. Try not to think of the crunch of that asshole's knee. And the other guy, the way his body went slack after I hit him, like something left his body.

I try not to think about those things, so of course, it's all I can think about.

Outside it's overcast but still a bright gray, the sun hollering from behind the clouds. I push the thoughts in my head around like furniture, try to focus on something else.

And it's now, sitting across from Crystal, in the smell of nicotine and citrus, I realize how much I don't know about her.

I've seen her naked more times than I can count. I know her areolas are darker than you would expect on such cream-white skin. She wears outfits cobbled together out of secondhand stores, and she strips to '80s pop, like Nena and Erasure and Soft Cell. So many dancers in Portland have tattoos, like it's required to get into the club, but she doesn't have any. People notice. Sometimes they come in and ask for the girl without the tattoos.

Music and her naked body. I know her in a way that's almost intimate and that still doesn't mean I know anything about her.

One thing I do know is that through this whole thing she's kept herself collected. Whether that's for her benefit or mine, I'm not sure. But only now is that desperation and frustration shining through the cracks. It makes me wish I was doing a better job. That I had a better idea than to go to a train station and hope by some magical fucking coincidence Dirk is there.

More than that, I want to find the kid.

Kids don't deserve drama like this.

The headrest pushes my hat into my eyes so I take it off and put it in my lap. Crystal drives like we're in a rocket ship. We approach a four-way stop and there are two cars sitting across from each other, the drivers waving at each other, trying to let the other go first, and she weaves around them without pausing.

We drive past streets that are familiar, until she ducks down a side street and we're in a whole new part of town. I try to remember the turns, the landmarks, the storefronts. Figure this place out.

She asks, "So what is it you ran from?"

"What do you mean?"

"Your friend said to call your mom. You didn't seem to want to."

"I wasn't running," I tell her. "Me and my mom love each other. There's a lot there in the valley in between us."

"Trouble with your dad?"

"Only trouble I have with my dad is that he's dead."

Crystal pauses. "I'm sorry."

"Nothing for you to be sorry about."

"Can I ask how he died?"

Shrug. "You can ask."

"All right. How'd you end up in Portland?"

"You ask a lot of questions."

"I'm panicked, so I'm talking to keep myself distracted, because if I don't keep myself distracted I'm going to fall apart. So can you just do me the kindness of dropping the stoic act? Sometimes it helps to talk about shit. Then we both win."

Her knuckles are still white gripping the wheel.

She steals a glance at me before looking back at the road.

"When I left New York I started out in Austin," I tell her. "Too hot. Checked out Los Angeles and I got a bad vibe. Heard good things about Portland so I came up here. It's pretty. Like a city grew out of the middle of the forest. And the coffee is good. But it's too quiet. I'm looking around for what's next."

As I'm talking there's a car in front of us doing ten miles under the speed limit. We're on a narrow residential block, so Crystal can't get around without going into oncoming traffic. She speeds up, practically riding the bumper, trying to get the person to drive faster, which isn't happening.

I point at the car. "That frustration you're feeling right now? Wanting the person in front of you to go quicker? It's like that. Being trapped inside that feeling. And the worst part is, this place still reminds me of the worst parts of New York."

"How is this anything like New York?"

"It's like Williamsburg Junior. Same vibe. Goofy fucking hipster kids who are nostalgic for things they never knew."

"What does that even mean, to call someone a hipster? Isn't it kind of a meaningless term? If all it means is young and hip, you're a hipster, too."

"First off, I'm not hip. Second, it's like porn. You know it when you see it."

Crystal roots around for another cigarette, lights it. "You're full of shit, but I think you know that. How do you even have friends?"

"You mean Bombay?" I ask her. "We grew up together. He's good to me. I wish I could return the favor."

Crystal opens her mouth and inhales a gulp of air, like she's about to launch into something and stops herself.

We pause at a red light and she turns to me. "You seem pretty down on yourself. In a general sense."

I shrug at her. "Like I said, I'm not a good person. I'm trying to get to the next thing in one piece."

She nods. "You must be a real blast at parties."

A STEEPLE STABS UP into the sky before the full train station comes into view. Beige brick with orange roof and trim. It says UNION STATION on one side, GO BY TRAIN on the other. Crystal guides the car toward the entrance, where there's a mess of cars picking people up and dropping them off. No one is doing it in any kind of orderly fashion.

We're a couple of lanes over and Crystal says, "Can't get much closer."

"Find parking." I hop out and duck through the scramble, almost get creamed by something that looks like a cross between a trolley and a multi-person bike, kids perched around the edges of the spider-like contraption and pedaling like they're running from something.

I push through the doors, into the main room of the train station. It's big, lots of polished wood and brass and sand-colored marble. There are pools of people milling around the food vendors, staring at the arrival signs, vibrating with the apprehension of travel. It smells like French fries. I nearly trip over a group of crusty punks sprawled out by the door, a mess of mismatched luggage propping up a cardboard sign that reads: NEW TO TOWN. OUR DREAM TO OPEN A FOOD TRUCK. DONATIONS APPRECIATED.

They look at me expectantly. I keep moving, scan the crowd, not even knowing where to start. Crystal didn't have a picture, but she described Dirk to me. Sandy hair, goatee, thin, favors black. Lots of tats, but the most apparent being the noose tattooed on the side of his neck, which makes me believe that under different circumstances we wouldn't be friends.

I cut through the crowd, past the lacquered wooden benches,

not even looking at faces, looking at necks, for the splotches of black ink. Hope Crystal gets a good spot and gets in here quick because if he's here, she'll see him right off. I check my phone, thinking maybe she's texted me, and no, not yet.

Five minutes pass. Nothing.

This is insane.

Maybe we *should* go to the cops.

What the fuck does that even mean, that Dirk is going to sell Rose? Even though Crystal is convinced he's not that kind of guy, there's a level of desperation unique to heroin users. And anyway, this is already getting out of hand.

I'm not a detective. I'm just some asshole who's good at hitting people and can be occasionally clever. Every minute that ticks by makes me feel like I'm sinking lower into something and if I keep it up, I'm not going to have enough oxygen to get back out.

There's a bored-looking cop with a round ruddy face and a crew-cut standing at a post by the ticket window, staring at no one in particular.

Maybe Crystal isn't thinking clearly. Who even says she has to tell anyone what she does for a living? Maybe there's a way to get this around the cops without there being a problem.

She isn't here yet.

Fuck the Chicken Man. Dirk is a junkie idiot. It was probably one of his junkie idiot friends. What other explanation could there be? This whole spiel about the cops could have been a scare tactic. Something to keep us doing what we're doing: Making bad choices.

Executive decision time.

As I'm walking over to the cop, the noose passes my field of vision.

Dirk walks by me, just like that, a tattered green duffel bag flung over his shoulder.

It's him. I know it soon as I see him. My brain goes completely blank for a second. All this running around and he's standing right there.

Maybe I am good at this.

He's by himself. No little girl tagging along. He's got the vacant look and collapsed cheeks and waxy skin of a heroin user ready for another hit. I know that look. Seeing him, walking like it's no big deal, it stops my march toward the cop. I watch him walk into the bathroom. The door swings closed behind him.

You know what?

Fuck the police.

THE BATHROOM LOOKS like it was transported here from a high school. Subway tile and beige stall doors and urinals that stretch to the floor. One stall is taken. No one else inside. The door won't lock but there's a knee-high out-of-order cone just inside so I put it outside the door. Hopefully it buys me a couple of minutes.

There's an explosion of flatulence and a moan from the stall. I lean against the sink and wait for Dirk to come out. A few minutes pass. After some fumbling around with the toilet paper dispenser, he stumbles out and heads toward to the sink to wash his hands, tossing the duffel on the floor. I make like I'm playing with my phone. He doesn't even look at me, walks past to the hand dryer. It looks like one of the first hand dryers ever built and sounds like a jet engine when he presses the button to turn it on.

Soon as he puts his hands under it I get behind him and say, "Dirk."

He jumps away and I get between him and the door, to herd him back toward the sinks. He asks, "Who the fuck are you?"

"Where's Rose?"

His face goes white but he doesn't say anything. He's jittery, his shoulders clenching and unclenching. There's an angry red mark between the pointer and middle finger on his right hand.

I get close to him. "I want you to understand something. Are you listening to me?"

He nods.

Muscle memory takes over. My voice drops an octave. "You're going to tell me where she is. This isn't a question. It's not a debate or a negotiation. You're going to tell me now and I won't drag you over to that toilet you just befouled and stick your fucking head into it. Because I didn't hear you flush. Now, who did you sell her to?"

He shakes his head, puts his hands up in front of him, his eyes darting around the room. "It's not like that. I didn't sell her to some sick fuck."

"Tell me how it is. Right fucking now, or it's toilet time."

"It was a foster family. Off the books adoption. Some nice family got her. You think I'd fuck around with my own daughter like that? What the fuck did Crystal say about me? That fucking cunt—"

I stick my finger in his face, speaking loud so I know he'll hear me over the roar of the dryer. "Watch your mouth. You kidnapped a little kid, and that looks like a fresh track mark on your hand. You're not exactly in contention for father of the year."

Dirk's lip curls up toward his ear. "That bitch has you all wrapped up, doesn't she?"

The hand dryer is still going.

It's so fucking loud.

Why won't it stop? Is it broken?

"This isn't about you or her," I tell him. "It's about a kid. Give me an address."

"Listen, man, you got it all wrong. I'm looking out for Rose, okay? The old man said she'd be fine."

"What old man?"

Dirk looks up and past me, not listening, his eyes finally settling on something stationary over my shoulder.

The roaring of the hand dryer stops, replaced by the echoing sound of footsteps.

I try to turn around as something slams into me and drives me into a stall.

SIX

GOOD NEWS: THE stall I'm in is not the one Dirk had just occupied.

Bad news: Everything else that's currently happening.

I'm on my knees hugging a toilet, harried footsteps pounding away from me, my cowboy hat lying on the floor. I grab it and try to get out of the stall but the door swings inward, too close to the toilet, so I get stuck trying to squeeze around it. By the time I free myself the bathroom is empty. I duck out the door and don't see Dirk, just crowds of blank people. Not even a commotion.

They're gone.

My blood is pounding a drumbeat on the inside of my brain. Something hot and thick gathers on my forehead. I duck back into the bathroom and find a trail of blood trickling down my scalp, about to hit my eye. I can't feel the pain yet. I'm still too charged up.

I bend over the sink and splash water on it, watch swirls of pink disappear down the drain, then grab a chunk of paper towel and hold it against my head.

That's, what, two solid blows to the head in something like twenty-four hours? Three? I wonder how many points have been knocked off my IQ. As if I had that many to start with.

The door opens. An old man enters. He's shrunken and lost weight since he bought his khaki-sweater combo. He looks at me with the wad of paper towel pressed against my head and asks, "You okay, son?"

I nod at him, leave the bathroom. As I'm heading for the entrance I pass a newsstand, and you know what? Fuck it. If dumb shit is going to keep happening, I'm going to have a cigarette. I deserve it. And none of Crystal's slims. Not that I care about how they look. Phallic is phallic. I don't trust that they have enough nicotine for me.

There are three people in line in front of me, so it takes five full minutes to get up to the counter, which is staffed by a girl with a wool cap and facial piercings who moves like she's underwater.

When it's my turn she looks at the bruise on my face and the smear of blood on my forehead. She shrugs and asks me what I want.

"That's a loaded question," I tell her.

She shrugs again, so I ask for my brand and some matches. Cigarettes achieved, I duck outside, slap the pack against my palm, open it, take one out, and puff into the recessed filter to clear out the tobacco flakes.

I fire up, get dizzy straight off, hate myself, and feel a little like

I want to puke.

Man, did I miss this feeling.

The smell of it is like a key to an attic filled with dusty memories. Bleeding and smoking. I can feel pieces of my old life tugging at me.

I'm halfway through when Crystal comes running up. "Took forever to find parking and then I got into an argument with a meter maid... was Dirk not here?"

She gets a look at my forehead and her face contorts into a territory between confusion and fear.

"Sit down," I tell her, nodding toward a bench next to us. I fall into it. She perches, tentatively, on the edge. I run through what happened, everything Dirk said, and how I got rushed from behind. She listens and when I'm done she closes her eyes and exhales, folds her torso over her knees. Her fist goes up to her chin, her thumbnail to her lips.

"I don't even understand why he would do that," she says around the thumb. "Why would he steal my daughter and give her away?"

"He seemed pretty adamant that she was safe. Do you believe him?"

She doesn't hesitate. "Yes, actually. He wasn't a great dad but he wasn't a bad one. He hit me but he never hit Rose, never raised his voice to her. When we split up he pushed pretty hard to keep seeing her. Even threatened to get a lawyer, though he never followed though."

"I know you don't trust him, but do you trust him with her?"

"For as crazy as it sounds, yes, I do." She looks at me. "But that doesn't mean I'm giving up on getting her back."

"I wouldn't expect you to."

She digs down deeper on that nail.

"If you're hungry we can get something to eat," I tell her. "You shouldn't eat your hand."

She looks up at me, pulls her thumb out and stares at it, the top of the nail chalky, the skin around it red. It looks worse than it did when I noticed her chewing it in the coffee shop.

"Bad habit," she says.

I wave my cigarette. "These things happen."

With the hand she wasn't chewing, she reaches into her purse and takes out one of her skinny cigarettes and holds it in her hand for a moment before placing it between her lips. I strike a match and offer it to her. She inhales and sits back, blows out a plume of smoke and stares at it.

"This is the most I've smoked since I found out I was pregnant," she says. "I sneak one every now and again but I don't like her smelling it on me. And now it's like when you're a kid and you're rolling down a hill and you're picking up speed..." She waves her hand. "Forget it. What's the next step?"

I take off my hat, find the back of it is bent, so I twist the wire back into shape. "He said something about 'the old man.' Could mean his old man, like his dad. Do you know anything about his parents?"

"No. He never talked about them."

"Could be something, could be nothing. I'm going to ask Bombay to look into his background a little. Maybe he has family around here. That'd be a good place to start. I think we bought ourselves some time. He might hole up for a bit, try to hide, or find another way out of town."

Crystal contemplates her cigarette. We sit there and watch as it sends up a few desperate wisps of smoke. I dab at my forehead with the wad of paper towel. It comes back a little red, but not so red that I'm worried.

"Maybe it's time to actually call the cops for real," she says.

"What if, and it's just a thought, you got a lawyer? Someone who can be an advocate so shit doesn't get out of control."

Crystal huffs. "I can't afford a lawyer."

"There's got to be some social service organization you can tap into, right? Isn't there a sex workers' union?"

"Some strippers have unionized. I haven't. Didn't seem worth it."

"Maybe now it is. Can you talk to someone? Get some advice?"

Crystal nods. "Yeah. I can do that. I know some people who might be able to point me in the right direction." Her head dips back and she gazes up at the sky. "Nothing is every easy, is it?"

"Nope." I stand. There's a creak in my knee that I'm only now noticing. Might have banged it up in the bathroom stall. Might have banged it up in the garage. It's the most horrible guessing game ever. I stretch it out, swinging my foot forward and back, which doesn't help much. "C'mon. Let's go to the car. I'm on second shift. Tomorrow we find a lawyer. It's fucking Portland. It can't be too hard to find a sympathetic lawyer. We take it from there."

I begin to walk away and realize she's not following me. I turn and her head is tilted and she's staring at me. I tell her, "We should go."

Crystal asks, "Why are you helping me?"

Shrug. "You know how many karma points I'm going to earn off this?"

Her mouth is closed but her jaw pulses like she's clenching her teeth.

A YOUNG COUPLE COMES through the door, pushing aside the black velvet curtain and standing at the front of Naturals like they're waiting for something. The guy is wearing black jeans and suspenders and a white shirt with a huge pair of red lips on it. The girl is a blonde, her hair in a tight ponytail. She's wearing a full-body T-shirt like a dress, depicting a cartoonish, buxom woman in a pink bikini.

The fact that they're dressed like idiots doesn't give me pause. What does concern me is the fact that they're pushing a baby stroller.

I'm hoping they're using it to transport something, but as I get closer I can see that, yes, there is a baby inside, bundled in a blue blanket, waving its little monster hands and staring at the disco ball that's casting shards of light around the room.

Calypso is up on stage, fully nude, dancing to "Paradise City" by Guns N' Roses, so I position myself so I'm between her and the baby's line of sight. I don't know if the baby will understand what it's seeing, but still.

Fingers crossed they need to use the phone or something.

"Can I help you?" I ask.

The guy shrugs. "We just want to sit and get a drink."

"You have a baby."

He leans forward. "So? What difference does that make?"

Now I see what they were waiting for. Someone to challenge them.

"This is a strip club," I tell them.

"The female form isn't something to be ashamed of," the girl says. I can tell it's something she's wanted to say for a very long time.

I glance over my shoulder. Calypso is climbing off stage and things are quiet and people are craning their necks, looking over, trying to figure out what the hell is happening. Tommi must be in the back. I'm sure I don't need to get a ruling from her on this.

"Sorry, but you have to go," I tell them.

"What cause do you have to refuse our business?" the girl asks.

"You have to be twenty-one to get in and that baby isn't twenty-one," I tell them.

"We just want to have a drink," the guy says. "The baby isn't going to cause any trouble. What's the problem?"

As if on cue, the baby starts shrieking. That bone-grating cry that only a baby is capable of producing. This has to be an evolutionary thing. A survival mechanism. Nothing makes you want to drop what you're doing like a baby crying.

Now people are staring.

"The answer is still no," I tell them. "This is polite as I get. Don't make me be not polite."

The two of them hover, very visibly upset, wondering if they should press the issue harder. I've heard of people trying to bring babies into bars. I guess this is the next logical step.

After a few moments of grumbling and pursed lips, they turn to leave. The girl says over her shoulder, "I am going to give this place such a bad review on Yelp."

Control your anger before it controls you.

Inhale, exhale.

The couple leaves and the music kicks back on. Some punk-klezmer mix, which means Carnage is getting on stage.

Back to work.

Naturals is packed. Every stool is taken, every table filled, the front of the stage ringed with people waving dollar bills. There are three dancers tonight: Calypso, Candy Cane, and Carnage. The three of them different as can get.

Calypso has skin the color of espresso with a touch of milk and she's curvy with a lot of gold piercings in her face and a mane of hair like a lion. Candy Cane is a freckled redhead, white white skin with breasts so large and well-appointed you'd think they were bolt-ons, but no, she's blessed. Carnage is tattoos and gristle with a blank, harsh stare like she's accusing you of something.

That plus Crystal and Cacophony, the other regular girl, and I keep meaning to ask if the C-names mean anything.

When there's a lull in the crowd and Tommi is back behind the bar, she waves me over from where I'm nestled up in the corner, watching the crowd watch Candy Cane dance, and points to a paper plate on the bar in front of her. It's piled with nachos, coated in salsa and something that's glowing fluorescent in the black light.

"What the fuck is that?" I ask.

"My vegan nachos, hot shot," Tommi says. "Give 'em a try."

"They're glowing."

"It's vegan cheese."

"Tommi. Food should not glow."

"C'mon, I need the opinion of a carnivore. It's organic. It's made out of nut butters."

"I am not putting nut butters in my mouth."

"It's almonds and cashews, you goon. Just try it."

She pushes the plate toward me and I pick up a nacho, take a tentative bite. It tastes like salted liquid Styrofoam, so I tell her that, and she says, "Can't be that bad."

She picks up a nacho drenched in glowing nut butter fake cheese, chews it for a bit, and slides the plate across the bar and into the garbage pail.

"Back to the drawing board," she says.

Sergio comes out of the back in his starch white chef's coat that's probably a size small and still a bit big on him. His bushy brown hair is stuffed into a hairnet. He has a hopeful look on his face, but he sees the looks on our faces and his shoulders drop.

The crowd picks up some more and Tommi's a blur, slinging out drinks. A line forms at the bar. This is a weird social law in Portland that I broke when I first got to town. People line up for the bar like it's the bus or the deli counter. If you walk right up to the bar and order a drink, you don't get yelled at because everyone here is so passive, but you definitely get a lot of dirty looks.

With Tommi locked down I play utility, clearing empty glasses into the sink, checking to make sure the bathrooms are stocked, keeping an eye on the girls to make sure they're covered. I get into a nice groove. Concentrate on the work. Take a little mental vacation from the nonsense that's plaguing me.

When things slow down a bit, I take it as an opportunity to wave my pack of cigarettes at Tommi. She nods and I duck out front and ring up Bombay, hope he picks up this time. He gets me on the third ring, asks, "What up?"

"I need to get some background on a guy. Specifically his parentage." I run through the bullet points of the story, give him Dirk's full name.

"So is this how it's going to be?" Bombay asks. "You're going to travel the country, take jobs from people, keep me on retainer as your Watson?"

"Right. Except Sherlock gave Watson room and board, at least. I'm not even paying you. All I can do it treat you to my delightful personality."

"Very funny. You are so very funny."

"Look, man, I'm just trying to help someone who needs a hand."

"I get it. And hey, I do have some good news."

"Proceed."

"How do I put this? That friend you were asking me to locate for you? I can't remember his specific address but I do have some zip codes that are in Portland... so I would take that as a good signal."

Bombay does this sometimes. Gets nervous about talking on the phone about stuff like this, so he rambles and speaks in quasi-code. I take it from this that he traced Dirk's cell and while he can't pinpoint the exact location, he knows that it's within city limits.

That's good. That's very good.

"If it changes, I'll let you know right away," he says, verifying my guess.

"Thanks."

We end the call and I toss my smoke into a puddle at the curb and head back inside. Carnage is on stage dancing to what I think is Tool, and Candy Cane is giving some guy a private dance in the corner, her negligée a little satin pool on the floor.

No touching keeps the temperature down.

Most of the time.

The guy getting the dance—flop-sided haircut, scarecrow limbs, short-sleeved plaid shirt buttoned all the way to the top button—keeps reaching up to put his hand on Candy Cane's thigh. She keeps swatting his hand away. I stalk over and lean down to him, tell him to sit on his hands and if he reaches out one more time I'm going to break them off. His eyes go wide and he jams them between his jeans and the vinyl seat. Candy Cane winks at me. I smile back at her, try real hard to keep my eyes from wandering down to her bare breasts, do a not so great job at it.

Tommi calls to me from the bar, asks me to head down to the basement to get the new microbrew that she can't remember the name of but it has a picture of a pig in a rocking chair on the case. I head into the kitchen, pull up the corrugated trap door, and climb down the narrow ladder. The kitchen is tiny and Sergio can't move around much with the door open, so I swing it closed and when that happens the music cuts off and I'm alone in the quiet of the brick-lined basement.

There's a feeling of pulsating bass but that might be my heartbeat.

The basement is so small it's not worth keeping too much

down here, but we do have a Shanghai tunnel that spits out a steady stream of cool air, so the beer, at least, lives by the gaping black maw of it.

One day, fueled by boredom, I'm going to take a flashlight down here and explore a bit. I've always been curious. These things are all over the place. They're not actually Shanghai tunnels—no one got captured and sold off to China in them. But there is a system of tunnels connecting businesses to the waterfront, so that in olden times, goods could be delivered from the ships

I find two cases of the pig-in-the-rocking-chair beer— Rockingham, ha ha—and haul them up the ladder and into the kitchen, which is not easy because my knee still hurts. At least the cut on my forehead is on my hairline so it's hard to spot, and with the lighting in here, no one seems to notice my face is all bruised up. That, or they're ignoring it.

Sergio takes the cases of beer as I swing them up onto the kitchen floor. When I get up to the bar, things have emptied out a little, and Tommi is chatting with a few of the regulars, so I head out for another smoke. After a few drags the door swings open and Tommi comes out. "That's a filthy fucking habit."

"I've done worse."

"Did I hear right? Some assholes tried to bring a baby in here?"

"Yup."

Tommi laughs. "Not even the first time that's happened. This fucking town, man. I love it but it's not always easy. Anyway. Got an interesting phone call just now. Wanted to give you a heads-up."

"What was it this time?"

She pauses. "What do you mean 'this time'?"

"Fuck. I'm sorry. Some asshole called early this morning and said something about your dyke ass. I told him to come down here and something something beatdown. I don't remember. I should have told you. What happened?"

"Some heavy-breathing fuck, said some untoward shit about the girls and what he was going to do to them if we didn't pack up and go."

"This is weird."

"Tell me about it," Tommi says. "I called a couple of other clubs where I know people. No one's getting harassed. No one's getting threats. Wish you had told me, but still. Why us?"

"Could be some dickbag with too much free time and a couple of screws loose. Want to put me on the phone with him next time he calls? I can actually try to be scary this time."

Tommi raises her arms so they're close to her body and flexes. Hard lumps of muscle show through her tattooed forearms. "I'm pretty scary myself. He should be more scared of me than you."

"I don't know about that."

She laughs. "Tough guy, huh. That's funny, you being such a delicate flower." She lifts the corner of her shirt and shows me a white patch of skin on her side marred by a pink, mottled scar. "Knife wound from a bar fight. I don't fuck around, *Ashley*."

I consider telling her about the gunshot scar on my leg, figure that's best to keep to myself. Anyway, I'd end up having to take down my pants to prove I have it.

But the name thing, I can't let go.

"You know John Wayne's real name was Marion, right?" I ask.

"And he changed it."

"Real man sticks with the name his parents gave him."

Tommi nods at this, satisfied with my comeback. "One of the patrons said there's piss on the floor of the men's bathroom. Mind getting in there to mop it up?"

"We need targets in the urinals or something."

She laughs, pats me on the shoulder as she walks past. "Better piss than blood."

WORK FINISHED, BURNSIDE Bridge crossed, I stop into a market to get some beer, the white glowing buzz of it standing out like a beacon in the darkness.

Time to break another one of my self-imposed rules. I haven't been keeping alcohol in the house. But today is one of those days where I could really use a drink.

It's not like I'm pulling from a bottle of the hard stuff. Beer is barely a step above water. I need a six-pack to even feel a tingle, and by then I'm too frustrated to drink any more because I need to pee every ten minutes.

So this is barely breaking the rule. It's a technicality, if anything.

I'm still an okay person.

The beer case is an explosion of colors. Lots of artful labels, nothing that I recognize. I wander from one end to the other until I find a six of tall Guinness cans. That'll work.

I carry it to the counter and the guy working it, his Grizzly Adams beard reaching down to his navel, looks at my choice and asks, "Are you sure?"

"What do you mean am I sure?"

"We have a great selection."

"Cool. I'll get this though."

"I could recommend some really good microbrews. And our IPAs are really big right now. We have a double IPA that's amazing."

"Dude. Sell me this beer."

He sighs, pulls a small red Solo cup out from underneath the counter, takes a bottle of beer with no label, cracks the top, and pours a little into the cup. He slides it toward me.

"Try this," he says. "We make it here."

The smile on his face is big and broad, like he's letting me in on a secret of the universe.

Whatever. Free beer. I throw it back and it's so bitter it kicks my taste buds in the balls. I twist up my face and consider clawing at my tongue to get that lingering horribleness off, and somehow he completely misinterprets my reaction.

"Isn't that awesome?" he asks. "That's a sixty-eight IBU. That's like nuclear hops."

"I hate you," I tell him, trying not to gag. "Sell me the Guinness."

He rolls his eyes. "If you insist."

"Yeah, motherfucker, I do insist."

He runs the transaction through, takes my money, and even though I've got my hand out he puts the change down on the counter, turning away from me like I've insulted his mother.

IT'S OVERCAST SO I can't see the stars. Not that I could see them if it wasn't overcast. I figured New York had the market cornered on light pollution.

If it was daytime, from up here on the roof, I would be able to see Mount Hood off in the distance, the rest of the city unrolling toward it like a blanket. That view would be nice. Right now all I can see is yellow-tinted night sky.

I light a cigarette, already getting a bit of a headache because I haven't smoked this many cigarettes in a row in months. The pack is nearly empty and I only bought it this afternoon.

Bad habits.

I flip through the wad of bills in my pocket, the sum of what the dancers tipped out to me and what Tommi pulled from the register. A nice little haul for a night of work that was busy, but not so busy as to beat me into the ground. I stick the wad back in my pocket, alternate between the smoke and a beer.

I WISH YOU WERE here, Chell.

For a hundred reasons. A million. But right now, at this moment, it's because I'm getting to that place where I need someone to slap some sense into me. You were always very good at that.

Remember that time Good Kelli got attacked on the subway? She was coming home from work, right after rush hour, and that guy groped her on the platform. She fought him off, and when she went to report it she learned that this guy was a serial predator. She was the fifth woman he'd gone after. One of the girls he'd smacked up pretty bad, before someone came along and chased him off.

Kelli caught a blurry cell phone picture of the guy. The police put it out to the tabloids but it didn't help. Not enough of his face was showing. He was tall, wiry, scrubby beard, pale, sunglasses, hoodie. Could have been anyone.

Then he attacked a sixth girl. This one he nearly raped in a dark corner of the Prospect Avenue stop in Brooklyn.

The day I saw that, I got onto the R train. I rode it back and forth, from Forest Hills to Bay Ridge, the picture of him from that day's *Post* folded up in my back pocket. I was scanning faces, hopping between cars, looking for something familiar. The plan was to do it for a few hours each day until I caught him and did what I do best: Make him stop the bad thing he was doing.

It ended up I rode the train for nearly three days straight. I barely slept. Every now and then I'd get off to find a bathroom or something to eat. A few times I used bathrooms in subway stations, and I learned what rock bottom looks like. Sometimes I'd catch a quick nap between stops. Otherwise, it was sitting and waiting.

On the third day I was borderline delirious. That kind of tired where you feel like you're in a wind tunnel and you'll laugh at nothing, your internal circuitry on the fritz.

I was nodding off as the doors opened at Prince Street and I looked up and you were there, a brown paper bag clutched in your hand.

You were wearing plaid pants and a black T-shirt. That hair, red somewhere between the fire truck and the blaze it was rushing to put out. Those poison dart legs, and the smoke that billowed around the iris of your eye. A birthmark, you called it.

Nearly every head in the car turned. You had that kind of effect on people.

You sat down next to me, that smell of cigarettes and lavender flooding me, and you handed me the bag. It was a pile of chicken fajitas wrapped in aluminum foil from the Chinese Mexican place near my apartment. One of my favorite things to eat in the whole wide world.

This is a little silly, you said.

I ate two of the fajitas before I answered, *Good timing. I was hungry.*

Good timing? I've been looking for you for two hours.

How did you find me?

Lunette saw you yesterday. We put it together, what you were doing.

Someone's got to do it.

Why does that someone need to be you?

What else am I going to do with my time?

Sleep? Act like a normal human? Take up French?

Pause for another fajita. *He hurt Kelli. Kelli is my friend. He hurt other people. That's not the kind of thing I can abide.*

This isn't about you abiding anything. You're going to stumble across this guy? One freak in a city full of them? You're looking for a needle in a stack of needles. Understand the full scope of this analogy—the only person you're going to hurt is yourself because you are digging through a pile of needles.

Okay.

Do you get what I mean, about the needles?

Fajita. *Yes.*

Does it make sense?

Yes.

So will you let me take you home so you can sleep and eat like a normal human?

Fajita. *Okay. Yes. You're right.*

And you smiled.

That smile could punch through steel.

I wonder how long I would have kept riding that train. It would have been another day or two at least before I smelled bad enough the cops would have assumed I was homeless and tried to boot me to a shelter. And intellectually, I knew what I was doing was ridiculous. But I couldn't bring myself to get off, because I felt like if I did, someone else was going to get hurt.

Like whatever moment I chose to leave, I'd be going up one stairwell and he'd be coming down another. And it wouldn't really be my fault, but it would feel that way.

I remember trying to explain this to you on the walk back to my apartment. It didn't sound so eloquent, because by that point I was having trouble stringing more than six words together at a clip.

But you got the gist.

After I was done you said, *Ashley, you've got a big heart and I respect you for that. But you can't save everyone who needs it. All you'll do is kill yourself trying.*

Which is true, in the end.

I couldn't save you.

Does that mean I should stop trying?

The cops did catch the guy, eventually. He attacked three more women between the time I stopped looking and they picked him up.

I CLIMB BACK THROUGH the window, into the apartment. Open up my laptop and turn on some Ella Fitzgerald. A little something to fit the mood. I stare at the map on the wall for a bit. I've got enough money, maybe, once this thing with Crystal is done, to get the hell out of town and set up somewhere else.

So, where to?

New York, LA, and Austin are all out. Houston and Dallas, too. Anything in the Bible Belt, obviously. I've heard people say nice things about Ann Arbor in Michigan. Detroit would be interesting. Cost of living would be low, at least.

I look at the insert for Alaska. That could be cool. Someplace remote. I don't mind the cold. Maybe I can get far enough north to where it's dark most of the time. And there would be fewer people to annoy the shit out of me.

Throughout all of this, Ella Fitzgerald is singing "I Want to Stay Here."

Godfuckingdammit, Ella.

Portland. It's a goofy town filled with goofy people who try to bring goofy babies intro strip clubs.

And Crystal.

I poke at the stack of community college brochures next to me. The ones I picked up on a lark and convinced myself I was going to read. Even if I don't stay in town, which I'm not planning on, at least maybe they'll inspire something. I should give some kind of thought to making something of my life, other than cleaning up piss and scaring kids trying to cop a feel.

The brochures have too many words. I toss them back onto the counter.

Climb outside for another smoke. It feels nice to be outside. I'm happy I found an apartment where outside the window is the wide expanse of a roof. That feeling of the breeze, the alchemy of the cigarettes and the alcohol, those together are like a wormhole furrowed through my brain.

Sitting on the fire escape of my apartment, looking out over First Avenue.

Wandering around the East Village in a haze, ducking in and out of bars.

Working jobs for people, acting like a private eye, pretending I was the King of New York. The thing I didn't know then that I know now is that you can't own a town like that, no matter how much it feels like you do.

You're a detail. A cog in a grand machine, not valued, easily replaced.

Still. I miss it.

Christ, I get precious when I'm melancholy.

My phone buzzes in my pocket. I pull it out, don't recognize the number, nor do I care. It stops. There's a sound from inside the apartment. Tapping? I climb up and listen. Knocking. The phone starts ringing again. I answer and Crystal says, "Let me in, please."

Her voice sounds panicked. I climb in through the window and open the door and she's standing there with her shirt half tucked in, her hair mussed into a tight nest, her left hand hanging limp at her side, covered in blood.

SeVeN

CRYSTAL'S EYES ARE phased out, like she's looking through me. I grab her arm and pull her into the apartment, pry open her fingers to find there's nothing in there, no open wound, just the blood, so I bring her to the sink.

I put her hands under the running water, and I hate to be thinking it, but it's the first time I've touched a woman here in a way that's not a handshake or accidental brush, and I'm taken by how warm and smooth her skin is. I put that out of my head and take the dish soap and squirt green globs of it onto her hands.

She snaps out of it a little and begins to rub her hands together, the blood turning the water red-pink, the white-pink of her skin showing through. Definitely no cuts or nicks on her hand. I ask, "What happened?"

"There was a rat nailed to the wall inside my house. It was...

still alive."

"Fuck."

"Yeah."

When her hands are clean I give her a dishtowel and pull a beer out of the fridge, crack the top, put it in front of her. She looks at the beer and instead walks to her purse, takes out a white legal envelope, and places it on the counter. Then she picks up the beer. "There was this, too."

I open the envelope and place the items inside onto the counter.

A letter.

Two pictures of a happy little girl on a play set.

And a wad of cash.

"Five thousand," Crystal says. "I counted. Read the letter."

It's one paragraph, typed in small print on crisp white paper.

```
Dirk wasn't lying. The girl is safe.
She was placed with a family who
was very carefully vetted and she
will be well cared for. We are not
monsters. She'll have a good life.
Take the money and leave town. If
you stay, if you go to the police,
if you continue to run around with
McKenna, we cannot guarantee your
safety—or hers.
```

I read the letter four times, put it aside, and pick up the pictures. They're black and white. Rose is wearing a dress and her long hair is splayed out by the wind as she swings on a swing. There's nobody else in the photos.

The play set is anonymous, with nothing that betrays a location—no cars, no landmarks, no sense even if it's a private yard or a public playground. The photos were taken from far away. Across the street, or sitting in a car.

There are timestamps on the photos from earlier this afternoon.

That's something. That could mean she's close.

Crystal takes a long swig of her beer and puts the can down, folding the money and photos into the letter, sliding it back into the envelope. She places it on the counter and picks up her beer again.

The silence builds between us, filling up the room like smoke. I tell her, "Air would be good. Want to go sit outside?"

Crystal nods, and I climb through the window that leads out onto the roof, offer my hand, pull her through. We settle on the tar paper and light cigarettes and sit there for a bit, each of us pulling on beers, staring off into the night sky. The only sound is the wind and the quiet.

Finally she says, "I know it says to stay away from you but I didn't know where else to go."

"You did the right thing."

"I don't even know what to make of this. Who am I, that someone would do this? This is… none of this makes sense."

"I don't know."

"Why me? Why Rose?"

"I don't know. But I'm going to find who it is. I'm going to get her back."

"They threatened us. And her."

"I know."

Crystal stubs out her cigarette on the rough surface of the roof, places the tip of her thumb between her teeth and chews. She looks up at me, then away, then at me again. "Why did you leave New York, Ash? And tell me the truth. Please."

"Why?"

"Because right now I feel like you're all I've got and I still don't know anything about you. I don't know if you're worth putting my faith in."

So much of me wants to hold it back, but I feel it pressing out. Really, the way her eyes get big and the way she's looking at me right now, like no one has looked at me in a long time, is what makes me want to tell her, so I do. "The woman I loved got killed and I went after the person who did it. I made a lot of mistakes in the process."

"What happened?"

"It's a whole thing. Short version is he's in jail now. I found him, turned him over to the cops." I linger on the kicker and figure, may as well. "I really wanted to kill him and I got damn close, but I couldn't go through with it."

"Why?"

"Blood doesn't wash out blood."

"The woman. Was she your girlfriend or something?"

Pause. "No. Not that I didn't try. I mean, I loved her. I would do anything for her. She wouldn't love me back. Not the way I wanted her to."

Saying that out loud makes me feel like I'm shrinking.

Crystal makes a noise, like she's clearing her throat, or she wants to make a comment on the thing that I said but she also doesn't want to offend me. I ask, "What?"

"Just... I don't want to be a dick, but all that 'friend-zone' bullshit. It's such a fallacy. It's predicated on the idea that it's the woman's fault for not liking you."

"I gave her everything. Everything she could have wanted."

I hate the sound of my voice when I say it. The words are so much sharper than I mean them to be. Crystal shrugs.

"Women aren't slot machines," she says. "You don't put in good deeds hoping a prize comes out."

"It wasn't like that."

"What was it like?"

Her eyes poke at my exposed skin like needlepoints. I stub out my cigarette, take a long pull of beer, light another smoke. Use the things in my hands to fill the holes in the conversation. Try to formulate some clever retort and realize I can't.

"Let's not wallow in shit that's done," I tell her. "You should stay here tonight. Take the bed. I'll sleep on the couch."

Crystal makes another sound like she's clearing her throat, or like she's noting the fact that I am forcefully and quickly changing the subject. She says, "I couldn't take your bed…"

"I fall asleep on the couch more often than I fall asleep in the bed. The bed has a little more privacy anyway. This is not a debate."

Crystal takes a deep breath. "I didn't mean to say something to upset you. About the girl."

"It didn't upset me. That part of my life is far away and a long time ago."

"What was her name?"

Inhale, exhale.

"Chell. Like cello, minus the 'oh.'"

"That's a pretty name."

"Yeah."

"Ash… what are we going to do?"

"Sleep on it. Tomorrow morning we come up with a plan."

I get up and offer her my hand, pull her to her feet, but she's small and I pull her almost into me. The smell of her, that citrus scent, fills my head. We look away from each other, climb back into the apartment, and I point to the far end, where the bed is pushed against the wall and piled with blankets. "Top drawer, there's some T-shirts and shorts, if you want to change into something comfy to sleep in."

She nods, wanders over to the dresser, and pulls open the drawer. With her back turned to me, she pulls her shirt over her head, revealing her bare back, not wearing a bra, and she roots through the pile of shirts. As she turns I catch the swell of her breast, and I realize that even though I've seen her naked plenty of times, there's something about this that seems very inappropriate, so I duck into the bathroom and brush my teeth, take a piss, drink some water, wonder if the sheets are an appropriate level of clean.

When I get back out she's waiting for her turn, in a black T-shirt and my shiny blue basketball shorts. The clothes are so big on her it makes her look thinner than she really is. She's barefoot, one foot planted, the other drawn back behind it, toes spread on the floor, her hair tied back into a tight ponytail so that it shows off the part of her head that's shaved down to stubble.

"Thank you," she says.

"No problem. If you need anything in the middle of the night and you can't find it on your own, let me know."

She nods and disappears into the bathroom. I pull off my shirt, pull on a tank top, jump into a pair of shorts, and turn on the small lamp next to the bed, switch off the overhead. Just enough light for me to get to the couch. I try to settle in. Truth is, it's not terribly comfortable, and it's only two cushions long, but I'd feel bad sticking her onto the couch. It seems rude.

When Crystal is finished in the bathroom and walks past me I pretend I'm already asleep, although it seems a little absurd I would fall asleep that quick. I listen to her settling into the bed, and then the sound of her breathing.

Think about what she said about Chell.

I know the way I chased after Chell wasn't the right way to handle that. And I know that when she died she was upset with me because I let how I felt poison me. But no one's cut through me like Crystal just did. Made me feel so silly about something so big.

And it's not even a bad thing.

Task at hand. I consider the new puzzle pieces. Can't figure out how they fit into the picture. But I do remember what Chicken Man said.

I can find you anytime, anywhere.

When I'm sure Crystal is sleeping I get up and put on a pot of coffee and hope he was bluffing.

A CLATTER IN THE sink brings me out of sleep. Crystal is standing by the coffee maker, her hair slicked back and wet. She doesn't see that I'm awake. For a second I think she's staring out the window, but I see her reach her hand up to the spot over the sink where I keep the photo of my dad pinned. The picture of him in his bunker gear, standing outside his firehouse in Bensonhurst.

She touches the photo. After a few moments of looking at it, she turns and disappears into the bathroom.

When she comes out a minute later I'm sitting up, but haven't committed to standing, even with the promise of the coffee she set to brewing. My back feels like it was twisted into a knot.

I stayed up until morning light poked through the window, and something about seeing that made me feel a little safe. Safe enough to sleep. So I got two hours, maybe.

Crystal says, "I hope you don't mind. Took a shower."

"It's fine. How long have you been awake?"

"Not long. How'd you sleep?"

"Good."

I head into the bathroom to clean up, climb into the shower. Think about the beautiful woman on the other side of the door, because I can't help it. How could I not? It's been a while.

After the shower I towel off, find a crumpled pair of jeans in the corner, recycle my shirt, head out, and she's got a cup of coffee waiting for me, steam curling off the top of it. She's leaning up against the counter, asks, "No cream or sugar?"

I open the freezer and pull out the ice tray, plunk a cube into her coffee and mine. "I don't usually entertain."

"No food either."

"There's a loaf of bread in the fridge. Toast is food."

She puts down her cup. "So. What's the plan?"

The ice cube is melted so I swirl the mug a little and take a long draw on the cup. "We both have to work tonight. So how about until then we drive around. Look for people Dirk knows, or places he might be hiding out."

"What about the letter?"

"I don't think they're going to hurt her. Us maybe, not her."

Crystal puts the mug down. "I'm not going to gamble with my daughter's life."

"Chicken Man could have killed me. He could have waited in your apartment and killed you. Instead he threw five grand at you and tried to set you at ease. So there might be a line he's not willing to cross. All he has so far is threats. Nothing more than that."

"And you're still on board."

I smile at her, thinking maybe it'll make her feel better, to pretend like I'm not a little scared right now. "I told you, that douchebag still has to reimburse me for my phone."

Crystal nods. Takes a swig of her coffee. "Okay, wiseass. Can we get something to eat?"

DOWN THE BLOCK there's a place that does egg sandwiches. Not the egg sandwiches like back home, where you get a smashed white roll with an over-fried egg, a slice of American cheese and some paper-thin bacon, served up at the back of a bodega from a griddle that hasn't been cleaned since the place was built.

These things are beasts. Artisan bread, fluffy eggs, some kind of molten fancy white cheese, like gouda. Real actual bacon, thick as a piece of heavy cardboard.

The whole walk there my head is on a swivel, watching the block, the cars going by. There's not much to see. This neighborhood is generally empty in the morning. Even the people who are out, no one pays us any undue attention. Inside the restaurant there are a dozen people in line ahead of us, which means it's going to be a while. Rather than make several sandwiches at once, like an employee at any normal business, the girl at the counter with a shaved head and a brain full of THC first takes an order. She gives that order to the sandwich maker, a pale kid covered in nautical-themed tattoos, who makes the sandwich and sends it out.

They do this one at a time.

"So," I say to Crystal. "How did you and Dirk hook up?"

"We were both doing a lot of heroin. So, like that."

She doesn't volunteer any more information, which seems unfair, considering how much she wants me to share my feelings. But I let her have it.

"What if he left town?" she asks. "Maybe we should have stayed at the rail station."

"Shit, I forgot to tell you. Bombay tracked the signal. Not specific enough to get a location, but he'll know if the phone leaves city limits. If it does, he'll call me."

Crystal punches me in the shoulder. "That would have been nice to know."

"I got a little distracted by you showing up at my door covered in blood."

"You could have texted me."

"I didn't have your number programmed into my new phone."

She laughs. "I'm starting to understand why you say you're not a professional private eye."

"Wow. Really?"

She smiles.

We get to the counter, and girl gazes at the two of us like she's expecting us to break into a dance. We place our orders and I reach for my wallet, and as my hand is in my pocket, Crystal puts her hand on my wrist, her grip tight, and says, "If you're not going to let me pay you, at least let me buy breakfast?"

The clerk tilts her head at that comment but doesn't say anything about it, just accepts some bills, makes change, puts the order in. Crystal gives her name and we pour ourselves some coffee from the self-serve station. We grab an open table and wait.

We sit there, the expanse of the red-and-white checkerboard tablecloth between us. I pull out my phone and look at it, not knowing what to expect. Maybe a message from Bombay, or at least a distraction, but there's none to be found.

"So," she says. "Ashley."

The way she says it is the way everyone says it when they're trying to figure it out.

"It used to be a boy's name," I tell her. "Good Irish name. Until Ashley Abbott in *The Young and The Restless*. It first became popular as a girl's name the year after I was born. So, bad timing."

"Really? Because it sounds like your parents had a sick sense of humor."

I don't mean to, but I can feel my face twist into something unpleasant. She asks, "What did I say?"

"I'm sorry, it's nothing."

"I saw the picture of your dad. I know it was your dad. You two look alike. How did he die?"

The words leap from my mouth before I have a chance to stop them. "The towers."

Crystal arches her eyebrows. "The World Trade Center?"

I nod, not looking at her.

"Oh god, Ash. I'm so sorry."

"I hate when people say sorry. No offense. You didn't kill him, you know? What do you have to be sorry about?"

"Because it doesn't take much to see that you loved him," she says. "And I'm sorry that he's not here. He was a firefighter? Was he working that day?"

"He was off. But the FDNY issued a total recall. Everyone had to report, whether they were working or not. He got there in time to die."

Crystal nods. "Wow. Fuck."

"Yeah."

"That's just... wow."

I don't know why, but I keep going.

Maybe it's because I haven't spoken about this with anyone in a while, and it feels good to get it out, acknowledge it as a real thing that happened, and not some thing I have to carry hidden inside me. "It's a weird thing, being a kid, getting used to the idea your dad might not come home from work. Anyone's dad could not come home from work, you know? An accountant can get hit by a bus. But my dad went to a job where the chances of him not coming home on any given day were much higher. He put his life at risk so someone else would get to keep their dad. And the way he died, it was just... no reason. Mistakes other men made and he's the one who paid for it. It's a big, fucked-up thing. I don't know where to start with how I feel. Even all this time later."

Pressure builds behind my eyes. I blink it away.

"You want to know something? You want to know what I believe?" Crystal leans forward, smiling. "I believe that one day, the firefighters who responded that day are going to be like the knights or samurai of our generation, you know? Our definition of what it means to be a warrior."

The way she says it, the smile that dances across her lips, the light in her blue-green tempered glass eyes, something big and invisible fills my chest and it's all I can do to keep breathing. I fight to keep my voice level, say, "I never thought of it like that."

The woman behind the counter calls out Crystal's name. She jumps up and grabs the tray, brings it to the table. I pick up my sandwich and jam it into my mouth, try to eat. It singes the top of my mouth and my throat is thick so it's a struggle, but I'm thankful to have something to hide behind.

Needing to move onto another topic, I tell her, "I know it's a little rude, because not a lot of the girls like being asked this, but I figure... it's different now, right? Is it okay if I ask your real name?"

She looks up, unblinking, her face straight. She swallows the bit of sandwich that's in her mouth and says, "My name is Crystal."

CRYSTAL SWINGS HER car up a tight incline, flashing her lights and pounding on her horn. Multiple signs plastered on the walls suggest she do this. The parking garage for Powell's is terrifying. The ramp is a hard blind turn that's big enough to barely fit one car and it's meant to go two ways. I grip the car's oh-shit handle the whole way.

We get up into the lot unscathed and she pulls the car into a free spot. After dropping the keys off with the attendant we head inside to find that the entire store is wall-to-wall people. The Strand in Manhattan is like this, constantly packed so it's hard to move through the stacks, but this place is humongous. Like a warehouse, sectioned off and full of books. So big the rooms are color-coded.

It's a good place to waste a day, wandering, drinking coffee, flipping through books for snippets of stories, and best of all, being alone in a crowd. Everyone's attention is otherwise occupied so you can become anonymous in these aisles. Coming here is the closest I've felt to being home.

"So what are we getting again?" I ask.

"Every week I get Rose a new book," Crystal says, leading me through the throng. "I have to have a new book ready for her when we find her. She'll be upset if I don't."

We get to the kids' section and Crystal stops, staring ahead, watching little kids run around and laughing with their parents. I think she's upset to be seeing that, so I put my hand on her shoulder because I think maybe that's what she needs. She moves a little bit toward me, almost like she's going to press herself against me, and then she doesn't and we're just standing there.

The moment passes. She steps away and I ask if she wants coffee and I think she shakes her head no, so I wander in and out of the rooms, trying to remember where the coffee counter is. A half dozen times I've been here and I can never remember. I stop in the blue room for a couple of minutes—literature—because I know that's close, and I browse, check out the staff picks, see if there's anything interesting.

I catch the sign for coffee, which is in the gold room—genre and graphic novels—and make a mental note to remember that for next time. I head there and order a small to go. The barista smiles at me in a way that I'm worried might be flirting, so I nod and take the cup from her, leave my change in the tip jar. The coffee is blazing hot, so that I have to pass it between my hands every so often. I see the sign for crime and mystery books. I guess that's relevant to my interests. I walk the lane and grab a random book off the shelf. Bright yellow cover with the silhouette of a big tattooed motherfucker on the front. *The Hard Bounce*. I thumb through it. The passages I skim are funny. Though the author is probably a puny nerd who's never seen a rumble in his life, acting out some fantasy of power. Most of these authors are doing that, I figure. Still, it looks interesting enough, and I've got nothing new to read. I tuck it under my arm, take another tentative sip at the coffee, and it's still too fucking hot.

I return to the kids' section and find Crystal flipping through a stack of books, one foot curled back behind her so she's balancing on the heel of the other. I come up alongside her and ask, "What kind of books does Rose like?"

"Stuff about girls, or animals," she says, not looking up. "Adventure stuff. I like to buy books with strong female protagonists."

"What's it like?"

"What's what like?"

"Having a kid."

Crystal steps away from the shelf, moves to the next one over. "It's fucking hard. I didn't plan to have her. She just… happened. Given what I do it's not always easy, but we make it work. Until

114

now, I guess. But I don't regret it for a second. She's the best little girl in the world. Every parent says that about their kid. Every other parent can go fuck themselves, because it's true about Rose." She pauses and looks up at me. "Do you want kids?"

"I never really gave it much thought. When I first got here I thought of getting a dog. Now that I have an apartment that's a little bigger, and there's all this space, parks everywhere, I thought, dog would be cool. I came close. But I didn't because it was something I had to be responsible for. And if I'm not responsible enough for a dog, I know I'm not responsible enough to have a kid."

"Well, the beautiful thing about having a kid is everything takes so long, you get used to it. The pregnancy lasts long enough you get used to the idea of being a parent. The kid can't walk for long enough that you can get used to the idea of having some insane little person running around your house like Leatherface. By the time Rose could walk I had a pretty good grasp on it."

She stops flipping books and pulls one out, a small rigid book with a cartoon girl in a spacesuit on the front. It's called *Abby the Astronaut.*

"This is perfect," Crystal says.

We head down to the register and pay and the girl behind us in line, a white girl with a bindi, looks up at my hat and asks, "Where did you get that, man?"

"Texas."

"Are you Texan? You don't sound Texan."

"New Yorker. Born and raised."

"Oh god, you're from New York? That's so cool. I'm dying to check out Williamsburg one day. You know, fingers crossed."

"That's exactly what Williamsburg is missing. Williamsburg is missing you."

The girl tilts her head and her face scrunches into an awkward smile.

"You are such a dick," Crystal whispers. But she laughs after she says it.

WE DON'T GET lost this time as we roll toward the DXM house where I first had the pleasure of meeting Thaddeus. Not exactly someone I'm looking to revisit, but the day has been nothing but a series of strikeouts.

None of Dirk's friends have seen him. We stopped at two heroin dens. An apartment downtown and a ranch-style home way on the outskirts of town. Both places looked about the same on the inside—people sprawled out, floating between this reality and another. Unpleasant, stale smells heavy in the air. No one had seen him recently enough that it was of any use.

We stopped at a pizza place where Dirk worked for a week before he got fired for stealing out of the register, and a warehouse where he worked as a porter. Whiffed at both.

I get to see a lot of the town at least. Learn a little more about how it's put together. See some more bad driving. Though I spent a lot of the time looking out the side view mirror, to make sure we weren't being followed.

Our last hope today is Thaddeus. Maybe he's seen or heard from Dirk, and he's sober enough to relay that. Maybe there'll be someone else there. Maybe he has something, some kind of clue that will indicate where he's gone.

And hopefully nobody is touting a shotgun after having dipped into a stash of hallucinogens that were processed with tools from underneath a kitchen counter.

It's been a quiet day between us, otherwise. Crystal's words are bouncing around the inside of my chest like fireflies. I feel like I've been sitting in the fucking dark for so long, locked in a room with this part of myself that I hate. And talking to her has made me feel things I haven't felt in a long time.

Maybe there's something to this being-human thing.

As we get closer to the DXM house, I smell something burning.

It's not uncommon to smell things burning around here. Lots of leaves and fireplaces and fire pits in backyards, emanating that warm, comforting smell of burnt wood.

But this is acrid. Harsh and chemical and black.

My father would have been able to say exactly what it was. When I was a kid, we would be driving, or I'd be at the firehouse, riding along to a call, and he'd take a sniff and say, "Oh, that's a polyester couch." The way he said it was like, *why doesn't everyone else know that?*

And as we turn the corner on the block, we're greeted by a cavalcade of emergency vehicles clogging the street, their lights spinning and flashing. There's a crowd of people watching from behind green police sawhorses.

All of them are staring at the gutted, smoking remnants of the DXM house.

EiGhT

WE SIT THERE for a little while before Crystal says the sensible thing, which is: "We need to go."

She puts the car into drive, swings out a wide U-turn, and heads back toward Chinatown. Driving slowly this time, no more juking around the cars that are aimlessly drifting around the road like clouds.

"What the fuck?" she asks.

"Got me."

"Do you think this has anything to do with the people from the cartel?"

"They were processing drugs with stuff they probably got at the local hardware store," I tell her. "That seems like a good recipe for going ka-blooey."

We stop at a light and Crystal looks at me. "Do you really

believe that? That it was an accident."

"Not really, no."

We drive in silence the rest of the way to the club.

SOON AS I walk in the door Tommi pulls me aside and asks me to grab some cases of beer from the basement and mop up both bathrooms because she didn't have time to get to them today. Crystal scurries off to the back and Tommi realizes we came in together and she narrows her eyes.

"You two carpooling now? You're buddies?" she asks.

"I'm charming."

"Right. Get to work."

So I do, on autopilot, my hands hauling the beer and wringing out the mop, and I know they're my hands, but I feel disconnected from them. My brain is spinning too hard, so it doesn't engage with the rest of me, like a gear that's come loose.

Okay. Think it out.

Dirk takes the kid, gives the kid to a foster family. But he's insulted at the idea he's not invested in her well-being. He's not selling the kid into anything hellish, or so he says. Another party, presumably not Dirk, is telling us that everything is okay and to fuck off.

So why take the kid in the first place?

This would make some kind of sense, maybe, if Crystal was a bad mom and he was trying to save the kid, which I've got no indication is true. Dirk may have had designs on being a dad but he lacked follow-through, and this whole thing sounds like Rose is with a complicit third-party. She'd have to be. How do you make a kid disappear like that?

So Dirk is trying to leave town and we stop him—I think we stop him—but someone was meeting him at that train station. Someone who didn't want me talking to Dirk. Most likely Chicken Man.

Maybe it's connected to the DXM lab, maybe not. If it is… maybe someone's trying to erase Dirk? If the explosion at the lab was set off on purpose, that makes sense, a little. Like someone is wiping their arm across a chessboard and knocking off all the pieces.

Unless it was a random explosion related to drug manufacturing, and then who the fuck knows?

My head hurts.

The crowd ebbs so I belly up to the bar and Tommi puts a glass of ice water in front of me. I consider asking for something a little harder but figure she wouldn't want me drinking on the job. Hood doesn't drink—I don't know if that's by design or what. I take a sip of the water and watch as Carnage finishes collecting the piles of bills at the foot of the stage and grabs her clothes in a tight wad against her bare chest and Crystal replaces her.

Her black hair is pulled into a tight ponytail, so tight it looks painful, showing off the shaved part of her head. Red red lips on white skin. She's wearing a sheer black thing and big leather boots that go up to her knees, with silver zippers running down the inside. Black gloves that look like velvet.

Once she's on the stage she makes a big exaggerated smile and winks at a scruffy-looking guy with big glasses sitting at the foot of the stage, and Carnage cues up Crystal's songs on the way back to the dressing room

First up is "Faith" by George Michael.

Crystal spins around the pole, contorting her face into pleasant shapes.

In the car, in my apartment, she's small and sharp with an iron shell.

She's a completely different person up on stage. Big and magnetic. Beckoning to the crowd, wanting to bring them in on a secret, but a secret they have to earn first. I take another sip of water, feel a rush of heat course through me.

She's beautiful. Not the way she looks. That too, for sure, but there's something about her that puts me at ease. And I haven't felt at ease in a long time.

The way she carries herself, the way she looks at me, the way she says the thing I need to hear. She cuts through my bullshit in a way like Chell did. I don't know if that bodes well or not, but it's still nice.

As George Michael sings she tugs at her gloves, slowly getting them off, twirling them around, tossing them back toward the mirror behind her, and she goes at the black sheer thing, peeling it from her body like tape, and it won't come free easy. Like it's trying to keep you from that thing you want.

Fuck that sheer thing.

She dips her right thigh and pops back up, rotating her entire pelvis like greased-up gears, perfect revolutions all the way around, and it near knocks me off my feet.

By the end of the song she's naked save the boots, which I

know she won't take off, and she looks up, in the gap between the words, and she sees me staring, and I want to look away because this feels rude. But I don't. I hold her blue-green tempered glass eyes and smile and she winks at me.

The way she winks.

Fuck.

The second song comes on. "This Must be the Place" by the Talking Heads. Dammit, she's got great taste in music. And this wouldn't seem like a song that's made for stripping but on Crystal it fits like racing stripes. She drops into a split, driving her pelvis into the ground, but I'm suddenly less interested in what she's doing, and more interested in the two guys sitting in the far corner of the stage by the back wall.

One is heavyset, with short, curly black hair, like he's got a pad of steel wool glued to his head. Thick in the chest and the arms with skinny legs that look like tent poles. The other is scrawny with a patchwork beard that's probably supposed to be cool but really makes him look like a rat.

Brillo Head and Rat Face are going back and forth, talking intently, glancing around like they're playing the angles of the room. A couple of glances over at me, too.

The one thing they're not looking at is the knock-ass gorgeous woman who is twirling in front of them, naked for the world to see.

Every now and again some asshole comes in and ignores the girls, acts like he's too good for them, but really it's a game. Like maybe if he acts like he isn't interested it'll make him seem mysterious.

This doesn't feel like that. This feels like something else.

The song is winding down and Crystal is spinning faster, and I put my hat down over my drink and cut around to the high-top table behind these two knuckleheads, because maybe I can listen to what they're saying, or else at least I'll be in position if they pull something.

Which, in fairness, this all might be paranoia.

There's a lot going on and it's not entirely unexpected for me to start jumping at shadows.

As I reach the table the song ends and Crystal drops to her hands and knees, picking up the dollar bills that made their way onto the stage, and the two guys are getting to their feet now, so I push past them and start picking up bills too, like I'm trying to help, but really I'm putting myself between her and them.

She looks up at me, confused, but doesn't stop picking up the money.

One of them taps me on the shoulder. I turn and it's Brillo Head. He says, "You bumped into me."

"Please accept my sincere apologies."

He laughs like a cartoon bear, says, "I don't appreciate your tone."

I think he's kidding, playing at being a tough guy, and his hand wraps around my neck before I have the chance to get my hands up. Fuck, he's fast. My lungs scream from the sudden lack of oxygen. I reach for him but he pushes his weight into me, slams my head against the mirror. The panel cracks and I fall to my knees.

Someone screams.

There's no music playing now because it's between sets, and I look up and Rat Face is scrambling up on stage, where Crystal is holding the remnants of her clothing in tight fists.

I manage to reach over and hook my hand into Rat Face's belt and I pull him back down, and he barrels into me and Brillo Head. The three of us tumble into a pile on the floor. I roll away, extricate myself from the mess, and jump to my feet. Rat Face seems like the easier of the two to handle, so I jab him in the nose, enough to break it and make it bleed, and he gets all worked up over that, which lets me focus on Brillo Head.

We're both on our feet, squaring off, and he looks like he can handle himself. Like maybe this won't be easy.

At the same time, my body is telling me to hold back.

To not give myself over to that feeling.

Control your anger before it controls you.

Inhale...

Brillo Head charges. I sidestep. The punch he throws glances off the side of my head. It hurts, but I've had it worse. I get behind him and use his momentum, push him into the wall. He spins around and I duck, but not well, and he body-checks me. I hit the ground and curl up as his foot slams into my ribs.

Something shifts that shouldn't shift and breathing suddenly becomes so difficult I think it's better to not do it.

I roll onto my back, try to brace myself, and that's when I see Crystal, reassembled in her sheer outfit. She's above us, lifting one of the bar chairs above her head, and she brings it down on Brillo Head. The chair splinters but doesn't break.

Same with Brillo Head. He splinters, doesn't break.

But it distracts him long enough that I can throw my fist into the back of his knee, and he buckles, almost comes down on me, and it would be a little funny if that's the thing that ends up killing me. Big dude falls on me. Hell of an epitaph.

But he stays on his feet, and Rat Face, blood cascading down his face, is grabbing at him, pulling him toward the front door. They stumble through it, nearly pulling down the black velvet curtain in the process.

Seems they've had enough of kicking my ass.

I stare at the ceiling.

It's made up of tin panels. They look nice.

There's a huge crashing sound and glass is raining down toward me. I squeeze my eyes shut, turn over, and roll away, right over the brick they threw through the window.

I keep rolling, until there's dirty purple carpet under me and I can get up without slicing myself on something, my body knitted together with bolts of pain. When my feet are sturdy underneath me I turn and find Tommi on the phone, Crystal holding the broken bar stool, everyone pushed up to the far corners of the room, as far away from the mayhem as they can get.

The mirror behind the stage that isn't broken shows that I've got blood smeared around my face. The mirror that is broken shows me how I feel right now.

THE CHANGING ROOM for the dancers feels like an overpacked storage closet. Which is essentially what it is. Since there are only three girls on rotation at any given time, it's outfitted with three crumbling vanities and a desk that was salvaged from a curb somewhere. The vanities are for the girls and the desk is for me and Hood to split, not that we keep anything there.

The vanities are overflowing with feather boas and see-through underthings and messy piles of half-used makeup. Each one has a mirror that Hood attached to the back with scrap wood and assorted screws.

As I'm sitting at the vanity farthest from the door, I try not to look at my face in the mirror across from me. Crystal dabs at it with a towel, her tits showing through the sheer thing she's wearing. It strikes me as not cool to stare. Can't look at my face, can't look at her tits. I don't know what to look at. On the makeshift desk Hood and I split is a box set of *Battlestar Galactica*. I focus on that.

"That was some beating," she says.

"I'm a popular guy."

"You were holding back."

"I did the best I could."

Tommi peeks her head through the door. She can't come in because there's so little room. She looks at Crystal and asks, "How's my delicate little flower doing?"

Her words are so drenched in disdain it's dripping off and pooling on the floor. That hurts worse than anything else.

"I'm fine, Tommi," I tell her. "Guy got in some lucky shots. And there were two of them."

She doesn't acknowledge me, just ducks out.

The wet towel in Crystal's hand comes back from my head pink.

"Do you think that has anything to do with what's going on?" Crystal asks.

"Those two assholes? Maybe. I think maybe. They were looking for a fight."

"Why?"

"It looked planned. Like they were specifically looking to stir shit up."

Crystal leans forward to get a look at my face. She puts her hand on my chin and pushes my face to the side to look at my cheek. Says, "Want to make sure the glass didn't get you."

She leans in close, and her red red lips on white skin are close, and there's a tug of gravity between us. I can feel her breath on my face. I stop just shy of pressing my lips to hers, because it feels wrong, what with everything going on.

Crystal verifies that wrong feeling when she turns her head away from me. "I'm sorry."

"I know. Don't apologize. I'm sorry."

She turns back, looks me in the eye. "You're a good guy, Ash. I like you. It's on the radar." She looks down and laughs. "I don't know what it is about me and guys who are so good at getting in trouble."

"Guess broken people are just attracted to each other."

Crystal's blue-green tempered glass eyes frost over. She punches me in the chest, hard. She sticks a finger in my face. "You think because I'm a stripper I'm broken? That's a shitty thing to say."

"I didn't mean it like—"

"Yes you did. You meant that because I made some mistakes in my past and I take my clothes off for money I'm, what, it takes me down a couple of notches? I make good money and I own my decisions. I own my body. Don't fucking treat me like I need fixing."

Before I can say anything, and it's not even like I can think of anything to say, Tommi pokes her head back in. "Cops are here. Do not use the word 'bouncer,' okay? You don't have a license and I don't need the trouble. I've got some people ready to back you up that it was all self-defense."

I nod, turn to Crystal. "How do I look?"

She doesn't say anything, just stares at the back of the room. I get up and squeeze past, make my way through the silent bar, a slight breeze wafting in from the broken window. On the way I take a sip of my water, the ice melted, and pop my cowboy hat on.

The two cops waiting for me out front are young guys. Tight buzz-cuts. Their nametags say Queally and Kurtz. Other than the color of their hair—Queally's is jet black, Kurtz's is sandy—it would be hard to tell them apart at a quick glance. They carry themselves wound up, ready for what's coming next. Like two young Marines home from the front. They look me up and down and they don't bother to introduce themselves.

Queally says, "You're the guy."

"I'm the guy."

"Want to walk us through this?"

I recount the story, give them a rough approximation of what the two guys looked like. Leave out the information about how maybe they're connected to some insane fucking conspiracy about a missing kid and a cartel and the blown-up house of a drug manufacturer. I wonder whether I should come clean and tell them about Rose—and if I was smarter, probably I would—but I keep that card hidden in the deck.

The two of them listen but don't move. I can't get a read off them and it makes me uncomfortable. When I'm done Kurtz says, "So you're hanging out, they attacked you, that's it."

"I got the sense they were here to cause trouble. I got up in between them and the girl."

"Why do that?"

"I'm nice."

"Want to hand over some identification?"

I pop out my driver's license and hand it over to Queally. He looks at it, says, "New Yorker." He pokes his buddy. "Dude's name is Ashley."

"I'm the modern-day boy named Sue," I tell them.

They both look at me with mixed-up expressions.

"Forget it," I tell them.

Fuck, man. You can't trust anyone who doesn't get a Johnny Cash reference.

Queally hands back the ID, asks for some contact info, so I rattle off my cell phone number and he writes it down in his palm-sized leather notebook. I ask, "Any of the other clubs dealing with problems like this?"

That was a stupid question. Their antennae go up.

Kurtz puts his hands on his hips. "Why would you ask that?"

"I'm a curious guy."

They know I'm not curious. That there's something bigger in there. I suddenly am extremely not thrilled about them having my contact information. That puts me on a record somewhere. In a file. Findable.

They don't dig, thankfully. Queally shrugs and says, "Haven't heard anything."

Kurtz looks around to make sure it's the three of us standing out on the sidewalk. He leans close, and in a quiet voice says, "Well, you must be looking forward to a nice night."

"What's that mean?"

"You saved that girl, that's worth at least a blowie, isn't it?"

"That's not why I did it."

Kurtz smiles. "Right, man." He turns to Queally. "Maybe we ought to come by after shift? The gashes always go nuts for a badge."

Queally forces out a smile. The kind of smile that says: *I need to agree but I kind of don't want to*. So I figure he's not a complete scumbag. Emphasis on the word *complete* because he chooses to say nothing. Leaving me wide open to make this worse.

Kurtz sees something in my face because he says, "Aw, I was just messing around. Don't be so sensitive. Save it for a better class of pussy."

Control your anger before it controls you.

Inhale, exhale.

I take a small step toward Kurtz and say, "Doesn't matter if you're kidding or not. That's a shitty sentiment."

His face darkens and his voice gets heavy with authority. "You have a problem, kiddo?"

"I have a problem with people saying disrespectful shit."

"Who the fuck are you, talking to me like that?"

"I'm the kind of guy who doesn't hide behind a badge or a gun. That's who I am."

Kurtz purses his lip and steps toward me. I tense my shoulders, waiting for whatever he's planning—a shot across the jaw or a pair of handcuffs. He's ready to do something. It's it in his eyes. He's used to the respect that comes with his position, and doesn't like when that respect isn't bestowed upon him.

Queally pushes into the space between us, puts his hand on my chest, tells me, "Back away."

To Kurtz he says, "He's not worth it."

Kurtz looks over Queally's shoulder. "Maybe I should dump the badge and gun in the car. See if you're still a tough guy?"

"You're setting a sterling fucking example for the local police force. I hope you know that."

"Motherfucker..."

Queally pushes Kurtz hard. "Get in the car. Two strikes, remember?"

Kurtz huffs, gives me some stink eye, and walks away.

Queally looks back at me. "You didn't need to provoke him."

"He doesn't need to be a dick," I say.

He starts to say something and stops, clamps his mouth shut. I turn to the bar, feeling much better for not having brought up Rose.

Naturals is empty now, just Tommi cleaning up and Carnage and Calypso sitting in the corner at a table, pulling on glasses of wine. I sit at the bar and Tommi says, "Some hell of a bouncer you turned out to be."

"Tommi, look..."

She puts her hands up. "It is what it is. Can't help it if those two hammerheads are intent on trouble. You didn't bring them here."

I'm not so sure that's true, but it's still nice to hear.

"Want me to do something about the window?" I ask.

"Hood is out getting plywood and we'll get the window covered up. That'll have to do for the night."

"I'm not fired?"

"No, you're not fired. But whatever you said to Crystal back there, be sure to make it right. You getting your ass kicked is one thing. You fuck with the girls here, that's for sure I'll beat on you worse than those two idiots. Then I'll fire you. Then I'll kick your ass again. Now take off. Go home and clean up."

I head for the back room. Crystal has changed into a black T-shirt and purple jeans, lacing up her sneakers. She looks up at me and her face is a flat line.

"Want to get out of here?" I ask.

She walks past me like I'm supposed to follow her. I think. Maybe.

As we get outside the front of the bar my phone buzzes. I pull it out and it's Bombay.

As soon as I answer he says, "I'm going to text you a phone number. Get to a pay phone and call me back from there."

"Fuck do you mean? Tell me what you found."

Crystal stops midway to lighting a cigarette, watching me.

Bombay says, "Ash, I'm serious. Pay phone."

NINE

YOU DON'T KNOW how hard it is to find a working pay phone until you actually need one.

Crystal trails after me as we zig-zag through Chinatown, where the occasional crowd stands outside the occasional bar, but otherwise the area is deserted.

Neither of us speaks.

What is there to talk about?

I know what I want to say. It starts with an apology and spirals downward from there. What I said was shitty. I thought it was clever or thoughtful, like I found a common thread connecting us. But she's right: It was an unfair assumption to make.

At the corner of a half-empty parking lot I find a bank of three phones. The first, the receiver is missing. The second seems to work but I pick it up and it screams static at me. The third, there's no sound. There's still a mess of adrenaline built up in my blood and I slam the phone against the receiver and Crystal jumps. The handset cracks and, satisfied I've made my feelings clear, I place it back in the cradle.

She puts her hand on my shoulder. "Relax."

Control your anger before it controls you.

Inhale, exhale.

We walk some more.

Crystal struggles to keep up. "You walk too fast," she says.

"I walk normal."

"Fucking New Yorkers."

"Making jokes now? Are we friends again?"

I slow my pace a bit so she can walk alongside me. She doesn't speak for half the length of the block. We stop at a corner to let a car drift past and she says, "It was a dumb thing to say."

"I know. And I'm sorry."

"Good."

We turn the corner, and there, lit by a streetlight like a beacon, is a single pay phone on an otherwise empty block. I grab it off the receiver and get a dial tone, dig into my pocket.

No change.

I'm about to slam the phone against the receiver again when Crystal holds out a handful of quarters. "For laundry."

I plug them in, dial the number Bombay texted to me. The phone rings. Across the street there's a mural, big bright rainbow-colored cartoon characters working on a community garden. Christ, even the graffiti here is lame.

Bombay picks up. "Dude! The fuck took so long?"

"Do you know how hard it is to find a working pay phone? Anywhere in the world?"

"There's one right down the block from me. I'm on it now."

"How does that help me?"

"Admittedly, it does not."

"What did you find out?"

Bombay clears his throat. "Couple of things. I got some information on the cell phone. There's this guy I work with who owes me a favor and doesn't ask questions. Though, truthfully, he likes the challenge and probably would have done it anyway. But I figured, if there's a kid involved, I'd do what I can."

"Thank you."

"Let's not make a habit of this. It makes me uncomfortable. So the cell is in Portland. I can't tell you exactly where, only that it's pinging between a couple of local area codes. I've got an alert set up so that if it leaves those area codes I'll get a notification. Good so far?"

"I got that much from your weird coded nonsense earlier, yes." I kick the metal base of the pay phone. "What else?"

"There's a phone number that's been calling this guy a lot in the past week. Two dozen times, about. The number came back to a woman named Ellen Kanervisto. She's a local activist with a group called Keep Our Water Clean."

"That is... strange."

"I can only tell you what the numbers tell me. I found something about her in one of the local papers. She's speaking at a civic meeting tomorrow. Something about a chemical the city wants to add to the water supply."

"That it?"

"That's it. I'll text you the time and address," he says.

"Oh, now you can text me? Why not do that in the first place, instead of sending me trekking through fucking Mordor to find a pay phone?"

"Dude, first off, you're being melodramatic. Second, you do know we had to break a whole bunch of laws to do this, right? You understand that because I come from a Muslim background and I work with computers, the chance of my phone being tapped is not outside the realm of reason, right? This is called being safe."

I kick at the metal base of the pay phone a little more. "Fair enough. Thank you, Bombay. I really appreciate this. I know it's a lot to ask."

"Don't go killing anyone."

"That much I can promise you," I tell him.

He pauses. I wonder if we've been disconnected. Then he says, "That's good. That's very good to hear."

"Okay. Love you, brother."

"Love you, too."

Click.

I hang up the phone and run through the new information with Crystal. She doesn't recognize any of it, or have any ideas of why an environmentalist might be trying to get in contact with Dirk. We light cigarettes, stew over things for a few minutes, and I shrug. "So we go to the meeting tomorrow. Maybe talk to this Ellen woman and see what's up?"

Crystal exhales a cloud of smoke. "I have a better idea. We steal her cell phone. Maybe we can trick Dirk into telling us his location. Because what if we talk to her and she doesn't want to give him up, or tries to warn him or something?"

"That's a terrible idea. Let's do it."

"So... I should go home."

She gives me this look when she says that, and I don't know what the look means. All I know is how far she's standing away from me, which is far enough that if I put my hand out I would barely miss being able to touch her. That's the only thing I can tell right now.

"Maybe you should stay at my place again tonight," I tell her. "Just to be safe."

Crystal narrows her eyes at me. "I'm not going to fuck you."

"I'm not asking you to fuck me."

"That sounds like a back door invitation to me fucking you." She laughs, lowering her voice to a deep purr. "Oh, baby, I just want to keep you safe. Come on by tonight, and if you want to be a little more comfortable, take your panties off."

"I'm not that kind of guy. I promise. Just... let's go. I just need to stop at the club real quick and pick something up. Then we'll go back. Okay?"

Crystal pauses. Looks past me, above me. Seems to consider a lot more than what I'm asking her.

Finally she says, "Okay. Let's go."

A N HOUR'S WORTH of research later, and my head hurts.
This meeting tomorrow night is taking place in a school, and it's hosted by the feds, and it's about some kind of chemical

additive that's supposed to be dumped into the river.

Portland has a rep for being a green and clean hippie-dippie city, which is a little funny considering the Willamette River, which cleaves the city in two, is filthy. Part of it is a Superfund site, which means it's so dirty the federal government has given it a special earmark required for cleanup.

The riverbed is apparently a sludge of agricultural waste, raw sewage, heavy metals, and industrial run-off. Not as bad as the Gowanus in Brooklyn—a waterway so polluted I'm convinced you would melt if you fell in—but it's still pretty bad.

That's the riverbed. The actual water is a bit cleaner, thanks to conservation efforts. Apparently it's safe enough to swim in because the levels of E. coli are below hazardous levels.

Personally, I feel like any E. coli is too much E. coli, but I don't judge.

So as part of the Superfund cleanup, the feds are testing a new chemical with a name half as long as my arm. According to extensive studies, including animal trials, it's completely safe, and has successfully eliminated a lot of the contaminants present in controlled conditions that are similar to the Willamette. Something about ionization and chemical binding and blah blah yawn science.

On the whole, it seems like a pretty good idea, but here's the funny thing about it: Ellen Kanervisto and the Keep Our Water Clean group are protesting the use of the chemical that's supposed to keep their water clean.

They don't want chemical additives in the water, even if that chemical additive is meant to clean the river. Her and the other members of her group are sure that there's some kind of conspiracy abounding, and point to a discredited study saying the chemical creates mercury-like compounds.

This meeting is part of the environmental review process, in which the government will explain why it's a good thing, and people will complain about it. It sounds like literally the most boring thing I might ever have to sit through in my entire life.

There's a scrape and a bump from the front of the apartment, and Crystal comes through the front door carrying a box of pizza. My stomach drops. "I thought you were picking up Thai?"

"Everything's closed. I know a late night pizza place. Only option."

"That's not pizza."

Crystal plops the box down on the coffee table next to my laptop. "What do they say about beggars and choosing?"

"I'd rather go out and beg on a corner for food than choose to eat this pizza?"

"Ha ha."

I close out the windows I'm reading, shut the laptop, and bring it over to the kitchen counter so I can plug it in to charge. When I get back Crystal is already in the same basketball shorts and T-shirt from last night. She sits on the couch and opens up the pizza box. I put a beer down in front of her.

"What do you think?" she asks.

"Doesn't look right. Doesn't even smell right."

"Just try it."

I sit across from her and take a piece. It's smaller than a slice of pizza is supposed to be, and thicker. Can't fold it right. The cheese has weird dots of yellow, like there's cheddar in the mix. That makes my heart hurt.

She takes a big bite of her slice and smiles. "C'mon. It's been a rough week. We earned some carbs."

I contemplate the slice a little more. "And why couldn't we order in again?"

"Because if we were lucky enough to find a place that delivered to this neighborhood, which we probably wouldn't, it would take two hours and there'd be a service charge. Easier to go out and get it."

"Do you ever feel bad about the fact that you live in a fake city?"

"Do you ever feel bad about the fact that you're a whiny fuck? Eat."

I gird my stomach and take a tentative bite. The sauce is sugar sweet, and the cheese is a weird texture. It doesn't pull like regular cheese, coming off in a clump. These people have never heard of oregano. Greasy, too, leaving a film on the inside of my mouth.

Crystal smiles. "Good, right?"

"I refuse to call this pizza. But it's food, and I need food."

"You fucking diva."

We sit and eat, me mostly cramming it down my throat. It's not entirely unpleasant if I don't think too hard about it. When there are three slices left in the box Crystal takes it and puts it in the fridge, comes back and falls into the couch. She puts a fresh beer bottle on the table and nods down toward the glass of whiskey I poured for myself earlier, which I have yet to touch.

"You going to drink that, or is it for display?" she asks.

I poke at the glass with my finger and it slides across the table a little. The thing I had to pick up from Naturals was a bottle of Jim Beam, which I had to settle for since there was only one bottle of Jameson but plenty of Jim sitting in a carton in the basement. I figure Tommi will understand. I'll pay for it, even if it means paying what she would have earned on it rather than what it's worth.

I pick up the glass and hold it under my nose. It stings a little, but it also smells warm.

"Been so long since I had a drink like this," I tell Crystal. "A real drink."

"Why did you stop?"

I put the glass down. "I didn't like the person it turned me into."

Crystal arches her eyebrow. "Why did you need to start again?"

"I wanted to have it. I don't know. I don't know what to say."

"Ash…" She sits back into the couch, like she's settling in for something. "Tell me again why you left New York. I know you told me, but I feel like there's more to the story. Like there's something you're not telling me."

"What does it matter?"

"Because it looks like you're carrying something heavy."

The glass has beads of sweat running down it, the ice cube I dropped in long since melted, lightening the color of it from dark amber to light bronze. I pick up the glass and hold it to the light and press the rim of the glass to my lips and take a sip. It's not the whiskey I drank, but it's whiskey, the smell and sting of it breaking open something that was closed.

I put the glass down. "Chell. The girl who died. I didn't kill the guy who murdered her. But I came close. I'm glad I didn't. I made a decision about the kind of man I want to be, and that's someone who's doesn't kill people. But between Chell and my dad, that place was hanging over me like a burden. My dad being dead... I felt like there was something I needed to live up to. He was this grand ideal of heroism and here's me, doing drugs and getting drunk and beating the shit out of people and thinking I'm somehow making good on that example. And I wasn't. I was just a stupid asshole. Still am. I'm not a good person. I don't understand anything about myself and thought getting out of town would help."

Crystal wraps her lips around the rim of the beer and takes a long swig. "So that's what this is about? You're trying to prove something to yourself?"

"Yes. And no. I don't know."

Crystal nods, slowly. Sneaking up around the edge of something. "I want to ask you something else. It was the question you didn't answer the other day."

I take a sip of whiskey. She takes a sip of beer. We place our drinks down on the coffee table, amidst the wet circles where they previously sat.

"Okay," I tell her.

"When we went to the garage, I asked you if you had a death wish and you didn't answer me," she says. "And, honestly, this whole thing is insane. You've gotten beat up. Someone pulled a gun on you. You could have gotten killed in that garage..."

I put my hand around the glass. Don't pick it up. Feel the cool condensation on my hand. And I don't say it to Crystal, I have to say it to the glass. "I don't want to kill myself, but I'm indifferent to the concept of dying. I feel like if I did it would be like dust blowing away in a strong wind. Does that make sense?"

I pick up the glass and finish it in one gulp, the burn of it filling me with warmth. I get up from the couch and go to pour myself another, prepare to finish the bottle and smoke a hundred cigarettes, like I used to when I wanted something to be numb and gone, but find Crystal is standing behind me. I turn to her and she reaches up and puts her hand on my cheek and says, "You are broken, aren't you?"

"I don't know what I am," I tell her. "The only thing I know is that I don't like the way I am."

She nods, pulls me into her, into the crook of her neck. I inhale, hard, that smell of citrus. She always smells like it, even though she's showered here and is wearing my clothes, and I wonder if it's something in her purse that she puts on, or if she always smells like that.

I press my face into her smooth skin, feel her small, tight body against mine, and wonder if I'm going to be able to get through this without crying.

Yes, I think so. Maybe.

Crystal pulls away from me. She moves her face close to mine and I think she's going to kiss me, but she dips her mouth and presses her forehead against my lips. She asks, "Will you sleep with me tonight? No fucking. Just… share the bed?"

I nod, nothing left to say. No witty rejoinder. I'm hollowed out. The physical toll of honesty.

She steps away from me and takes my hand. I reach back for the bottle of Jim, to bring it with me, and she shakes her head. "You don't need it."

I shut out the lights, so there's only the soft amber glow of the lamp on the bedside table. She leads me over to the bed and climbs in, pulling me after her. She lays down facing away from me. We slide under the covers and I cross my right arm under my head, and I don't know what to do with my left arm, so I press it against my side as I stare at the back of her. She's still facing away from me and she says, "You can put your arm around me."

Her voice is so small.

I slide toward her and place my arm over her waist. She takes hold of it with both hands and pulls it close, like a teddy bear. I can feel her hands, and her breasts pressing through her shirt. Her black hair falls into my face and it tickles my nose.

"How did Rose get her name?" I ask, because she's asking so much about me, and I want to know something about her.

"When I found out I was pregnant, me and Dirk decided we needed a fresh start," she says. "Get off the drugs, live a better life. So we moved here because we heard it was pretty and we didn't have any hookups. It worked out for me, not so much for him. Anyway. When we first rolled into town, we were in the car, and I was sleeping. I was only a few weeks along at that point, but I knew it was a girl. From day one, I knew. And I woke up and there's this neon rose. It's over one of the buildings downtown. And as soon as I saw it I just knew. Rose is a part of this town as much as she's a part of me. She was the new thing we were going to have in a new place. A blank slate."

Her voice catches a little at the end.

"What's wrong?" I ask.

"Rose has this recurring nightmare. There's this thing that stalks around the outside of the house, and when it crashes through the window to come after her, she wakes up. I had her draw it for me. It's a big man wearing a luchador mask. Like a Mexican wrestler. I don't even know where she learned what a luchador mask is. So she would have the dream and wake up and come get in bed with me. We'd sleep like this, with me behind her and her curled up into a ball, like a little pill bug."

Crystal makes a noise that sounds like a sniffle. Like maybe she's clearing her sinus, or crying. I can't tell which without her looking at me. She grips my arm tighter, wrapping herself around it.

"I hate the idea of her being somewhere right now and maybe she's having that nightmare and I'm not there to comfort her."

Crystal brings her hand up to her face, probably to chew on that ragged nail. I take her hand and intertwine my fingers with hers. She lets me.

"It's going to be okay," I tell her.

"You're not a bad person, you know," she says. "A bad person wouldn't care."

She kisses my hand.

Now is when I'm glad she can't see my face.

TEN

A KID WEARING A dingy rainbow poncho, with a mustache that curls up on the sides like a silent-film villain, walks up to the microphone. He puts his mouth directly on it to speak so that there's a blast of static. He makes a face, leans back, tries again. "Sorry. So, I think we need more bike lanes in Hazelwood? Also in Hillsdale, and Mill Park, and Wilkes..."

The moderator, a middle-aged, beer-gutted man, his skin shiny with flop sweat, sighs. He glances at the glossy boards surrounding him, displaying colorful graphs and pictures of the river. He shrugs at the stenographer at his side, a doe-eyed brunette in a pink sweater I'm sure he fantasizes about, given the creepy glances he's been throwing her way.

The moderator leans into the microphone perched on the table in front of him next to a blank paper coffee cup. "Sir, this is a public forum to discuss the Willamette River. Do you have any comments about the river project?"

"I thought this was a public forum?"

The man wants to laugh, I can see it stalking around the edges of his mouth, but he stops himself, knowing how well that would go over. He says, "Yes, about the river project only."

"Uh… maybe we need more bike lanes along the river?"

"Okay, sir. Noted. Thank you for your contribution."

The man in the poncho smiles, looks around, confused a little about where he is: A public school auditorium, the place a third full, the crowd spread out along the worn wooden seats that are bolted in rows to the floor. Voices echo off the hard surfaces. Ellen Kanervisto is in here somewhere, I hope, but I can't see her. I pulled up her profile on Facebook, found a girl with big brown eyes who looked Hawaiian or Malaysian, with a sloppy wool cap and a warm smile. Crystal and I don't have much choice but to sit and wait for her to get called to the mic.

Which, hopefully, will be happening soon.

I dig a finger into my leg to try and keep myself awake. This is boring. So far one person has spoken in favor of the project, and I'm pretty sure that person was a plant, because she was dressed too neatly and sounded rehearsed. Like she was reading facts off a card.

The rest of the people who've spoken have all been against the project, deriding it for releasing another chemical into the river. Every time someone speaks against the project, little cheers erupt from around the auditorium. Every time those cheers erupt, the moderator sinks into his seat a little.

In a general sense, I would never trust a man wearing a suit, but I feel a little bad for the guy.

Crystal's head dips back. I turn to her and she yanks it back up, opens her eyes wide. "Sorry," she whispers. "Tired."

Her being tired makes me think of this morning, when I woke up, rolled over and away from her, completely out from under the blanket, which she had wrapped around herself like a cocoon. I felt good. Better than I have in a while. I stayed like that for a half hour, staring at the ceiling until she woke up.

Then we got out of bed. Got food. Checked on the club to make sure things were okay, and to see if Tommi was still mad at me. Which she is, a little.

Then we came here and it's been an hour of people droning on about bullshit I don't care about.

Pretty dull, compared to the last few days.

The moderator shuffles through the pile of cards in front of him. We were invited to fill out a card if we wanted to speak— both of us declined. He takes the top card and holds it up and squints, like the handwriting is sloppy, and says, "The next speaker is Ellen... Kanvista?"

Ellen pops up from her seat across the auditorium like she had a spring underneath her. She's slim, in a black sweater and gray tights, with a shock of electric blue hair. That's why I didn't recognize her. Her hair wasn't dyed in her Facebook profile. She strides to the microphone and says, "Thanks for giving us this opportunity to speak out against your plan to rape our river."

Crystal drops her head into her hands. I laugh at that, loud enough that a couple of people turn and shoot me dirty looks.

I lean over to Crystal. "She didn't bring a purse up with her to the mic. She was sitting by herself. See if her phone is in there. Grab it and we go."

Crystal nods and gets up. I expected a bit of pushback. But no, she is very enthusiastic to commit petty larceny.

Ellen is leaning into the microphone, so closely there are little bursts of static. "What you're doing is removing from us any ability to make a choice here. You're going to dump chemicals in the river and hope it fixes other chemicals. Well, what happens when you turn up something wrong with this chemical?"

Not a terrible point.

The moderator looks like he wants to argue back, but he's not allowed to.

Crystal is making her way to the seats just as Ellen says, "I know you've already made your decision and this whole thing is a charade, but if you have any decency you'll consider what everyone has told you tonight. We don't want this. Thank you for your time."

Fuck. I was hoping she would talk longer.

She turns as Crystal sits in the seats behind where Ellen was sitting. Crystal disappears from view, presumably to reach underneath and dig through Ellen's purse, but Ellen has finished walking along the front row and has turned down the aisle. The moderator is sifting through the cards so I climb up onto my seat and put my hands in the air.

I scream, "Attention, everyone!"

Everyone in the auditorium stops and looks at me, including Ellen. The top of Crystal's head appears and disappears again. Good girl.

"I am a clever diversion!" I yell.

The man in the poncho starts clapping and smiling. I look back at him and he throws me a thumbs-up. I bet he's high.

The moderator looks desperately toward the back of the room, at a heavy-set rent-a-cop who's struggling to get out of his folding chair and is furious he's been called upon to do something.

Crystal pops up from behind the seats, cradling something in her hand, close to her body. She looks at me and nods. Seems like something finally went our way. I tell everyone, "That will be all. Please continue."

I hop off the chair and head for the back, everyone in the place staring at me.

IT'S TURNING TO night when we get outside. That place in twilight when it's not dark enough for your eyes to adjust, but not light enough to make things out. Crystal is holding a small black thing in her hand. "Got it. What the hell was that?"

"What was what? My clever diversion?"

"That."

"I had to give you more time. Ellen was headed back to her seat."

"Did you have to say it was a diversion?"

"Does it matter? Let's do this quick."

We get to Crystal's car and climb in. I leave my door open so the dome light stays on and take the phone, press the button on the top. A grid of icons slide into place over a picture of a sunset. It's not password-protected.

"We ought to buy a lotto ticket later," I tell her.

I click into the recent calls, and then into contacts, but don't see Dirk's name. Same with the texts. I click through deleted messages. Nothing.

"That's weird," I tell Crystal.

She takes the phone out of my hands, checks a few more things. "No deleted voicemails. Nothing. But this is the phone."

"Is it?" I take it from Crystal and check for the phone's number. I find a pen and a scrap of a receipt in the center console and jot it down.

Crystal sighs. "Now what?"

"Take the phone back. When the forum is over she'll be looking for it. Hand it to her and tell her you found it between the seats and that she must have dropped it."

"Why do I have to do it?"

"I look way less trustworthy than you."

Crystal squints at me, says, "Yeah, you do."

We get out of the car and I'm rooting around in my pockets for my smokes when Ellen and another guy come around the corner. They're not looking at us, they're both looking down at a phone, their faces glowing with a faint blue light. There's a soft chime on the phone in Crystal's hand. She looks at me, looks down at it, and holds it up. There's a text message that says: *Stay where you are. We're tracking you, asshole.*

"Great," I tell her, taking the phone out of her hand. "Get in the car and go. I'll figure something out."

Crystal hands it over and heads toward the driver's side. I don't wait for her because Ellen and her friend are turning toward us, and I don't want them to make the connection to her. Crystal pulls away in the opposite direction and I dart down a side street and start jogging. Good thing I started smoking again.

Now what?

I really want to get her phone back to her but would rather not have the conversation about why I have it. Something about her melodramatic performance at the forum tells me she won't accept it quietly. I get to the corner and turn. I'm in a residential neighborhood, all houses and cars and bikes and square angles. I have no idea where I am. I hate not knowing where I am.

Another block, and down the way I can see a yellow bike rack that's shaped like a giant pair of eyeglasses. There are a dozen bikes chained up to it. I bet there's a coffee shop nearby. I trot toward it and find that, yes, there's a little café tucked into the street between the homes.

I duck inside and grab a napkin from the counter with the milk and sugar, wipe down the phone, and place it on the counter. A girl with a black trilby on her head and a smattering of facial piercings turns to me and puts on a forced smile.

"Found this right outside on the sidewalk," I tell her. "Maybe the owner will come back for it."

She reaches for the phone and I spin around and practically run out the door. She calls after me but I don't want to stop so she can get a good look at me, and hopefully Ellen and her friend can track it back to here.

Not ideal, but she'll have her phone back and I'll feel like less of a dick.

The street is still empty, so I run off and turn the corner.

Straight into Ellen and her friend.

Fuck. Wasn't thinking. Should have gone the other way.

I put my head down, mutter an apology, and keep walking. But I hear them mumbling behind me and Ellen yells, "Hey."

My clever diversion, it seems, was not that clever.

I keep walking but there's a crunch behind me, and the fall of footsteps, so I take off without looking back, because I know I'm in the wrong here and I don't have too many other options than to get away as quick as possible.

Something hard hits me in the back and throws me forward and I hit the ground, skid across the pavement, arch my back to keep my face from bashing into the sidewalk. My knee comes down hard. I try to roll over but there's something on top of me, crushing my lower back and my stomach so that I want to puke and can't breathe at the same time.

A male voice yells, "Where's the phone, motherfucker?"

My face is pressed onto the sidewalk so I twist and try to push the words through my compressed sternum. "Coffee shop."

He pauses. A little bit of the pressure comes off and it gets easier to breathe. He says, not to me, "Go to the coffee shop. I'll hold him until we know he's telling the truth."

Footsteps recede and enough pressure comes off that I'm able to get out from under the guy and scramble to my feet. He stays close to me, holding onto my wrist, and he's strong. Trained in something, because he's not exerting a whole lot of effort and my arm hurts like crazy.

I still can't get a good look at him, since he's mostly behind me. He says, "Whether she comes back with the phone is irrelevant. I can't decide between calling the cops and kicking the shit out of you. One of those things is going to happen."

"Look. I know you're pissed. You have every right to be. It's a long story but I promise you we were about to bring the phone back. This got a little out of hand…"

The pressure increases. I bite my lip and twist my body to follow the arc of my shoulder. Feels like something tears. He gets close to my ear and I can feel his hot breath exploding on my skin. "Shut the fuck up, asshole. You keep talking and you're going to get that beating."

"Man, it's just a phone. C'mon. Control your anger before it controls you."

"What kind of Buddha bullshit is that? You know what? Some people need to get smacked around a little. It's the only way they learn to not do stupid shit."

"I got the phone!" Ellen calls out from the bottom of the block.

The guy releases his grip on me a little so he can turn to look, and I take that opportunity to spin around and plant my elbow into his eye socket. He backs up, folding in half at the waist, his hands up at his face, but doesn't drop. I tell him I'm sorry, then I step back, put my boot into the crook between his shoulder and his neck, and push. He goes sprawling back and I'm running in the opposite direction before he hits the ground.

MY LUNGS FEEL like papier-mâché, ready to shred. I stop in the shadow of a tree that hangs down and creates a shade of black deeper than the night sky. There's some movement at the end of the block so I duck through a high wooden gate, into someone's backyard. Put my hands above my head to give my lungs room to expand. Take big, greedy breaths.

Stupid. So incredibly, monumentally stupid.

That guy was doing what I would have done in that situation. What he thought was the right thing. But a beating wouldn't have turned out well, and calling the cops would have been even worse. The latter being the more likely conclusion. I can't afford to end up sitting in a cell. Too much to explain now, and too few good answers to actually explain them.

As per usual, I am the cause of my own suffering.

Once my heart has slowed to acceptable levels and my eyes have adjusted to the darkness in the backyard, I can make out a rail-thin old man in a gray sweat suit and black wool cap doing yoga. The backyard is sunken, and he's a couple of tiers below me, down big concrete steps framed by hanging branches. Legs spread, back arched, and hands spread up to the night sky. There's a koi pond gurgling next to him. I have no idea how the hell he hasn't realized I'm here.

So of course I cough. Not on purpose.

He turns and looks at me. I look back at him.

"Get the fuck out of my yard," he growls.

I know in my bones this guy is from New York, which makes me want to laugh. It's right there, in the accent, the attitude, the steel gaze. I want to make a comment about us having this kinship, but I realize me intruding on his yoga time is not a great ice breaker.

So I say, "Okay." Back out of the yard, close the gate, and find that the street is clear. I should probably call Crystal but instead

I call Bombay. Get that clarified first. He answers and I tell him, "Your intel was bad."

"What do you mean?"

"It wasn't her."

Silence on the phone. "Look... maybe we should have this conversation another time..."

I'm so deep in the burbs right now, there probably isn't a pay phone for miles. And anyway, I don't want to spend the night trying to find one. I walk to the corner so I can figure out where the hell I am, and tell him, "I think I copied that phone number down wrong. The one for your friend I'm supposed to get dinner with. Can you read it off to me?"

Silence. Then he catches on and tells me the number.

Definitely not the one I saw in Ellen's phone.

"That's a start," I tell him. "It seems I copied the address wrong, too. The place I went to, my friend wasn't there. Do you think you can get me the correct address?"

What I mean is: What's the address where the phone is registered?

More silence. I'm really hoping Bombay will indulge me here. There's a difference between being paranoid and being safe. I'm generally in favor of being safe, but right now I feel like he's being paranoid. I get to the corner and there's not a car or a person out, and another stretch of homes and trees, and I wonder if I'm going to have to comb all of Portland to find another pay phone. There's a shuffling of papers and he says, "Here it is." And he reads off an address that I repeat to myself a couple of times so I can commit it to memory.

"Thanks. And did you ever find out about my friend's family? I had asked about relatives and stuff?"

"Nothing solid. I need more to go on."

"Got it. Okay. I'll see what I can get. And Bombay, listen..."

"Don't worry about it," he says. "I have to finish up something for work. Let's talk soon."

He's annoyed with me. The edge of his voice is knife sharp. It nicks off bone, even through the tiny speaker.

"You know I'm trying to do the right thing here, right?"

Bombay sighs. "The problem is the same as it always is. Your definition of the word 'right.'"

Click.

THE CAB DROPS me off in front of Naturals. Across the huge piece of plywood over the front window, spray painted in sloppy green letters, is: *Yes, we're open.*

Inside it's quiet. I think it's a weeknight so that makes sense. Calypso is dancing for the three sole patrons to Janis Joplin singing "Son of a Preacher Man," wearing a little white thing that doesn't cover up a whole lot. Tommi is behind the bar straightening up and when she sees me, I can't tell in the dim light if she's smiling or frowning.

I sit on the bar and she pours me a glass of ice water without saying anything. I stare at it for a little bit and want to ask for a Jameson, but I don't want to feel too much like I used to. Like if I drink a Jameson right now on top of everything I'll be admitting to something. So I ask for a tequila rocks and she shrugs. "You're not working."

She places the small rocks glass in front of me, poured from the well bottle. It tastes like it ran down the back of the bathroom wall on its way to the glass.

Still no answer from Crystal. I'm hoping she's on her way. I dig a handful of bills out of my wallet and toss them on the bar. She says, "I can get you a drink."

"I stopped in last night and grabbed a bottle of Jim to take home." Tommi's face points south. "I'm sorry. The liquor stores were closed. If that's not enough, you can take it out of my paycheck."

"You know there's another option than just taking liquor from the bar?" she asks. "Don't drink. If you're the kind of person who has a drinking problem then I don't need you working here."

"Tommi… I don't have a problem. I'm making good on it. You know… just, sometimes you need a drink."

"You've been working here months now and you haven't touched anything but ice water to your lips," she says. "Now you want the hard stuff. I've been around the block, kid. That smells a bit like a relapse."

"I do not have a problem."

She shakes her head. "I don't know what the fuck is going on with you. But I've got enough shit going on here. What I need is your help. I don't need you diving into a bottle or crapping out on me."

Tommi picks up the wad of bills and looks at it, and sighs as she begins to straighten them out and place them in the register. She turns them so all the bills are face up, the presidents looking toward the front door.

She turns to do something else and I say, "I don't see Hood. I wasn't supposed to work tonight, was I?"

Over her shoulder Tommi says, "Quiet night. I sent him home. I'm trying to save a little money now that I've got a fucking window to replace."

"Any new developments on those assholes?"

Tommi's shoulders slump and she comes back to me, puts her thick arms on the bar. "Son of a Preacher Man" ends and "Atomic Dog" by George Clinton starts up. Calypso is naked now save her four-inch glittery heels, reflected in the mirror over Tommi's shoulder.

"I got another phone call," she says. "They said last night was a preview and it's only going to get worse. I called the cops. They don't seem to give a shit. They told me it's probably nothing and to call if anything happens. Fucking assholes. I've got a cot in the back so I can sleep here tonight. I have a bad back. I don't want to sleep here. But I've got so much money dunked into this fucking place. Do you know how that feels, kiddo?"

"Let me stay here tonight," I tell her.

She pauses. "Why?"

"I'm stressed out, and when I'm stressed out I don't sleep well and... I'm not going to be sleeping much tonight anyway, I may as well do it here."

She pauses, stands up a little. "I can't pay you overtime or anything..."

"Not asking for you to pay me. I want to help."

She nods slowly. "Okay. Okay, thank you."

"And I'm sorry about the booze."

The song ends. It gets real quiet in the bar. In the mirror over Tommi's shoulder I can see Calypso picking up her clothes, two of the three guys picking up their stuff to leave. Their chairs scuffing against the floor. Calypso is speaking in Spanish. It's mostly gibberish, not that these guys know, but it sounds sexy as fuck, and they toss an extra couple of bucks on the elevated dance floor.

Tommi says, "It's been a rough week. I'm sorry if I was short with you."

"Don't apologize. Lots of fucked-up shit going on right now."

She looks at something over my shoulder. The third patron is getting up to leave too, so that the place will be empty. Tommi walks over to the iPod hooked into the speaker and turns Elvis Costello on low and goes back to wiping down the bar.

Calypso waves to me as she ducks into the back and Carnage comes out in a studded leather bondage bikini and looks around before disappearing back inside. Within a few minutes both the girls come out in thin robes and sit at the bar. Tommi pours white wines for both of them.

Calypso and Carnage set off into a private, whispered conversation. Sergio comes out of the kitchen with a couple of plates. He places one down in front of each girl, one for Tommi, and the last plate in front of me. It's a cupcake, dark body under a white cap of frosting.

"Vegan red velvet," Tommi says. "Let me know what you think."

I take a bite. There's an odd sourness to the icing, and it's also grainy. The cupcake itself tastes like sawdust with some chocolate flavoring. So dry I have to take a big swig of tequila to get it down, and the tequila tastes like shit, so this whole thing is not turning out well for me. I put the cupcake back onto the plate and push it away.

Sergio comes out again and looks at the half-eaten plates, does a full-body sigh. He comes over to take mine.

"Too dry," I tell him. "Sorry."

Tommi takes a bite of her cupcake, frowns, and pushes it away.

"I swear, my fucking kingdom for a good vegan cupcake," she says.

"You know the trick to vegan cupcakes?" I ask her.

"Are you a chef now?"

"The trick is you'll never make a good vegan cupcake because all the structural stuff you need, like butter and eggs, is not vegan. Why try to make something into something it's not?"

"I'd still like to give it a shot," she says. "Who knows, maybe we'll figure it out."

There's a sound from the front and Crystal comes in. Everyone nods and waves at her and she sits next to me. Tommi pours her a glass of red and goes back to whatever she's futzing with.

I run Crystal through what happened. I tell her I left the cell phone at the coffee bar, completely omit the part where I got into a little rumble with Ellen's friend. Then I go through the phone call with Bombay.

"So..." Crystal says. "What does this mean?"

"It means it's a dummy account or something," I tell her. "I don't know. But I know Dirk hasn't been calling that particular phone and I wouldn't be surprised if she has no idea who he is. So tomorrow we to go the address that's listed with the phone. Much better chance of the address being correct. The bill has to go somewhere."

"Why not now?"

"I told Tommi I'd stay here tonight. With the threats and stuff, we just want to play it safe."

"Okay. I'll stay with you."

I shake my head, take a sip of tequila. "Better if you go back to my place. No one's showed up there yet. I don't have any roots here so I figure I'm harder to track. Let's use that to our advantage. I don't want to have to worry about you and the bar."

"I'll hang out for a little bit. How about that?"

"Fine. For a bit."

WITH EVERYONE GONE and Crystal in the back straightening up her station, I can't think of anything to do but busy myself cleaning. It's silent in Naturals, the disco ball still twirling and throwing shards of light around. There's something about an empty strip club that feels vaguely apocalyptic. Like something's not right with the rest of the world. I like it.

By the bathroom there's a piece of mint-green gum stuck to the wall so I grab a putty knife from the toolbox under the bar and think about all the things I'd like to do to the asshole who stuck it there while I try to pry it off.

The lights dim further. The speakers come to life.

"Jane Says" by Jane's Addiction.

I turn and Crystal is standing by the door to the kitchen, outlined so I can see her silhouette. She lets the door close and now I can make her out better. She's wearing a sheer black shirt and a pair of boy's cartoon underwear. Ninja Turtles, I think. White with red trim. Her feet are crammed into high heels, her hair pulled back into a tight ponytail.

I put the putty knife down as she walks toward me, my heart beating like a hummingbird, so hard I'm nearly floating off the floor. She reaches her hand and pushes me down onto a red leather seat where white cushioning spills out of the gashes like it's bleeding.

"What is this?" I ask.

She stands over me, her legs spread, and she begins to shake her hips in time to the song, slowly to the right, slowly to the left, jerking a little at each ascension, like there are invisible threads pulling on her. She puts her hand on my shoulder and dips toward me. Her ponytail whips around and brushes across my face.

I ask again. "What is this?"

My voice is so low I'm not sure she could even make it out over the song. If she's even listening. Her blue-green tempered glass eyes are far away gone.

She lowers herself onto my lap and she grinds into me a little. Her body is so warm, like she just got out of a hot shower. My hands graze the smooth skin of her thigh. Her eyes come into focus and she says, "No one touches. Don't you know that?"

I drop my hands and lower my head to the side, close to her neck, her rocking her hips, take a huge breath of that smell of citrus.

"We're all made of atoms," she says. "Electrons on the outside. And electrons repel. So what you're feeling right now isn't touch."

She straightens up and reaches her arms behind her, shoulders twisting at odd angles, and the sheer thing billows and falls away, and she's naked from the waist up. She presses herself into me and I can feel her nipples through my shirt.

"What you're feeling is resistance," she says. "That space in between."

She straddles me tighter and lowers her mouth to my neck and kisses it and my body lights up like a firework. My instincts tell me to sit on my hands, to be good, to abide by the rules.

Even though I think that maybe I don't have to.

I know it's wrong of me to ask, but I do it again. "What is this?"

Crystal leans back from me, the weight of her shifting away from me but still connected to me, and says, "Shut the fuck up."

The song changes over to "Thank You Boys" as she presses her mouth onto mine and I can taste red wine.

THE WATER TAKES a couple of seconds to get warm. When it does I wash my hands and splash some of it on my face. Look into the mirror. I usually hate what I see in the mirror.

Tonight I don't hate what I see.

I finish washing up and step back into the bar, go hunting for my shirt, which is not easy, because it's a black shirt and it's still dark in here. I can still taste red wine in my mouth, Crystal having planted a deep kiss on me after she had dressed and left, me still lounging on the corner of the stage, because I figured I earned a couple of minutes of lying around and basking in the moment.

The shirt is balled up in a pile underneath the chair. I pull it back on and step outside, light up a smoke, look around at the empty street.

This fucking town, man.

It's a little goofy. Weird people doing weird things. Nothing's open late and the pizza sucks. I can't get around anywhere and I get lost so easy. No one knows how to drive and everything I know how a city is supposed to work, I can't find here.

But some of the food is really good. The quiet can be nice. I like the way things smell. That smell like it's always just about to rain. Petrichor.

Some of the people are nice, too.

THERE'S A SOUND at the front door. I jerk into a sitting position and use the stripper pole as leverage to get to my feet.

It's nearly pitch black inside because the only source of light is coming from under the kitchen door, and a little bit from the street coming around an edge of the plywood over the window. It's enough that I can make out shapes, but not much more than that.

There's a small red LED clock on the bar. It's a little after six a.m.

The front door creaks open.

It might be Tommi. It might be Crystal. I consider saying something and realize it might be neither of them, so best to use surprise to my advantage, just in case. I slide down behind the stage where I set up Tommi's sleeping bag, so whoever's by the door can't see me. Good thing I was too lazy to set up the cot.

The curtain up front that separates the club from views on the street is moving. Whoever's there is standing and looking around, probably letting their eyes adjust to the darkness before moving inside.

Yeah. This isn't right. If it were Tommi or Crystal they would have said something by now.

I'm a step ahead here, so I move over to the bar, toward the light switch, and the gun with the blanks that's under the bar.

Not ideal, but better than nothing.

The curtains part before I can get over to the gun, but I'm close enough to the light switch that I can hit that, and whoever it is will be momentarily blinded. So will I, but at least I'll be expecting it. I throw the switch and harsh light fills the room and my eyes sting. I have to force them to stay open.

Standing inside the curtain is Chicken Man, a handgun hanging down at his side.

Fuck.

He throws his hands up toward the glare. I squint through it and dive for the kitchen. There's no way out in the back so I pull up the grate that leads to the basement and I don't have enough time to climb down the ladder so I drop through and land hard, roll to the side.

There's a clattering sound somewhere above me, Chicken Man trying to navigate the ladder with that mask probably impeding his vision.

Only one place to go.

I run into the enveloping darkness at the mouth of the Shanghai tunnel.

ElEvEn

THE LIGHT THAT streams in behind me gets crushed to nothing ahead of me. I can't even see the end of the tunnel. I pull out my cell, click the top button to light up the screen, and it shows a tight, slightly curved corridor of aged, brown brick. There's a wall ahead and another pool of darkness to the left. I head for it and turn around the corner, hold my breath, listen hard.

There's a shuffling sound, grunting. A flash and an explosion at the same time, followed by a bit of the wall exploding, spraying brick and mortar at my feet. Chicken Man is firing blindly from the mouth of the tunnel.

"Missed me, motherfucker!" I yell.

I'm pretty sure my voice doesn't shake when I say this. Probably the adrenaline. Truth is, I just peed a bit.

I pull out my phone, do a quick check, and it seems that the tunnel extends for a while. I put my hand along the wall to keep braced and inch away from the main corridor.

"You're making this harder on yourself," Chicken Man calls out.

"Put down the gun and fight me like a man," I tell him. "We'll get this settled straight away."

"This is getting out of hand," he says. "So I'm going to kill you, and I'm going to go back and kill the girl, and that's when this will be settled. I warned you to keep to yourself, asshole."

"Yeah, well, I'm not that smart."

After a few seconds there's the sound of scrambling, and the crunch of dirt. I'm far enough in now that the sound is echoing, so it's tough to pinpoint the origin. I keep going, into black like I didn't know black could be, so dark it seems to be pulling me forward. I try to move quickly, keep my hand out so if there's an impediment my hand will feel it before I run into it.

It smells like dank and wet. Mildew. The sounds are getting softer behind me. I have to hope he's taking it slow, worried this might be an ambush. Like I actually have any idea what the fuck I'm doing. My hand hits something cold and metal. I move my hand around and feel it get caught between something. It takes a moment to figure out that there are iron bars blocking my path.

Okay. Getting him to follow me may have been the worst idea I've ever had. I try to squeeze between the bars but they're too close together. I'll get stuck before I get through.

There's a breath of air to my right. I reach over and feel a hole, give it a quick blast of light with my phone to check, and find a gaping maw in the brick, like something pushed itself out, bricks tilted toward me like shark teeth. There's enough room that I can squeeze into the gap. I push myself through as the footsteps draw closer.

It's tight. Bricks come loose and fall and threaten to trip me, but I get to the other side and step into an open space. Wetness in the air so thick I can feel it on my skin. There's a steady drip of water in here somewhere. I flash my cell phone. It's a small room, with a half-broken chair in one corner, and the way the light plays off the walls and the low ceiling and the wooden beam in the middle of the room, it looks like there might be someone sitting in that chair. I know it's not true but I can't scratch that image from my head when the cell phone light clicks off, and suddenly I need to be out of there.

I can't remember the last time I was this afraid. And not afraid like how you're scared of dying or letting someone down. Not afraid like there's some asshole chasing you with a gun and maybe this plan wasn't a great one. I mean that childlike fear of there being monsters in the dark. Like a razor-nailed hand is hovering at your neck, barely brushing your skin. My heart is pounding so hard my chest hurts.

There are two options: I can stay and fight. In a tight corridor I stand a chance. I could get close enough to him before he sees me that I could get the drop on him before he gets a shot off. Unless he has a flashlight or is using his cell phone like mine. I'll be a giant target that's easy to hit, either straight on or by ricochet. He's even got the added bonus of body disposal. He could leave me down here and it'd be a long damn time before I'm found, probably.

So it's that, or keep going.

There was a door across the room, I think. One more shot of light from the cell phone. There's a wooden door on the far end. It looks more like a piece of plywood on metal hinges. Tan and weak, and even if there's a lock on it, I bet I could bash clean through it.

A beam of light dances somewhere in the darkness, flitting on the edge of my vision, and disappears. He must be using something for light, and if he's close enough that I can see it, I better decide now. I head for the door, picturing it in my head, dance around where I think the beam is, and lead with my shoulder.

The door isn't locked. It doesn't even really stay closed on its own. It swings and I stumble forward into the darkness, and I hit the ground and my hand gets caught in something wet and slimy, and I want to cry out but I stop myself, get up, keep moving forward, my hand on the wall, trailing my fingers through decades-old grout that brushes off at my fingertips. Desperate to find some kind of exit.

Another flash of my cell phone. I think I see a figure ahead of me, the vague outline of a person in the distance. I jump a little and the cell phone goes dark.

I think that before it went dark, the figure moved.

I'm scared and my mind is fucking with me. That's all this is.

I can't hear anything behind me so I risk the phone again and there's no figure ahead of me.

Breathe deep.

Off in the distance I can see brick that indicates the termination of the tunnel. There's another door to the right of me now, this one heavy and wooden and seemingly new, so I go over and push but it's locked.

I put my shoulder into it, not slamming up against it as much as bracing and pushing, trying not to make too much noise. It takes a couple of tries but finally the door groans and gives way. I push into another dark space and trip over something, and there's a crashing noise as glass breaks on the floor around me. I put my hand down to break my fall, right onto something sharp that rips into the soft skin of my left palm.

This time I do yell out, jumping to my feet. The room smells like beer. The light from my cell reveals stacks of beer crates, some of which I knocked down, the floor scattered with spent beer and brown shards of glass. That explains that.

The basement of another bar. Okay, that's workable. I head for the ladder and reach for the bars and grab a rung and a jolt rocks my body as I realize there's still a piece of glass stuck in my hand.

I shine the phone on the half-moon curve of brown glass sticking out of the fat pad under my thumb. I yank it out and searing hot pain rushes in to replace it as blood weeps out. My hand feels like a piece of meat sewn to my arm. I hide the pain in a box in the corner of my mind and climb the ladder, pray that this guy doesn't suddenly appear behind me and open fire, pray harder that the grate won't be locked.

I have to assume it won't be locked. I have to. It's too easy for someone to get trapped in basements like these on accident. That's why we don't lock the grate at Naturals.

Anyway, it'd be nice if something went my way.

Since I'm climbing in the dark I don't know how far I have to go, and so when my head hits the trap door I nearly fall off the ladder, but manage to maintain my grip. I push up and out and the door moves without too much trouble. Climb into a darkened kitchen, the stainless steel glistening in a dim nightlight plugged into the wall by the stove. I close the hatch quietly and lay on top of it for a minute. It's heavy metal. It's got to be bulletproof. I can take a second to rest.

The more I rest, the more I breathe, the more the pain creeps up on me like a hungry animal.

My hand is still bleeding at a nice clip. I climb up and find a kitchen cart, roll that over the hatch, in case the guy is going to follow me. I root around in the kitchen and finally find a first-aid kit. Turn on the light and wash my hand in the sink, and it's deep, probably deep enough that I need stitches, which is not great. I hold my breath and run a finger through it, to be sure it's clean of glass. Without meaning to, I scream and double-over.

I take a minute to recover, breathing through my nose, and turn to the counter. The kit is old. The rusted tin and the stenciling make me think of World War II. But I open it and there's fresh gauze and bandages and even a tube of crazy glue. I check the wound again as thoroughly as I can, sucking in air through my teeth and thinking about puppies and Christmas as I pry the two halves of my skin apart. It looks clean. I give it a good rinse in the sink and dump some crazy glue into it, pinch the sides together, and wrap it tightly in gauze.

My head is getting muddy from pain. I think of Crystal.

The way her skin was warm. How it felt pressed against mine. The way she gripped the back of my neck, like holding on would keep her from drowning.

That helps.

My phone buzzes. My mom.

Dammit. Gross.

Her timing is pretty terrible, but I made her a promise when I left New York: I would always answer the phone when she called. Always. She encouraged me to go, could see that I needed it, but still I know it hurt. I'm all the family she has left in the world. And I'm way too guilty about it to break my promise.

I put the images of Crystal's naked body out of my head, grab the phone with my good hand, say, "Hey, Ma."

"Ashley? What's wrong? You sound like you're out of breath."

"Just out for a jog."

"If you're busy or you're just getting in…"

"Ma, c'mon. I made a promise. Though it's really early in the morning. I wish you would get a better sense of the time difference."

She laughs. "I don't always think about that. And maybe if you called me every now and again, I wouldn't feel the need."

There are spots of blood in the kitchen, on the counter, around the first-aid kit. There are big smears around where I climbed in through the hatch. Plus white dust and dirt everywhere. I grab a hand towel and go to work wiping it all up, and ask, "So how are things?"

"Good. Quiet. How about you? How's the bar you're working at?"

"It's good. I'm making some money. Meeting nice people."

"And are you still looking at the colleges around there?"

"Kinda. Here or something else, I'm going to go and finish my degree and get a grown-up job. Make you proud."

"I'm always proud of you."

The towel is getting heavy with blood so I walk to the sink, turn the faucet, and wet it a bit. The water is searing hot right off and the red blood goes pink.

"Are you still thinking about leaving?" she asks. "Last time we spoke you were thinking about going somewhere else."

I'm about to answer when the words get caught in my throat. I don't exactly know how to answer that one. Sure, a couple of weeks ago, it was simple. On to the next thing. Now I feel a tug.

"I'm not sure," I tell her. "Figuring things out."

"Oh, I see. You met a girl."

"Ma…"

"Oh, come on. I have to ask."

"There's a girl."

"What's her name?"

"Crystal."

"That's a stripper name."

"Ma!"

She laughs. "Kidding. Is she nice?"

"She's terrible and ugly and she treats me like dirt."

"Good boy. One day I'm going to have a conversation with you where you take me seriously."

I kneel on the floor to get the blood around the hatch. I bled a lot. I'm also feeling a little faint, but that might have more to do with not eating any food or drinking any water or getting much sleep since sometime yesterday.

"I always take you seriously," I tell her.

"Of course. I want to know you're happy, is all."

I lean back and sit on the floor, toss the towel up into the sink.

"I am. I'm good. For the first time in a long time, and despite a lot of extenuating circumstances… I'm feeling okay."

"I'm so happy to hear that, dear. Sometimes a change of scenery is exactly what you need to reset. Why do you think I didn't put up a fight when you left?"

"As always, Ma, you were right. Listen, I do have to go. I love you, okay?"

"I love you too. And it would be nice if you were the one who called me sometime."

Click.

I survey the kitchen, and it seems I got all the blood and dirt. There's still a mess down in the basement but I need to live with that. No way am I going back down there right now. I pick up the towel, which is now varying shades of red and black and brown. I wring it out, run the water in the sink for a bit, and fold up the towel. Probably best to dispose of it someplace else since it's coated in my DNA. I step to the front and into a restaurant with heavy wooden chairs and tables. Farmhouse-chic. Gray light sneaks in through a curtained window at the front.

There's a group of people smoking cigarettes across the street, so I don't want to go out that way. I go back through the kitchen and find a back door, check around the frame. It's wired for an alarm. This makes me nervous, so I go back through the restaurant to see if there are any security cameras, and mercifully, there are not.

So I guess I *am* going for a jog.

There's only so much you can do sometimes.

I go back to the door in the rear, kick it open, and a shrill alarm screams at me. I run down the alleyway to the street and cut a hard right. The smokers will see me but only from behind, so hopefully it won't be enough to identify me.

Once I'm a couple of blocks away I slow down a little, cut down another alley, and stand behind a garbage bin, where I dump the towel. I take out my phone and text Crystal: *Where are you?*

No answer. She's probably sleeping.

Wait.

Chicken Man said "go back and kill the girl."

Not go kill her. Go *back* and kill her.

I am suddenly not comfortable with his choice of words.

I SCOPE OUT THE front of Naturals for a couple of minutes. I need to make sure the place is locked up before I leave. The car Chicken Man had crammed me into isn't there. The street is nearly entirely devoid of cars. No people, either.

What I do end up seeing is Tommi's black pickup truck coast to the curb outside the club. She hops out and heads for the door and fuck, what if he actually is still inside? I tear down the street after her and manage to get into the door as she's made it to the middle of the room, a look of fury on her face.

"Ash," she says. "What the fuck happened here? Why aren't you in the bar?"

"One second."

I push past her, check both bathrooms and they're clear, then head for the kitchen and find the grate is still up. I get on the floor and hang my head down, which as I'm doing it I realize is massively stupid, but the basement is empty. There's dust on the rungs of the ladder. The same dust that I was covered in after I came out of the tunnels. So it's safe to assume Chicken Man climbed back out.

Safe, but not a guarantee. I close the grate and drag the corner of the prep table over it so it can't be opened from underneath and Tommi is standing over me. She grabs me by the collar of the shirt and pulls me all the way up onto my feet. "Tell me what the fuck happened, right now."

My head spins.

"Can I sit? Please?" I ask.

She throws me up against the doorjamb. "No. You can't. Tell me what's happening."

"I was getting chased through the tunnels by a guy in a chicken mask who was trying to kill me."

Tommi's face scrunches up. She takes a step back, looks down, picks up my left hand and frowns. There's an uneven splotch of red in the middle of the bandage. She puts my hand down and shakes her head. "The fuck is going on?" she asks.

"I don't know for sure. I'm thinking it might be tied to Crystal."

"How so?"

"How much do you know about what I'm doing for her?"

"Barely anything. I know she needed a hand with her asshole ex, so I hooked her up with your Pollyanna ass."

"Okay, well, things have gotten complicated."

"How can I help?"

"You don't want to get involved in this. You're already in the crosshairs as it is."

She goes rigid. "Listen to me carefully. No one fucks with my girls. So I'm in this now. What do you need?"

"Get me to my apartment. Crystal is there, and I'm worried the asshole with the gun knows that."

TOMMI HAS BARELY stopped the pickup truck when I jump out of the passenger door and bound up the stairs to my apartment.

The door is ajar.

It would be smarter to go in quiet but I'm not in smart mode right now, so I dive in with my shoulder and the door crashes against the wall. I nearly stumble over my own feet but catch myself on the counter.

The tray table I use as an island is kicked over, the window to the roof wide open. There's a coffee cup smashed on the floor. In the middle of the kitchen is my one chair, thrown onto the side, broken at the joints. There are piles of white rope lying on the floor. Someone was tied up.

There's no place to hide in the apartment, so after a quick glance toward the bed I check the bathroom and it's clear. Hoist myself up out the window, and the roof looks clear too.

As I'm looking around the kitchen for a note, a clue, anything, something on the counter lights up.

Crystal's cell, notifying her that she has a missed text message.

The one I sent her.

Where are you?

TwElVe

I HALF-WALK HALF-STUMBLE DOWN the stairs, trying to keep my feet moving right, but I'm dizzy from this. There was no blood as far as I could see, but other than that, I couldn't even make a guess at where Crystal is.

No trail, nothing.

I tried to protect her. Tried to do the right thing. Tried to keep it bloodless. I should have killed that motherfucker in the chicken mask in the parking lot when we first met.

Instead I let Crystal down.

Like I let Chell down.

Like I let everyone down, ultimately.

All because I thought I could be something I'm not.

The haze of morning has mostly burned off and the sun peeks through a mess of clouds. Disappearing and reappearing like it's sticking its tongue out at us.

I climb into Tommi's truck and shut the door and the dome light goes off. Sink into the seat. Feels like someone reached a hand up my ass, gripped the first thing that felt solid, and yanked.

"She's gone," I tell her.

Tommi doesn't move, just stares forward, her hands gripped on the wheel.

"Where do you think she went?" she asks.

I hold up her cell phone.

"What do you think…?" she asks.

"I don't know."

Tommi pulls out her own phone. "Time to call the cops."

"Fair enough," I tell her.

She's right. Time to stop playing at this.

Before Tommi can finish dialing there's a smacking sound on my window and for a second I think what I'm seeing can't be true, but it's Crystal. Alive, eyes wide, pressed up against the glass, smiling, like we're not sitting there thinking the worst. Like she went around the corner to the market and came back to a funeral.

She jumps back as I throw open the door and slide down to the pavement, my throat seized up. Crystal crouches besides me, in a pair of flip-flops and basketball shorts and one of my too-big T-shirts. I grab her and pull her close, pulling in that scent of citrus, like I was empty without it.

After a second she squeaks. "You're hurting me."

I back off the hug a little. "Sorry."

Tommi is standing over us, not sure what to do. Crystal jumps up and wraps her arms around Tommi, who lifts Crystal clean off the ground. "You had us worried there, kiddo. What the hell happened?"

I climb to my feet, light a cigarette with shaking hands, something to calm me down and settle my stomach, as Crystal tells the story.

CHICKEN MAN WAS standing in the kitchen when she opened the door.

He was all tough-guy bluster, waving the gun around, demanding to know where I was. She told him to fuck off, so he tied her to a chair. He had brought his own rope, so clearly he had some semblance of a plan.

Then he set into interrogating her. He wanted to know where I was, what we knew, where we were getting our information, why we didn't take the money and go. The whole time, she said, he was stalking the room like an animal. Furious that I wasn't there. Crystal kept telling him to fuck off, until Chicken Man got in her face and said he'd kill Rose if she didn't cooperate.

Again, she apologizes to me profusely, but she couldn't take the risk that he would.

I tell her I don't blame her and that she should keep going.

She told Chicken Man that we've been following crumbs—the cartel garage, the DXM house. He asked how we knew to go to the train station. She told him it was a guess, and he said something like: *That asshole is smarter than I thought.*

I guess he means me. Aw.

So Chicken Man wanted to know where I was and Crystal

offered to call me, to tell me to come over, figuring she would tip me off somehow. She would think of something clever to say so I would know she was in trouble.

Which isn't that original a plan, apparently.

You'll tip him off somehow, Chicken Man said.

That makes him smarter than I thought.

She didn't want to give up my location. She really didn't. She swears. But she had to weigh that against the safety of her daughter, and the weight of the gun sitting inches from her face.

And, truly, I don't blame her for telling him I was at the club.

My life versus a kid? I would have picked the kid too.

So she told Chicken Man and he left. She planned to get out of the chair and call me to warn me, but she was tied up pretty good. First she tried to tip the chair over, but she didn't have enough leverage. Then she scooted over to the counter to find something sharp. Maybe she could knock a knife down into her hand or something, like in a movie, but there was nothing within reach.

For a little while she screamed her head off, but the apartment across the floor is vacant, and the soundproofing between my apartment and the apartments below me is pretty spectacular. And that early, there's no one in the restaurant or the yoga studio. So that didn't work either.

She was finally able get a foot free enough that she could kick the chair onto its side. She collapsed into a heap and bruised herself up a bit, but the chair broke enough that she was able to get free. The problem was, the ordeal of getting free took so long that by the time she did, she heard footsteps out in the hallway, and afraid it might be Chicken Man, ducked out the window before she could grab her phone.

And she was right. Chicken Man came in, walked around, picked up a mug, and smashed it on the floor. She ran to the other end of the roof and hid behind a vent. Luckily he didn't think to explore the roof. The window had been open anyway, since it gets pretty warm in here, so it being open wasn't suspicious.

After a few minutes she heard something down on the street and peeked over the side of the roof, and watched Chicken Man get in his car and drive away. He had the mask off, clutching it in his hand, but she couldn't get a good look at his face, which was blocked by a tree. Just a flash of golden blond hair.

A few minutes later we pulled up.

She went down the fire escape on the other side of the building, not realizing I was going to bolt and tear ass up to the apartment. And she got jammed up trying to get the ladder down.

And here we stand.

Me shaking, Crystal smiling, Tommi wondering what the fuck she got herself into.

TOMMI HOLDS OUT a hand and looks down at my packs of cigarettes. I light two—one for her and a new one for me. Crystal looks at her and says, "I thought you weren't a smoker, Miss High and Mighty."

"It's been a long week. We're all falling into bad habits."

"Five minutes," Crystal says. "Let me put on some clothes and we'll lock up and get out of here."

We both head upstairs, me ahead of her, and we get inside the apartment and I shut the door and push her against it and kiss her hard on the mouth. She kisses me back and says it again: "I'm sorry."

"Just... I thought I let you down."

"I didn't mean to dredge that up."

We untangle from each other and she heads toward the bed, picking her clothes up off the floor and changing out of my clothes. I pick up the blue plastic broom and dustpan and go to work on the coffee mug shattered across the kitchen floor. It was a plain white mug but I liked it a lot. Chicken Man is an asshole.

He needs to learn about controlling his anger before it controls him.

Crystal stops at the counter and puts her hand over her phone. She looks at the text message and stuffs the phone into her pocket, struggling to get it to fit against the tight pull of her jeans.

"Do we need to talk about... before?" I ask. "At the club?"

She shakes her head, like I asked if she wanted some yogurt. "Nope."

"Because..."

Crystal flashes those blue-green tempered glass eyes. "Ash. We fucked. I think we both needed a little release. Let's focus. We shouldn't linger here."

"Okay."

She smiles as she moves toward me, and places her face close to mine.

"I will say this. You have pretty eyes," she says, and she presses her lips softly to mine. "And you're a pretty good lay, too."

I want to say something clever to that, but I've got nothing.

TOMMI IS SITTING in the truck with the engine running. We climb in and she pulls away and says, "You two can come to my place. Figure that's the safest thing. Then we'll call the cops."

"We can't," I tell Tommi.

"That seems pretty fucking stupid," she says. "In fact, I still don't know why you didn't go to them already."

Crystal holds up her hand, one finger extended. "One, what if they give me shit about being a dancer and decide because of that I'm not a fit mom." She sticks up a second finger. "We were explicitly told by the kidnappers or whoever to not go to the cops." Third. "I don't trust them."

Tommi nods her head at me. "And you trust this jackoff?"

"Hey," I tell her.

Crystal pauses for a moment. I hold my breath.

She says, "Yes. I do."

"You have people to back you up, you know," Tommi says. "Just because you're a stripper doesn't mean you're a bad mom."

"Think about me, and child protective services, and this whole fucking mess," Crystal says. "And please tell me you believe they'll give me my daughter and go? At the very least they're going to make me get a new job, and what then? I make good money dancing."

"What's your degree in?" Tommi asks.

"Medieval English literature."

"Jesus," Tommi says. "What were you thinking?"

"I love Chaucer. And Rose is safe. Dirk says it and I believe him. I know it sounds ridiculous, but he'd never let her get hurt. For all the bad shit he's done, for as much as I hate him, I know that. It's a matter of finding her."

185

Tommi throws a glance at me. "What do you think of this?"

"There are good cops and bad cops," I tell her. "It's luck of the draw. Wrong cops responds, some asshole with a chip on his shoulder, and you're fucked. And it'll always be a stripper's word against a cop's. There's no winning that fight. Plus we still don't know if this guy in the mask has hooks in the cops. If he does, that's a big problem. I think Crystal is Rose's mom and I'll follow her lead."

"What about the cops who responded the other night? They seemed okay."

"One of them referred to the girls as 'gashes,'" I tell her.

"Motherfucker!" Tommi yells, slamming her fist onto the steering wheel.

That seems to be good enough for her, because there's no more talk of calling anyone.

We drive in silence, Crystal sitting shotgun, me in the back, heading through twisting tree-lined streets. The farther we get, the more trees there are, and fewer houses. We pass something that looks like a junkyard and at the last second I realize it's a bar.

There are enclaves of food trucks set up in empty lots and big beautiful homes that look like they've come out of picture books and then there's nothing. Road and woods like we're in back country.

And then we're in a small neighborhood with quaint cafes.

This town exists in stops and starts. Like little islands of activity on a long, quiet lake.

As I'm reaching for my phone to check the time because the dash display is broken, Tommi cuts the wheel and swerves down a road that doesn't even look like a road. Gnarled trees crowding in and looming over us.

Every few minutes I catch a glimpse of something man-made through the trees. A window. A roof. A car. There are homes out there, hidden by the trees, spaced far apart, set back from the road, separated by huge stretches of woods.

Tommi swerves again and we're on a dirt path barely big enough for the pickup. Branches rap at the windshield.

Then we're in a clearing, like we were never on a road. Dropped off the edge of the earth.

There's a huge cabin in front of us, two cars parked in front of a detached garage. One is a beaten white hatchback, the other is a freshly waxed silver Jag. Opposite ends of the car spectrum.

The cabin is two stories of dark wood with green and red accents. Tommi kills the engine. The pieces of the sky I can see through the canopy are washed gray. I step out of the car and it smells green, and it's quiet, save for things moving through the brush, insects making insect noises.

Crystal says, "This is friggin' huge. And beautiful."

"This is why I married a real estate agent," says Tommi.

We get to the front door and Tommi pulls her keys out. She says, "Try to be quiet. Monique might be sleeping in."

The living room is drenched in yellow light. It really does look like you would expect the inside of a cabin to look. Big, heavy furniture. Afghans and minimal artwork. It smells like the inside of a cedar closet, and there's a cast iron stove in one corner and packed bookshelves scattered about.

Standing by the door that leads into the kitchen is a statuesque black woman in a fuzzy pink bathrobe, her head shaved, her eyes puffy and tired.

She's about to say something but then she sees us and pulls her robe tighter. "I didn't know we were having guests."

Tommi crosses the room and has to reach up. They kiss briefly on the lips, Monique not taking her eyes off us. Tommi says, "They're friends, and they're in trouble, and they need a place to stay."

Monique twists her face. "You were smoking." Tommi stammers, but Monique waves her hand. "I hate that smell."

"Momentary relapse. That's all, I promise." She jerks her head at me. "He's a bad influence."

"Hey."

Monique smiles. "Don't worry. I know she's trying to avoid the issue."

"Well, they've both been run into the ground," Tommi says. "They could probably do with a nap."

"That," I tell them, "is a wonderful fucking idea."

Monique arches an eyebrow at my casual use of profanity. I should watch that around adults. She asks Tommi, "Everything okay at the club?"

"Everything is fine."

I step to Monique and offer my hand. "Ash," I tell her.

"Your name is… what?"

"Ash. Short for Ashley. It's a girl's name."

She nods. "Huh." She shakes my hand, her grip boardroom professional. She looks up over my shoulder as she lets go. "And you're Crystal. I remember meeting you."

"At Calypso's birthday dinner. Good to see you again."

"Yes, well..." Monique pauses, clearly not thrilled she's suddenly playing host. "There's a guest suite down in the basement with a bathroom if you want to rest and wash up. There are fresh towels in the linen closet. Though since there's two of you..."

"We can share the bed," Crystal says.

I smile a little at that. Monique sees me smile and the reaction intrigues her but she doesn't say anything. "Well, off to bed, kids. It does look like you need it."

CRYSTAL STRIPS DOWN to her underwear, tossing her sweater and jeans into a pile on the floor next to her purse. She climbs into the expanse of the king-sized bed, sinking down into the plush blankets.

The guest suite feels like a hotel room. Big bed, matching nightstands, a small desk and a flat-screen television. A painting of a sunset on the wall. But instead of a large window at the end, there's a small window that looks up at the driveway.

I guess we're past pretense here. I pull off my shirt and my jeans, toss them onto the chair next to the bed, and fall next to her, the blanket practically wrapping around me. Must be a foot thick. She leans up close to me and it's warm and soft where her skin touches my skin. We lay like that for a little bit, and finally Crystal picks up my bandaged hand.

"What happened to you?" she asks.

"Oh shit, I didn't tell you about my wild adventures in the tunnels beneath Portland."

I run her through my encounter with Chicken Man and my daring escape. At the end of it she shakes her head. We lay there for a little bit, dozing, and I think she's fallen asleep when she says, "I'm still sorry about before."

"You don't have to keep apologizing."

"How did you let her down? Chell? Or how do you think you let her down? Because I'm willing to bet you didn't and you're torturing yourself over nothing."

"Why do you ask me so many questions?"

She pauses, for so long I think maybe she's drifting off. Then she says, "Because it's always interesting, what you choose to reveal about yourself."

"The night she died, Chell called me," I tell her. "She thought someone was following her. She thought she was in danger and was calling me for help. I didn't get the message because I was blackout drunk. There wouldn't have been enough time to get to her. I know that. I could have been stone cold sober and a block away from her and maybe it still wouldn't be enough. But still. When I saw the chair and the rope it brought me right back to that morning. Waking up on the floor of my apartment and the whole fucking world was wrong and I failed someone else that…"

I catch myself.

Crystal twists so she can focus those blue-green tempered glass eyes onto mine. "That what?"

"That I want to help."

It's not a good save, and she knows it, but she lets me have it.

She presses her head against my chest and I lean back, listen to the sound of her breathing, and stare up at the acoustic tiles on the ceiling.

BRIGHT GOLDEN LIGHT trickles through the basement window.

Holy shit, there's sun in Portland. That must be a good omen.

The bed is empty, the covers in disarray but still in place. We never even got under them. The bathroom door is closed and the shower is running. I pull on my jeans and my shirt and head upstairs. The first floor of the house appears to be empty. There's a newspaper on the large oak kitchen table, an empty mug with the remnants of coffee at the bottom.

In the driveway are Tommi's truck and the white beater, but the Jag is gone. I follow my nose to the coffee and find one of those single-cup makers, where you stick a plastic pod into the top and it brews one serving. It's pretty wasteful by local standards, but I'm happy to see some caffeine, so I pick out a French roast pod, the only one that isn't flavored—flavored coffee always tastes like chemicals to me—and it takes a couple of minutes, but I figure the damn thing out.

When the coffee is done I stick another pod in and let it brew, figuring either someone else is going to want one, or I'll want a second. I grab a banana from the bowl on the counter and sit with the paper, flip through, looking for something that might be interesting.

A couple of pages in I find something that stops me cold.

It's a grainy picture of the auto garage where I almost got turned into a human balloon.

The story says that it was the front for a major meth operation—duh—and yesterday it was raided by the feds. Six people were arrested. Which is a relief, because I wasn't looking forward to seeing those guys again.

Now I'm sure of it: Someone is dismantling everything in this town touched by Crystal or Dirk.

The kid, her job, his job.

And their tactics are both varied and effective.

I check my phone. Nothing from Bombay. Which would seem to indicate that Dirk is still in town, if he's still got the cell phone trace active.

Crystal appears in the kitchen, her hair wet and flat against her skull. I point her at the coffee maker. She takes the steaming mug and dumps in some milk from the fridge and sits across from me. I slide the open paper toward her and she looks at it for a couple of seconds before zeroing in on the auto shop.

"Well," she says, taking a tentative sip of the coffee. "That's weird."

I tell her about my theory. She listens carefully and shakes her head. "Why would someone do that?"

"I have no idea. Dirk being involved with a cartel, that could be related. Who knows? The important thing is we have a next step. The address where the phone was registered. We should go check it out."

Crystal takes a long sip of her coffee and places the mug down.

"Let's do that. But maybe take a shower first. You look like you got dragged behind a truck for twenty miles."

"Thanks."

THE BANDAGE STICKS a little so I yank it off, find an ugly red gash crusted with dry, black blood. I get the water as hot as it'll go and climb in, take stock of my injuries. Besides the bruise on my cheek where I got pistol-whipped, I've got some bruising on my ribs and mid-section, from where Brillo Head kicked at me. Plus a lump on my head from the garage. A cut on my hairline from the train station bathroom. Maybe some more, too. I'm losing track.

Add those to the collection: The gulch a bullet dug through my left thigh one bad night in Hell's Kitchen. The scar that runs down the back of my left forearm. A thin, tight line most people might be surprised to know was patched up with a home sewing kit.

If collecting scars by means of stupidity were a hobby, I'd be ready to go pro.

I hold my hand under the jet stream of water. It stings so bad I have to force myself to keep my hand open. Arch my back and bite my lip. The blood washes away and I'm left with the gash. Once it's clean it doesn't look terrible. And it stays closed, which is a nice bonus.

All told, I'll live.

After I'm done in the shower and I feel halfway human, I root around in the medicine cabinet, find a tube of bacitracin and some gauze. I wrap up my hand and get dressed. I wish I had some clean clothes, but it feels nice to be showered, at least.

Back upstairs it's empty again. The kitchen smells like bacon and there are dirty pots on the stove. There's a sound from outside, people laughing, so I find a door leading out toward the back.

Tommi and Crystal are sitting at a table on a small covered deck, surrounded by high bushes. Tons of colorful flowers, reds and purples and blues and yellows that I don't know the names for. Behind them are woods as far as I can see.

They're eating and smiling, talking about something that isn't drug cartels and missing girls. Beams of sunlight pass over them before disappearing behind the clouds.

I stand there and watch for a minute. Which is probably a little creepy, sure. But there's also something nice about this.

The two of them together.

I know I care about Crystal. That's easy. But I'm coming to care about Tommi, too. Her opinion matters to me. What she thinks of me. I want to make this whole mess stop as much for her as I do for Crystal, as I do for Rose. This whole little unit of mine, this little slice of my life, is starting to function. I feel less like I'm this vague idea of a thing held together by tape.

And it's now I realize that feeling—that any moment I'm going to have to pack my bags and go home—is gone.

Has been for a little while now, I think.

Tommi looks over and sees me and waves. "Food is on. Let's go."

I cross over and sit at the free chair, find a plate piled with bacon and over-easy eggs. The banana barely made a dent, and I want to jam the plate into my face. There's a little stack of toast in the middle of the table next to a pat of butter. I take a piece and spread some on, use that to attack the eggs.

"You do good breakfast," I tell Tommi. "Even though it's nearly dinnertime."

"Breakfast is about all I know how to cook."

I shove a piece of bacon in my mouth and realize what I'm

eating, ask, "I thought you were vegan?"

"Me? No, fuck that," Tommi says. As if to verify this for me, she reaches across the table and picks a couple of strips of bacon off the plate. "Monique is vegan. I'm not vegan."

"Why the vegan club?"

Tommi shrugs. "Seemed like a good idea. And we're in Portland, so you have to play to the market. Shit like that, people pay attention to. The only problem is I had the idea years ago, before any of the other vegan strip clubs opened. So it looks like I'm a copycat. But I had the idea first."

"Well, cheers on that," I tell her.

And I eat some more bacon, because bacon is good.

"So Crystal filled me in on your theory. It's not completely insane, but at the same time, it's a little nuts. I don't know. What I do know is that I'm going to keep a closer eye on my business and make sure it's okay. Here's the caveat. Another two or three days tops, then I'm going to the cops. All of us are. So go out, play detective, but come the end of the week, if this isn't fixed, we're getting it fixed. Fair?"

"Understood," I tell her, finishing off the toast.

"You can take the hatchback in the driveway," Tommi says. "Better you're driving around a car that isn't Crystal's."

Crystal says, "Thank you."

"So tell me," Tommi says to me. "How are you adjusting?"

"With what?" I ask.

"This whole country living thing."

"It's coming along."

"You know what I miss the most? Christmas in New York. I'm

not even a big fan of the holiday. But there was something fucking magical about that city during the month of December. Like the whole place was filled up with light. And everyone was slightly less of an asshole. It's the only month of the year that strangers actually acknowledge each other when they pass on the sidewalk."

"Wait… you used to live in New York?"

"For a long time." Tommi smiles at the memory. "From when I was six until I was in my late twenties."

"I can't believe we've never talked about that."

"Well, maybe if you talked a little more instead of sitting around so sullen all the time, you grumpy fuck."

"And you've been here ever since?"

"Ever since."

"How do you handle it? All this fucking quiet?"

"Are you kidding?" she asks. "That's what I left for. Do you know why people leave New York, kid?"

"Why?"

"Because eventually, you need to chill the fuck out. This is a pretty good place to do it. See, here's the problem with New Yorkers. You've all got a superiority complex, and sooner or later, you've got to get over it, or you'll find you can't function in the outside world. Yeah, our pizza isn't as good and last call is a little earlier. I miss good bagels too. But you know what? You can get a good fucking meal here. And the people are nice. And you can drive a half hour outside town and stand under a waterfall. If you want to wear that sarcasm like a suit of armor, go ahead. But you've been working for me a few months now? At least admit that you're still here for a reason."

She pats me on the arm, hard.

Crystal smiles at me.

It's the kind of smile that looks a little like a sunrise.

And for the second time in twenty-four hours, I've got nothing clever to say, and sitting there like that, in the silence of expectation, is too much. Everyone's plates are cleared so I get up and grab them, stack them up.

"I'll handle the dishes," I tell them.

Tommi says, "You don't have to do that."

"Sure I do. I owe you for a lot more than this."

"Make them shine then."

"Sure thing, boss."

Tommi and Crystal both laugh a little at that.

THE HATCHBACK GROWLS like a hungry animal, but it runs. I retrieve my cowboy hat from Tommi's truck, get in the car, and Crystal turns us around and drives slowly down the path. The sun is gone now, because it's always gone when you feel like you might need it.

I repeat the address to Crystal and she nods. "I got it. That's not even far from here."

Once we're on the street, it's only a couple of turns and we're on a hilly stretch of road with a lot of traffic. Everything around us is super fancy. There's a Starbucks, but the outside of it looks like a quaint country inn, the architecture matching the surrounding businesses.

"Where are we?" I ask.

"Lake Oswego," says Crystal. "Also known as 'Lake No-Negro.' I'm sure you can figure out why."

"Classy."

"Yeah, well, fuck this neighborhood. This is ground zero of what's ruining this town."

"What's that then?"

"All these rich assholes, moving here and ruining the character. Knocking down historic homes to put up some boring modernized cube. I swear, this town used to be so beautiful, and people are destroying her, inch by inch. Nothing is sacred."

"That's funny."

"What's funny?"

"It's the same way in New York. The reason a studio apartment rents for three thousand a month is because there's some asshole willing to pay it. That drives up the property values, which drives out businesses. Then these big, beautiful buildings get torn down so some spiritless monolith can go up in its place."

"Well," Crystal says, rooting around in her purse for a smoke. "Bullshit is bullshit, no matter where you are." She pulls one out and goes to light it, pauses. "I shouldn't smoke in someone else's car."

"Crack the window."

She considers this for a second, puts the cigarette down in the cup holder.

"So do you miss it?" she asks. "Do you think you'll ever go back?"

"I don't know if I have a good answer for that. The city's in my blood. I'll go back eventually. My mom is still there. My friends. I don't know what the terms will be."

"I've never been to New York."

"You should go."

She glances at me sideways. "Maybe you can show me and Rose around. We can all go together."

I smile. Catch myself smiling, but don't stop. "That'd be nice."

We drive a little more, down a few more busy streets clogged up with traffic. There's nothing holding up the traffic, just the roads are so narrow and it's so hard to make a left turn, so we spend a lot of time sitting and waiting.

I'm dozing off when Crystal turns down a street and says, "This is it."

We pull to the curb and the numbers next to me show it should be on the other side of the street. I hop out of the car and light a cigarette before I'm even fully standing, stretch my legs, and look across the road.

Crystal says, "Holy shit."

Across the street from us is a storefront with a big sign up top, deep French blue with white lettering.

The sign says: *Committee to Elect Mike Fletcher to Congress.*

ThIrTeEn

CRYSTAL PUTS A cup of coffee next to the keyboard.

"Black no sugar," she says. "I don't know how you drink it like that."

"I like coffee to taste like coffee. Not a milkshake."

She pulls a chair over to the computer terminal. The computer banks at the Multnomah County Central Library are empty, given the place is about to close.

I pull up Fletcher's Wikipedia page so Crystal can take a look. There's a picture of him against an American flag. He's looking vaguely off to the right. He's got chubby cheeks, a goatee that's starting to show gray, some salt and pepper in his dark hair. A grin like he's trying to sell something that's broken.

"So what have we learned?" Crystal asks.

"Mike Fletcher. A city commissioner. Made his money in real

estate before running for office. He's a little shady, some questionable donations, but from the tone of what I read it's nothing egregious, and probably par for the course. He's running for Congress and is considered to be the favorite for the seat."

Crystal leans back in her chair, picks up her coffee, takes off the lid. It's a light mocha brown, and she blows across the surface before taking a sip, legs crossed, one canvas sneaker kicked into the air.

"So what do we know?" she asks. I'm about to answer when I realize it's rhetorical. "We know a cell phone was calling Dirk, a lot, within the time that he took Rose. We know that the phone is registered to this guy's campaign office under another person. Why Ellen?"

"That," I tell her, pulling up another screen. There's a picture of Fletcher at a rally for Keep Our Water Clean. He's got his arm around Ellen. She's got a look on her face like she's tolerating him. He's got a look on his face like he wants to fuck this cute little thing he's got his arm around. "She did some volunteer work at his office."

"So the phone was used to communicate with Dirk because whoever was doing it knew it could be traced back to her, and it would be harder to make the connection to Fletcher?"

"It wasn't foolproof," I point out. "We made the connection. But it would definitely slow down whoever was looking. It looks like it was a smokescreen. Maybe she signed something without looking at it."

Crystal leans forward and puts her cup down. "So Fletcher, or someone connected to Fletcher, wants me and Dirk gone. Why?"

"He announced his campaign two months ago. Maybe

someone working for him is trying to clear his closet of skeletons."

Crystal shakes her head. "This is a little heavy. Who the fuck am I?"

"This is very fucking heavy." I pull up another photo of Fletcher. "Look at the nose. Do you know what Dirk said to me in the bathroom? He said something about what the old man told him. What if this is his dad? They kind of look like each other."

Crystal squints, her eyes opening slowly with realization. "You think this guy could really be Dirk's dad?"

"His profile says he's got three kids and his wife is his high school sweetheart. I have to imagine that he wouldn't be as viable a candidate if people knew he had another family."

"So he's trying to disappear any trace of me and my daughter so he can run a political campaign?"

"Maybe."

Crystal puts the lid back on her coffee and looks at the screen. "So where do we find him?"

"What do you mean?"

"Let's go to his office and find out where my fucking daughter is. Right now. I'll beat it out of him."

"Bad play," I tell her, bringing my voice down to a whisper, hoping she'll match. "Watch this."

One more screen, and this is the one that scares me. It's a picture of Fletcher with the head of the police union, on a news article in which he's accepting the endorsement of just about every law enforcement union in the city.

Crystal reads for a couple of second and says, "Fuck."

"Right? It looks like Chicken Man wasn't lying. So besides the fact that someone may have been willing to kill me because of all this, you think he's going to be cool with us walking in to his office and demanding answers?"

"We go to the press, then," Crystal says. "Tell them everything."

I pick up my coffee and take a sip. Too hot. I put the cup down and tell her, "That's not a bad idea, actually."

CRYSTAL ISN'T HAPPY about it but she agrees to wait in the car after I point out that it's best to keep her face out of this. I finish my cigarette as I walk across the parking lot, toward the blank office building that looms out of the trees on a blank strip of buildings near the airport.

I check in at the security desk, where a catatonic white-haired security guard prints out a sticker for me to put onto my shirt. I crumple it up and shove it in my pocket and head toward the elevators. At the third floor, I find an empty receptionist desk and stand there for a couple of minutes, thumbing through old copies of *PDX Weekly*. I'm halfway through a story about a new trend called Bacon Mondays, in which bars are offering a free strip of bacon with every drink on Mondays, which actually sounds like a really great idea, when an old woman half my height but twice as angry storms over.

"Who are you here to see?" she asks.

"Molly Rivers."

She picks up the phone, hits a few numbers, and says, "Your meeting is here." She slams down the phone and looks up at me. "You can go back."

I don't know where "back" means, but I walk through the waist-high swinging door and weave through the empty newsroom, desks bounded in by cubicles of sea green felt partitions. There's a phone ringing somewhere in the distance.

At the far end of the room is something that looks like a nerve center—desks arranged into a giant square, computer terminals and papers and telephones scattered about. I head for that and see a young girl with red hair and freckles pick up the ringing phone, clearly annoyed to be doing it. "City desk, Molly Rivers... No, I'm sorry, we don't have the manpower to cover that event... If I leave to cover your garage sale there'll be no one here to answer calls from concerned citizens like yourself... No, fuck *you*."

She slams down the phone and looks up at me, says, "You're the guy who called?"

"I'm the guy who called."

The phone rings again. She sighs, picks it up, and slams it down.

"Let's walk," she says. "I need a smoke."

She gets up from the desk and doesn't wait for me to follow. Her hair is in need of a good combing, her clothes wrinkled in the back. She looks like she's been working for days.

She leads us through a cavernous warehouse, past what I assume to be a printing press, my shoes squeaking on the shiny concrete floor. I haven't seen a single soul yet besides her and angry grandma and the security guard down front.

We get to a door with a gray metal security bar and she pushes it and steps onto a gangway over a parking lot behind the building and pulls out a pack of cigarettes. I pull out my own and offer her a lighter as she's fumbling for hers. I cup my hand around the flame to keep it up in the wind and she nods and exhales.

"It looks a little quiet around here," I tell her.

"We're about to shut down. I'm not supposed to tell you that. I'm not supposed to tell anyone that. Thank god for my fucking journalism degree." She pumps her fist. "Hooray internet."

"I'm sorry," I tell her. "Is the job market that tough?"

"I got an offer from a newspaper in Wichita. Fucking Wichita. That's not even a place. I'll be covering cows. Fucking cows."

"That sucks," I tell her. "In the meantime, I was hoping I could ask you about Mike Fletcher."

She waves her hand, which sends a veil of smoke into my face. "What about him?"

"You've written a lot of articles about him," I say. "Clearly you've done some digging. I imagine there's got to be some stuff you're holding back. Maybe information that you couldn't verify. I was hoping you could tell me about anything you've found that you weren't able to print."

"I'm sorry, who are you again?" she asks, squinting at me. "Are you doing oppo for the Osborne campaign? I don't want to get involved in any of that shit. Do your own legwork."

"I'm not involved with any political campaigns," I tell her. "I'm just a guy trying to find some information."

"Like a private detective?"

"If you want to call it that."

Molly hugs herself. It's warm out but the breeze is insistent. "I shouldn't even be out here. Auggy won't answer the phones anymore. She sits there and knits. I'm going to get my ass reamed out for not answering the phones."

"By bosses who are about to let you go. And anyway, you've got Wichita."

She laughs a little. "What do I get out of this?"

"What do you mean?"

"Nothing's free. What are you digging into?"

"I can't say yet, but I'll make you a deal," I say. "If this shit turns out to be true, this will ruin him. Big time. I'll give you everything. You'll be able to have your pick of newspaper gigs."

"So," she says, sucking on the cigarette, exhaling a cloud of smoke. "This is about the love child?"

Something in my face gives it away, because she smiles and extends a finger at me. "That's what I call a loose confirmation."

"This might have to do with that. What do you know?"

"Rumors. He had a kid outside his marriage. It's not an uncommon rumor. Every unmarried politician is gay, every married politician has a love child. But I heard it from someone who knew him, that he got a load on one night and spilled to someone that he had a kid out of wedlock, but I tried to chase it down, couldn't find any paperwork. No birth certificates with his name on them besides those three little sadist goblins he calls kids."

"That's a pretty harsh way to describe someone's kids."

She tosses her spent cigarette down toward the parking lot. "They were running around at a campaign event and knocked me down and broke my recorder. He thought it was hysterical. They're monsters. So, can you confirm the love child?"

"I don't know what I can or can't do at this point," I say. "But

Fletcher is involved in some bad shit. And once I get it sorted you'll hear all about it. Is there anything else you can tell me about him?"

She nods. "He wants to be president one day. He's said that to me on more than one occasion. The guy's a power-hungry narcissist. Though, to be fair, every politician is a little bit of a power-hungry narcissist. I forget who said it, but politics is how ugly people get famous."

"Do you think he has a chance? At the president thing?"

"A lot of people think he doesn't."

"What do you think?"

"Bush Junior could barely string a coherent sentence together and he got elected to a second term. Nothing surprises me. Fletcher is smarter than most people give him credit for. He's not an incredible speaker, but he's cunning, and when he sets his mind to winning something, he usually does."

"Fair. Last question. Do you think Fletcher is dangerous?"

That one piques her curiosity. "Dangerous how?"

"Any way that might qualify."

Molly takes a full, deep breath, and lets it out. "Here's a rumor for you. One night, a friend of Fletcher's shows up at a hospital, beaten to ever-loving fuck. His sternum was dislocated. I didn't even know sternums could dislocate. The way he tells it, he got jumped by a bunch of kids. Couldn't identify them, didn't know why they did it."

"You think it was Fletcher?"

"I'm sure it was Fletcher. I had a source at the hospital who clued me in. But there were no charges, no incident report, no nothing. I asked the cops about it and they shut me down. As it happens, the president of the police union and Fletcher are childhood buddies. Welcome to politics. It's an incestuous clusterfuck."

Nice to see my suspicious are being confirmed all over the place.

"What makes you so sure it was Fletcher?" I ask.

"I was able to connect a couple of dots. Not nearly enough for a story. Just enough to get my ass sued into oblivion if I ran with it. But I saw Fletcher at an event and his hands were bandaged up. He said his tool rack fell over. Lying fuckface."

"A beating that severe, you'd think the victim would want a little revenge."

"Remember when Cheney shot a guy in the face, and the guy ended up apologizing to Cheney? Yeah. Fletcher has deep pockets. I'm sure that one didn't come cheap. Are we done now?"

"We are," I say. "This is all very helpful."

"You're welcome," she says. "Bring me what you've got when you're done. You can let yourself out."

She doesn't wait for me to say anything, just turns around and leaves me standing there on the walkway.

AFTER I'VE TOLD Crystal what I've learned—pretty much solidifying our theory that Fletcher is Dirk's dad—she asks, "What now?"

"Now you go to the club. And I find Chicken Man. Me and him have to have a conversation."

"That doesn't sound like a good plan."

"It'll be on my terms."

We drive for a bit in silence.

Crystal asks, "So what are you going to do. Like, beat the shit out of him until he tells you where Rose is?"

"I'd rather it not come to that. If I can end this without violence I'd be very happy."

"What if you don't have a choice?"

"There's always a choice."

"But what if there isn't?"

Inhale, exhale.

"When I went after Chell's killer, I took the bullets out of the gun," I say. "I brought a gun because I wanted to control the situation and make sure he listened, but I took the bullets out. I wasn't planning on killing him. But I also figured that if worse came to worst, I could have beaten him to death with the gun. In case I wasn't strong enough to let him live."

"Seems like it would take more strength to kill him."

I crack the window and go to light a cigarette but Crystal smacks my arm, so I hold it in my palm. "It would have been weakness. I have to believe there's a way to solve things like this that doesn't involve surrendering a part of myself."

Crystal shakes her head. "Some people, there's no talking to."

I don't know if she means me or Chicken Man. I don't think I want to know.

A FTER STOPPING OFF at my apartment to get a change of clothes, I drive Tommi's hatchback toward Lake Oswego. My stomach grumbles at me.

I pass a parking lot with a circle of food trucks, so I stop and pick out the Mexican cart because it has the shortest line. At the window a teen in a starched white shirt and a yellow bow tie takes my order of a cabeza burrito and a black coffee and disappears. There's the sound of pots moving and crashing and someone yelling at someone else, and he pops up with a burrito the size of my forearm, wrapped in wax paper, along with a small cup of coffee.

I load back in the car and drive to the campaign office, park down the block, far enough away that I feel safe but can still see the front. I don't know what the plan is. I don't think I have a plan.

Sit here, wait for asshole. That works. Hopefully he's here. There doesn't seem to be a lot of activity at the office. No one's gone in or out.

The burrito is a marvel of food engineering. It's thick and packed with meat but stays together as I dig through it. And I dig through it fast. For all my complaining, that's one thing the West Coast has on New York: Mexican food.

The burritos out here are killer beasts. Mexican in New York is risky if you're not in a legit Spanish neighborhood, like Port Richmond on Staten Island or Bushwick in Brooklyn. You pay for Portland burritos twelve hours after you eat them, but it's always worth it.

I pop the lid on my coffee, get settled into my seat. It's warm so I open the window and figure I'm going to be here a while. I risk a cigarette, think a little on what Crystal said.

I feel like a walking oxymoron. I go on and on about wanting to live a nonviolent life and now here I am, charging after a man who has literally tried to kill me. For a living, I work at a place where I am expected to hurt people as a problem-solving tool. I have no prospects, no thoughts on what I want to do when I grow up—who the fuck knows when that's going to happen—and I've made a promise I'm afraid I can't keep.

What if I can't find Rose?

What if I'm a fraud, leading Crystal down a disastrous path?

Crystal doesn't deserve this and Rose doesn't deserve this.

What Dirk deserves, I haven't figured out.

What do I deserve? I have no idea. I don't know that I deserve anything.

I drink my coffee, smoke my cigarettes, doing that thing I promised I'd stop doing because I'm supposed to be a different person now, which I'm not. We're always the same person.

Change is a fun thing to talk about, even more fun sometimes to take a stab at it, but there's still that coding, deep down in the bottom of us, that says what we're going to do when confronted with a crisis situation.

Fight or flee.

I want to flee, or be smart enough not to fight.

But I think I know what my coding says.

The sun dips down and it's night. I start to doze, and occasionally punch myself in the thigh to keep myself awake. For a little while I consider heading back to Tommi's house and catching a nap. Just as I'm pulling out my phone to text Crystal to see where she is, the door of the campaign office swings open. A man in a carefully pressed button-down pink shirt and navy slacks comes out. He looks like a catalogue model. Swimmer's build. Tall. Golden blond hair, like Crystal said.

Gotcha, fuckhead.

For all my hemming and hawing over the truth of my nature, you know what? I am pretty damn good at this kind of work.

He disappears into a Starbucks across the street from the campaign office, and I wonder if this might be a good time to confront him. He can't shoot me in a Starbucks. And it's important to note he's an asshole for going into a Starbucks. Their coffee is shit and this town is full of great coffee shops.

Probably better to wait. Maybe I can find out where he's keeping Dirk, follow him back there. That would make this whole thing a lot easier. After a few minutes he comes out with a giant cup. He crumples a piece of paper and tosses it into a trash can at the curb, walks to a dark sedan. It's the car he forced me into the night we first met. It's parked five spots in front of me, which I didn't notice.

Maybe I'm not so great at this work.

He pulls away and when I'm sure he's gone, I get out and cross the street. Linger at the trash can until it looks like the street is clear. When there are no cars and no people I push open the top and stick my hand in, straight into something sticky. I pick up the lid, see that my hand is halfway stuck in a melting ice cream cone, and the receipt is a little over to the left.

I pick it up, head into the Starbucks, and go straight for the bathroom, where I wash up and unfold the paper. He bought a large peppermint mocha—six fucking dollars!—and paid with a card. There's no name on the receipt. I was hoping there would be. The only identifying detail is that his card is a Visa, and the last four digits.

I walk to the register. The surfer-dude barista with white-guy dreadlocks nods up to my hat and says, "Yee-haw. What can I get you?"

"That blond guy who was just in here," I tell him. "I saw him come out and get in his car and drive away. I think I know him. Do you know his name?"

Surfer dude nods. "He comes in here a lot. Works nearby. His name is Chris."

"Last name? Anything else about him?"

The guy shrugs. "I don't know, man. He's a bit of a dick." His eyes go wide. "I'm sorry, man, I shouldn't have said that about your friend."

"Don't worry. He's not my friend."

That didn't pan out. I turn to leave and notice a fishbowl sitting next to the register. There's a sign on it: *Drop your business card to win a free coffee.*

"Hey, did he drop a card in here?" I ask.

"Yeah, but I don't think you can…"

Before the guy can stop me I reach in and pull out the card lying on top. It has a logo for the Fletcher campaign and the name Chris Wilson.

Hello, Chris.

A LITTLE BIT OF Google-fu between the names Mike Fletcher and Chris Wilson reveals a big fat nothing. I should have followed him. I know where he works, and that's nice, but now that I'm on a roll and I've hit a wall, I'm feeling antsy.

I dial up Molly Rivers. She answers on the second ring. "What?"

"Do you know a guy named Chris Wilson? Works for the Fletcher campaign?"

"Who the fuck is this?"

"Ash. The guy from earlier."

"I have enough shit to do. I was not put on this earth to act as your assistant."

"The faster the pieces fall into place here, the faster you get your story. Maybe you land someplace nicer than Wichita."

"God, if only." There's clicking on the other end of the line. Finally she says, "I met Wilson outside a fundraiser for Fletcher. Came by way of DC, but I don't know who he is or what he does and I didn't have a reason to dig. He was a cagey asshole and didn't say much more than that. It's all I have in my Fletcher file and that's all I remember. Don't bother me again until you've got something to give me."

Click.

Fair enough. I call up Bombay. He answers on the third ring.

"What up, brother?" he asks.

"Need a favor."

"You and the fucking favors, man! No 'How are you.' No 'I miss you, buddy.' You call me out of the blue asking me to do shit for you. C'mon man, can't we pretend like we're still friends here?"

"We are still friends. You're my closest friend."

"Make me believe it."

"Bombay... man. In all this world, there's no one I trust more than you. I love you. You know that. I would call more but... I'm not a phone guy." I climb out of the car, light a smoke. "I don't want you to take this personally or anything. I'm a little jammed up right now, and I need a hand, and the reason I call you is because I trust you to help me."

Bombay laughs. "Man, I was fucking around. But it's nice to know you love me."

"Asshole."

"What do you need?"

I don't want to play pay phone roulette again, so I choose my words carefully. "There's this guy I know I'm trying to meet up with. I was trying to find his address. His name is Chris Wilson. He's in Portland via Washington, DC."

"Chris Wilson? Are you kidding me? His name may as well be John Smith."

"Visa. Last four digits are six-six-two-three."

Pause. "Is this going to get me placed on a watchlist?"

"I ran into him, he left his Starbucks receipt behind. But I lost his phone number. Don't worry. We're pals. He'll be happy to know I found him."

Keyboard keys click in rapid succession. Bombay asks, "Did you hear about Tibo?"

"He okay?"

"Fine, yeah. You remember how he wanted to build a commune someplace? He did. Down in the woods in Georgia. It's a full-blown hostel and he's the manager."

"No shit."

"Yeah, man, and he's one of many. This place is really starting to empty out. You go into Dymphna's now, there's not a single familiar face."

"Who else is gone?"

"Well, me and Lunette moved out to Brooklyn. Bad Kelli is up in Astoria now. Dave is still in Manhattan, but that dude always has money and no one can figure out why."

"How's Margo?"

"She's good. I don't see her much anymore, but she's liking school, living the NYU college kid life."

"That's good. How are you holding up?"

Pause. "Good. Just bored, man. It kinda sucks not having you around."

"Aww. Do you miss me?"

"I do. Even though you're a fucking idiot and you're constantly getting yourself in trouble and you got my apartment trashed... at least you were fun."

"Sure, let's call it that," I tell him. "Let's call it fun."

"You think you might come back soon? Or you still on your journey of personal discovery?"

"Christ, don't say it like that. I'm doing a little traveling."

"Right. What's with the girl?"

"What girl?"

"The girl in your apartment the other day. The one you're helping out. You dig her?"

"Yes, I dig her."

"Did you do it yet?" he asks. "Did you do sex to her?"

"None of your business."

"So, yes then. You're not going to move there permanently, are you?"

"I don't know what the fuck I'm going to do."

"Man, you're digging on her hard, aren't you?"

"You got anything for me, Watson?"

The keyboard strokes fall silent. "In fact, I do."

He reads off an address, says, "I'll send it to you in a text."

"Thanks, man."

Click.

The address appears on my phone, the text of it highlighted blue. I click on it, and it dumps me into a map that shows a nice, clean, direct route to Chris Wilson's house.

WILSON'S CAR ISN'T on the block. I sit there for a little while, really make sure. Maybe he's out looking for me. Joke's on him.

I get out of the hatchback and walk toward the house, looking for signs of movement. It's small, one story. Light blue with yellow shutters. There's a tiny front yard and a large backyard that goes pretty deep. I can barely make out the rear fence from the bottom of the driveway.

I'm exposed where I am, standing out like this. Anyone in one of the houses across the street could see me, so I head toward the back, keeping an eye on the windows. No movement. No light.

The yard is empty. A little overgrown. There's a shed toward the back, and next to a sliding glass door there's a folding chair and a coffee can that's filled with swollen, brown cigarette butts.

I check the back door, press my finger against the handle. It slides without much resistance. Way to keep your door locked, dummy. I get it open, step into the kitchen, and close it behind me.

The kitchen is sparse. There's nothing but a toaster and a case of cheap whiskey sitting on the counter. Next to me is a recycling bin that's full of more bottles of whiskey, all of them empty. This guy likes to drink.

I case the house, but it's clear. Everything is very neat and arranged. There are no pictures, just small piles of personal belongings, a travel bag of toiletries on the bathroom counter. Like how someone would treat a hotel room.

The only books he has are by Ayn Rand. So I know for sure he's a degenerate.

I finish up in the house and step into the yard, unsure of what to do next. I could wait for him. Hole up in the house and ambush him when he comes in the door. The only reason he's had an edge on me twice now is because he's had a gun on me. Take the gun away and I think it's more than a fair fight.

There's a blue dancing light, like a television left on, in the sole window on the shed. That's weird. I cross the grass, keeping an eye behind me, making sure there's nobody who can see me, and get up against the white door. Listen. There's definitely sound on the other side.

This door isn't locked. I open it slowly and get smacked by a wall of stench. I breathe through my mouth. There's a pile of magazines, a case of beer, and a camping toilet propped up against one wall. A couch along the other, and a small battery-operated television on a milk crate.

And a sprawled figure on the couch.

I move in and find that it's Dirk, twisted up and snoring away. He's out. Doesn't stir as I cross the shed to him, my boots echoing on the wooden floor. I stand over him and kick the couch. He wakes up with a start, looking around until finally his eyes lock on mine, and they go wide with terror.

"Been looking for you," I tell him.

FoUrTeEn

I GRAB DIRK BY the collar and drag him outside. He doesn't put up much of a fight. There was a used needle lying on the floor next to him, which seems to indicate why. I figure on interrogating him in the yard because it reeks in the shed, but the neighbors could see, so I lead him to the house, toss him onto the couch in the living room.

"Not supposed to be in here," he says, mumbling like he's half asleep.

"Shut up." I pull a chair over and sit across from him. It's dark, the light from the street streaming in through the curtains. I reach over and turn on the lamp next to him and he recoils from the amber glow.

He doesn't look good. Eyes glazed over, skin sallow. He looks like a sorry piece of shit and that little black part of my brain, tucked away and hidden, wants to hit him. Not because I think it'll get me answers quicker, but because I think he deserves it.

I push that away.

"Let's start at the top," I tell him. "Where's Rose?"

"I don't know."

"You don't know where your daughter is?"

"I met the family who took her. They were a sweet family, man. I wouldn't send her off with a bunch of freaks."

"So this is a question for Wilson?"

Dirk nods slowly, a look of fear dancing across his face.

"I want to see how much I know," I tell him. "This is what I've figured out. Wilson is paying you to leave town, correct?"

"Yeah."

"And part of that payment was to pick up Rose so that she could be sent away with another family. An off-the-books adoption? There's probably no paperwork, so she can't be traced back to Crystal. Correct?"

"Uh-huh."

"And this scare campaign against Crystal and the club is tied up in that?"

He cocks his head. "What do you mean?"

"The rat nailed to Crystal's door. The threats to the club."

"Man, I don't know shit about that. I only know I'm supposed to lay low and Wilson says when the time is right he's going to drive me out of here. He said he had to drive me because you were too close to finding us."

I pull out two cigarettes and light them both, hand one to him. He stares at it for a minute, like it might be a trap, before he snatches it out of my hand and sucks at it greedily. He says, "We shouldn't be smoking in here."

"Wilson tried to kill me. I don't care if he loses his security deposit. Hey, also, quick aside, why the fuck did you rip off a cartel? That almost got me killed."

"Yeah... I fucked that up. I think it was three grand or something that I owed them?"

"The guy who tried to violate me with a high-pressure air pump said it was ten."

Dirk's eyes go wide. "Shit. That's fucked up. I'm pretty sure it was three though. Maybe four. They tack on a fat interest rate." He shudders. "They are going to kill me when they find me."

"They got shut down. Another domino that fell because of whatever the fuck is going on with you and Crystal. Which leads me to my next question: When did you learn Fletcher was your dad?"

"What are you talking about?"

"Fletcher. He's the old man, right? Your father? He's clearing you out of here so he can run for Congress."

"Man, you got that one wrong..."

I'm about to prod him for more when his eyes settle and focus on something over my shoulder. Something hard presses against the back of my head.

I am a fucking idiot.

Three times now. You'd think I would learn.

"You're light on your feet," I say.

Wilson laughs a little, and the gun retracts. "Get up," he says.

He's wearing the same outfit I saw him in earlier. Pink shirt and slacks, sleeves rolled up, every strand of hair spackled in place. A bemused smile stretched across his sharp face. He nods to Dirk to get up and leads us both into the kitchen, where he gets us into a corner, boxed in at a right angle by the counter and cabinets.

Wilson stands a couple of steps away, holding the gun between us like he can't decide which one of us to shoot first.

"How did you find me?" he asks.

"If I tell you, will you let me live?" I ask.

"Nope."

"Well, if I'm going to die either way, then you can go fuck yourself."

"Tell me, die fast," he says, moving the barrel of the gun from where it's pointed at my chest, down to my crotch. "Don't tell me, die slow."

I need to buy some time until I can figure out how to not get shot, so at this point, there's probably no harm in giving a little up. "The cell phone. It was registered under Ellen Kanervisto's name. The address was the campaign headquarters. You should have used a burner."

"Burners come with their own risks," Wilson says. "I thought having a name attached to it would obviate the problem, but I guess not. Good lesson learned. Thank you for that."

"You're welcome. So what are you, exactly?"

"A fixer."

"You fix... what, exactly? Dumb fucking assholes who want to run for office?"

"Essentially, yes," Wilson says. "I make sure nothing can come back to bite them in the ass. It's incredibly lucrative."

"And why did you come after me so hard? Throwing me in the trunk was a little much, don't you think?"

"Your history," Wilson says. "I ran a background check on everyone who works at the club. Routine thing. I wanted to know what I was working with. I found out you were tied up in some shit back in New York. That you were something like an amateur private detective."

"How did you even find that out?"

"That's my job. Finding things out. So that night she tried to hire you, I needed to shut it down quick."

"We were alone when she spoke to me."

Wilson nods his head back and forth. "I'm good at my job. Important thing is I heard you. I figured you were smart enough to back off."

"Well, guess what, asshole? I'm not. So does Dirk's dad know you're killing people, or did he tell you to get this done by any means necessary?"

Wilson tilts his head. "Who the fuck is Dirk's dad?"

"Fletcher."

Wilson laughs. "You're not as smart as you thought. Fletcher is the stripper's dad."

Fuck.

The eyes. The fucking eyes. I couldn't see them on that shitty library computer monitor. That's what I should have been looking at.

"So, you can't run for Congress with an ex-junkie stripper love child," I say, feeling it out. "But getting rid of her wasn't enough. You were going for scorched earth. Dismantle the club, blow up the drug house, knock out the cartel garage. It's not enough that Crystal is gone. You don't even want there to be a trail. All so this goofball could run for Congress."

Wilson shrugs. "It's a living."

"Killing people is a little extreme."

He gives me a grim smile, his lips creeping up his face until I can see his teeth. "Before I blew up that house I'd never killed anyone. Came close a few times but always worked my way around it. And that guy was an accident. I didn't know he was there. But you know what I found after they pulled his body from the wreckage?" He shrugs. "I didn't care. Truly, I felt nothing."

"Well, cheers to you."

"You're so fucking funny, you know that?" His face twists. "You think you're so smart. You're such a wiseass. Look at where it got you. You thought you could fuck with me? No." He's speaking so hard now he's spitting. "I have never failed at a job. Never. And I'm not starting now. So make a joke about that. Joke about the fact that in a second you're both going to be dead."

It's there, pulsing in his eyes. A radioactive level of pride, poisoning him. The worth of a human life doesn't outweigh his desire to be good at his job.

"Can you repeat that?" I ask. "I stopped listening."

He makes an angry little noise at the back of his throat, gargling consonants, and lifts the gun.

Then, to my complete shock, Dirk saves us.

He shakes off the heroin haze and yells at the top of his lungs, "You can't kill me, motherfucker. What about all that fucking money you owe me?"

Dirk takes a step toward Wilson, probably still enough drugs in his system so he doesn't realize this is a bad idea.

Wilson swings the gun toward him, giving me an opening.

I plant my foot and launch myself forward and slam into Wilson as he fires, knocking him to the ground.

The gun roars in the small space and leaves my ears ringing, like I've been standing next to a concert speaker. The gun flies into the shadows at the corner of the room and I jam my fist into Wilson's throat. He gags and gasps for air, reaching up to hold his neck, and I roll off and go to Dirk, who's been thrown against the cabinets, a spray of blood painting the white Formica behind him.

He's still standing. Maybe I threw off Wilson's aim enough that he'll live through this. But he's wearing a black T-shirt and black hoodie so in the dim light, I can't even see where the bullet hit. A blood-drenched hand is hovering near his left flank, which gives me a sense. I grab Dirk and push him toward the back as Wilson is struggling to get up.

We run through the backyard, me more dragging Dirk than him running, and I get him over the fence into the next yard. Wilson isn't chasing us yet, but I don't know for how long. I should have stayed. Incapacitated him somehow. Too late now.

The next yard is a huge swath of green grass with a big shed in the middle of it, and maybe there's something I can use in there as a weapon, because I don't think we're going to outrun Wilson, not with the way the color is draining out of Dirk's face. The way he's stumbling like he's drunk.

As we turn the corner into the shed I realize it's not a shed. It's a stable.

It smells like hay and manure and sweat. There are two horses in separate stalls. One is brown and small, one is black and huge. The brown one makes a horse noise and the black one stares at us.

So, new plan.

It's either the best plan I've ever come up with, or the worst.

Maybe a little of both.

I unhook the gate keeping the black horse penned in and wave over Dirk, who's doubled over, leaning up against a wooden post. He looks up at me and shakes his head. "No."

"We have to get out of here. Shut up and get on the horse."

He stumbles over to me and I lean down and cup my hands. He plants his foot and grunts. I pull up, and he's not too heavy and this might work, but the horse moves away from us. I've lifted Dirk high enough that for a second he's completely suspended in air, and he slaps against the dirt floor like he's doing a belly flop into a pool. He groans and folds in at the middle.

I laugh at him a little, because even though we're now on the same team—Team Don't Get Shot—I still don't like him.

The horse moves toward the back of the stall, away from us, clearly not pleased with any of this.

Okay. Maybe this was not a great plan. But we have to get out of here. I go over to the horse to try again but now he looks agitated, whipping his head back and forth and making grunting noises. I put my hands up and back away slowly and that seems to calm him down a bit. Dirk is trying to get up so I drag him out of the pen and lock the gate.

New new plan.

There's a two-by-four leaned up against the wall, so I leave

Dirk where he is, in full view from the open door, and stand by the side. Take a deep breath. I think I hear footsteps, the sound of something crunching underfoot.

I hold my breath.

There they are. Slow, tentative steps. He knows we're in here.

The second there's movement, I swing and catch Wilson right in the face. Something crunches and he screams.

That felt good. Too good.

The gun flies from his hand and he falls to his knees, clutching his face, and Dirk seems to have caught the plan, because he's on his feet and running at me now. I put my foot onto Wilson's shoulder and push him down, and kick his gun to the other side of the stable. I hold the two-by-four over my head.

I could turn him in. Go to the cops. But with Fletcher and his connections to the police, I don't know how far that's going to get us. Maybe we get lucky, maybe we get fucked.

I could kill him. Bring the two-by-four down and crush his skull. Problem solved. It was easy for him, to take a life. Why can't it be easy for me?

Such an easy solution, too. All I have to do is swing it. Won't even take much effort. I exert more effort getting out of bed in the morning. The two-by-four is solid in my hand. Solid enough to crush a skull.

I swing down, hard as I can.

The wood connects with his ribs with a dull thud. He folds in on himself, groaning, choking.

Nope. Not crossing that line. I'm not like him. I toss the two-by-four to the ground, satisfied with my smart, thoughtful choice.

It turns out hesitating over a moral quandary was a bad idea, because it gives Wilson enough time to bring his foot up into my balls. He catches them full on and my whole world explodes. Air rushes out of my lungs and I nearly fall to the floor, but manage to keep myself up. He turns and crawls toward the corner, already closing in on the gun. I throw Dirk's arm over my shoulder and lead him out and away, through a fence in the back and onto the street.

By the time we get to the car Dirk is slowing down a bit, but he's still on his feet. I prop him up against the side of it, look back to find Wilson turning the corner toward us. I toss Dirk across the back seat, climb behind the wheel, and peel out.

As I hit the corner and turn hard into it, I catch a glimpse of Wilson in the rearview mirror, pointing the gun at us but ultimately deciding not to take the shot.

MY STOMACH FEELS like it's trying to turn itself inside out, but without disengaging from the other organs it's attached to. The burrito I ate earlier is threatening to come back up. It's all I can do to concentrate on driving.

A few blocks away now, and Dirk is wailing like a dying animal. The adrenaline or the heroin or whatever must be wearing off. I got shot once, but it wasn't bad. Cut a little path through the meat of my thigh. As gunshots go, pretty convenient. Honestly, my ruined balls feel about on par with that.

A gut shot, I got nothing on that. I've heard gut shots are the most painful because they tear up a lot of soft tissue and you bleed out slowly. Maybe that's true. I don't know. All I know is he's in a lot of pain. People get shot and don't die sometimes, I guess?

"How you holding up?" I ask.

Dirk sputters. "Hurts."

"We'll take care of you. Just stay with me. Are you sure you don't know anything about the family that got Rose?"

"They were... the coast. That's all I know."

"And you thought that was a good idea, just give her away to some strangers?"

"They were... checked out. They were good people. I can't be a fucking dad, man. Crystal can't be a mom."

"How do you figure?"

"She's a fucking stripper."

"That doesn't make her a bad mom."

"Don't fucking talk to me... like you know what's better for my kid than I do. I'm trying to make things..." He takes a deep, wheezing breath. "... right."

"And you're making a mess of it."

"Who the fuck are you to say that?"

He's got me there, kinda.

I sneak a peek into the rearview mirror but can't see Dirk. He must be all the way down on the seat. "You're such a towering moral presence," I tell him.

Silence. Then, "I never... I never... fuck. Just get me to a hospital."

"I don't think that's the best idea," I tell him.

He doesn't respond. Whether he's passed out or ignoring me, I can't tell.

After a few moments, I hear what I think is weeping.

I pull out my cell, dial Crystal. Shouldn't be talking while driving. Fuck it. She answers straight away. I don't give her the chance to talk. "Got Dirk. He's been shot. What now?"

"Does he know where Rose is?"

"Not specifically."

"Is he dead?"

"Getting there. If you two check into a hospital then Wilson and Fletcher might be able to find you. But he needs medical attention."

Crystal says, "Get him to me. Meet me at your apartment."

"That's definitely not safe. Wilson might check there."

"Where then?"

"I know where we can go."

HOOD IS STANDING at the bottom of a walkway that leads up to a large Victorian-style house with four doors in a vestibule. He's in a light gray sweat suit and as I pull to the curb I can see that he does not look happy to see me.

He leans down into the car to look at Dirk, who's writhing around. "Why not meet in a fucking parking lot or something?" he asks.

"This wasn't exactly a well-formulated plan. We're in some serious shit now. I don't feel good about being outside. Can we go in?"

"Fuck no. My gram is sleeping."

Crystal pulls to the curb behind the hatchback. I yank Dirk

out of the car and look at Hood, figuring he'll help me carry him, and he shrugs. "I'm not getting covered in some motherfucker's blood. Cop sees me covered in blood he'll shoot me without even asking."

I'm about to insist on the help when Crystal comes flying at Dirk. She reaches back and plants a solid haymaker across his jaw. Dirk lands against the car and she pounds on him, screaming, "Why did you do it, you son of a bitch?"

She's crying now, big tears running dark rivulets of mascara down her face. Her entire body shaking. This is the first time throughout this whole thing I've seen her cry. It looks like her entire body is coming apart.

Dirk falls to the ground, fading fast. I pull Crystal off him. "Not the time or the place, okay? How do we get the gunshot taken care of?"

"Give him to me."

"Where are you going to take him? The hospital—"

"I'll get it taken care of."

As we're loading Dirk into the back of Crystal's car, his cell phone falls out of his pocket and clatters to the pavement. Hood picks it up and stares at the face of it and says, "Yo, guys."

"Hold on," I tell him.

"No, don't hold on."

I slam the door of the car and walk over and Hood holds up the phone.

"See that little arrow thingy there?" he asks.

I look at the screen and can't find it. "No."

He shows me the face of the phone and up by the battery

display is a little pointed arrow.

"Location services are active. Like a background GPS. That could mean someone is tracking this phone right now. In case that might be relevant."

"Fucking Wilson."

"So the motherfucker who shot this other motherfucker is on his way here? My fucking gram is here, man. What are we supposed to do?"

I'm thinking of an answer when my phone buzzes. Hood's phone buzzes too. We pull them out and we're both copied on a text from Tommi: *One of you get here now. Got a bad feeling about the crowd tonight.*

"Now, now, everything right fucking now," I say. I want to slam the phone against the curb, like that'll make the message go away, but it won't.

Control your anger before it controls you.

Inhale, exhale.

Inhale, exhale.

My fists are clenched so hard the bones in my hands are creaking.

I lean down to Crystal's window. "You go."

She peels away and I turn to Hood. "I'll go the club."

"Okay." He holds out a hand. "Give me the phone."

"I thought you didn't want to get involved."

He smiles at me a little. "Fuck it, man. Just go. I'll drive around a bit and dump the phone somewhere." Hood stuffs it into his pocket and turns to a gray Jeep, fiddling with a large set of keys.

"I'm sorry it got this far," I tell him.

"Community is all we got, son," he says. "Just make it right."

HERE'S MY PROBLEM: I spent so much time pretending I am something I am not.

What I am is a blunt instrument.

Point me at a job, I get it done.

So much about the life I tried to build has been stacked on an uneven foundation of lies and falsehoods. That I could change who I was. But nobody changes. We're all the same until we die, and all that matters is how we handle and channel those things inside us.

Who I am is someone who wants to do the right thing but can't do it without hurting someone.

Since I got to Portland I've felt like a tourist on a long vacation. That one day I'd toss everything in my bags and be on to the next thing. I had no real sense of permanence, no sense of place.

And now I feel like this is the kind of place where I can stay for a while, and that'll be all right. This might even be the start of something good. All that quiet that unnerved me so much when I got here, it's settled into my bones.

This isn't about me or my bullshit anymore. This is about people who need help, and might not get it because some asshole with delusions of power thinks he can stomp them into the earth to get what he wants.

That, I will not let happen.

I tear around corners, passing slow drivers, nearly cream three bikers who are riding in the middle of the street, cutting the lights on the side streets.

Finally, it feels like I know where I'm going.

FiFtEeN

THE PLYWOOD IS torn down from the front of Naturals. It's lying in the middle of the road alongside a barstool. Other than that the street is empty.

I slam on the brakes at the curb, don't bother locking the car, run through the open door, get caught in the black curtain that's still hanging down on the inside, and what I find past that fills me up with rage fast and hard, like water gushing into an empty space.

Calypso and Carnage are dressed to dance, huddled on seats in the far corner. Tommi is standing behind the bar, her hands up and behind her head.

Brillo Head is holding a bat up, the end of it pointed at Tommi. Rat Face is here too, a bandage across his nose. There are four other guys of varying type and size. So that makes six total, smashing stools, kicking mirrors, tearing things off the walls.

One guy has a rusted, beat-up canister of gasoline in his hand.

When I step through the curtain everyone in the bar stops, like it's a movie and someone hit the pause button.

Brillo Head grins. "I was hoping you'd be here."

Tommi looks at me and screams, "Run! Call the cops!"

There's a little pile of phone guts on the floor. Smashed to shit club phone and cell phones. Which explains why she hasn't called them.

I could call them. But some things it's better to handle yourself.

"You've got one chance," I tell the group. "Put down everything and leave. No one gets hurt. Stay and I'm going to hurt all of you real fucking bad."

Tommi groans. "Don't be a hero, Ash."

Brillo Head laughs. "Two of us handed you your ass the other night. You think you can take us all?" He steps away from Tommi and slings the bat over his shoulder. "Here's what's going to happen. We're going to beat the shit out of you, then we're going to burn this place to the ground. And we're going to have fun doing it." He points his bat toward Calypso and Carnage. "I've already called dibs on the goth bitch."

That black part of my brain reaches out a crooked hand and waves, desperate to get my attention. That part that rages at a world that took away innocent people—my father, the woman I loved—and shaped me into this sharp thing that hates with muscle memory.

I let it take over.

Maybe violence isn't not the answer.

Control your anger before it controls you?

Fuck that.

Anger is a weapon if you know how to use it.

"Do you know what I feel right now?" I ask Brillo Head.

"What?"

"Serenity. How fucked up is that?"

He tilts his head. He doesn't understand what I mean. I'm not sure I do, either. It's just the thing I needed to say right now.

Inhale.

One in the group, a guy in a tight black T-shirt and jeans, charges at me. He's small but building up a head of steam. I let him get close, dip down and lift him straight up, deadlift him into the low ceiling. Something cracks. I don't know if it's him or the tin plating. I step forward and he falls into a heap behind me.

I was using the guy's momentum. Barely even felt the weight of him. Still, it looked impressive. That seems to have gotten everyone's attention. A wave of fear ripples through them, everyone wondering which one is going to have the balls to step out next.

That trepidation passes and two more come at me, from the left and from the right. The one on the right, I jab him quick in the throat. He bends forward and I put my boot into his stomach and he flies into the bar. The one on the left crashes into me but I pivot and get behind him, use his momentum to drive his head into the wall next to the door.

The impact leaves a dent.

He hits the ground and goes limp.

Tommi ducks down underneath the bar, probably going for the gun. Calypso and Carnage leap up and grab at Rat Face. They throw him to the ground and stomp him, and unfortunately for

Rat Face, they're both wearing chunky platform shoes.

The guy holding the gas canister drops it, pushes past me, and bolts for the door.

Wuss.

That leaves me and Brillo Head, looming like a boulder in the middle of the room.

A big, seething boulder.

"Fair fight now, I guess," I tell him.

Tommi is up now, the small black revolver pointed at Brillo Head. He sees this and drops the bat and starts to put up his hands and I tell Tommi, "Stash that."

She asks, "Are you fucking kidding?"

"I am not kidding."

She drops the gun an inch, unsure of what to do, and Brillo Head seems to get what I'm aiming at, because he roars and charges me. I meet him head on, slamming into him and knocking him back. He's bigger than me, but his anger isn't bigger than mine, and I lift him off his feet and slam him on the ground, climb on top, pinning his arms down with my knees.

He thrashes underneath me as I slam my fist into his face.

His head thuds against the floor and his eyes go wavy for a second, but he focuses and tries to get up.

So I hit him a second time.

And a third.

Then I stop counting.

When his face looks like the inside of a pot of chili, Tommi grabs me, hauling me to my feet and yelling into my ear, "You're going to kill him."

The fog lifts and I look down at his face, the bloody ruined mess of it. He's alive, groaning. I don't think I actually did any irreparable damage. But that asshole will never be pretty again.

And I want to feel bad, but I don't.

My hands sting. I look down at my fists. Painted red, knuckles mottled black. I clench them and feel my fingers slide where they're slick with blood.

That feeling again.

Exhale.

"I'm sorry," I tell Tommi.

There's a grunting sound behind us and the guy I threw into the ceiling is charging toward us from the other end of the bar, a bottle in his hand. I put my arm around Tommi to get her out of the way when Calypso sticks her foot out and he goes sprawling, tumbling into the bar and cracking something. Then she and Carnage are on him.

I turn to Tommi. "Are you okay?"

"What the fuck is going on?"

"Too much to explain. Let me get the fuck out of here."

"Ash. Tell me what the fuck is going on *right now.*"

Sigh. "Crystal's dad is a politician who hired someone to wipe all traces of her off the planet so he can run for higher office. Crystal doesn't actually know this is her dad behind this so maybe don't tell her if you see her before me. He's also the one who's been fucking things up here so that there's no trail leading anyone back to her."

Tommi's eyes go wide. "Fuck."

"Right?"

"And what about you? I thought you were a pussy."

I don't have anything in the chamber for that one, so I shrug.

Tommi is about to say something when the smell of smoke hits us. We both turn and see a black cloud billowing out from the kitchen door. I nudge it open and see the guy I face-planted into the wall, his face covered with layers of thick maroon blood, is tossing junk from the changing room onto the top of the lit stove. Mostly lingerie and costume stuff, but also the *Battlestar Galactica* box set.

Hood is going to be so upset.

I grab the fire extinguisher off the wall and spray it with a burst of foam, turn off the burner, and jab the end of the extinguisher against the guy's head. He goes down and doesn't get up.

Back out front Tommi is talking on the phone, screaming at someone, insisting they send someone over immediately. Calypso sees one of the thugs stirring and kicks him in the head.

I keep walking out onto the sidewalk, pull out my pack of cigarettes, get one out, leaving red fingerprints on the white paper. I know I shouldn't be taking the time but I need something to tamp down the adrenaline. As I'm getting it lit Tommi comes up behind me.

"I need to get the fuck out of here," I tell her.

"Why?"

"This isn't over."

"Fuck. Fuck all of this. I called the fucking cops and I have a gun on me."

She pulls it out of her waistband. I take it from her hand and stick it in my pocket. It's small enough to fit but it's heavy and it pulls down on my jeans.

"Fletcher has ties to the cops," I tell her.

"We'll figure it out. He can't know everyone. I'll make enough noise that they can't ignore this." She puts out her hand. I give her a cigarette.

"Tommi… I'm sorry for all this."

She sighs. And then she looks at me, and her eyes are soft. She wraps her arms around me and pulls me tight, squeezing so hard I might burst. She pats me twice hard on the back and lets go, her hand on my shoulder. Her eyes are heavy with tears, shoulders even heavier with the weight of her dream falling to pieces.

"I'm going to get the guy who did this," I tell her. "Make him pay."

Tommi looks at me. Long and hard, trying to see past my face to the thing underneath.

She says, "Good boy."

IT'S A LONG drive to the hospital Crystal picked out. A half hour outside the city proper, and I get lost twice after I get off the highway, but eventually I find it. A big box on a tree-lined block. I park far away and walk over, stand under the tree on the sidewalk near the emergency entrance, light up. My stomach grumbles, residue from Wilson's parting nutshot.

"Ash."

I didn't even hear her come up behind me. I turn, and she's draped in shadow, moonlight curving around the edges of her face, washing it out someplace between blue and white. She looks tired. I get close and she hugs me and stays like that.

After a little while, she pulls away. "You smell like smoke. Fire smoke."

"Someone tried to burn down Naturals."

"Fuck."

"It's okay. He didn't do a very good job."

She looks at me a little bit closer. "You've got blood on you."

"Not mine, I don't think."

She steps back. "Ash... what happened?"

I want to tell her. I really, truly do. Because maybe if I can tell her, she can save me from it. But I've still got work to do, and I need to be this way for a little while longer.

I ask, "What's going on with Dirk?"

"He's going to live."

"What happened?"

"We dumped his wallet and ID. He gave a fake name. The hospital will call the cops, but out here they aren't too concerned with junkies, so they'll take their time. Even when they do show up, they won't put him under guard or anything. The plan is, once he's patched up we can sneak out."

"That's not a bad plan."

"Junkies can be resourceful. I've been to this hospital before, back in the day, and again with Rose once. They don't care much for checking IDs or guests. As long as you're quiet, they pretty much leave you alone."

"That's good. So... how much did Dirk tell you?"

"Everything."

"Everything?"

She looks away. "That Fletcher is my fucking dad, yeah." Crystal steps to the curb, looking down at her scuffed canvas shoes. She kicks at the sidewalk. "I never knew my dad. My mom told me he was dead."

She hugs herself, tilts her head up to the night sky.

"I can't believe he's capable of this," she says. "Not that it means anything. I don't even know him so how could I know what he's capable of? And now… I don't know what we're going to do. We go to the cops, who are they going to believe? We still have the same problem."

"I've got a plan."

She turns to me, one eyebrow raised.

"I'm going to surrender to Wilson tomorrow," I tell her. "Meet him someplace safe and secluded and he's going to tell me where Rose is. Then you and I are going to get her."

"That's a terrible plan."

I smile. It's a weak, sad smile, but it'll have to do. "I can be persuasive."

"He'll shoot you."

"No he won't."

"Are you going to take a gun or something?"

"I don't do guns."

That I'm saying this with Tommi's gun weighing heavy in my pocket is a little beside the point.

"Ash," she says. Gets close to me and takes my hand. "I want my little girl back, more than anything in the world, but I can't let you kill yourself to do it."

"No one's getting killed. I told you, I have a plan. I'm going to find out where she is and then I'm going to stop Fletcher. I'm going to do those things and you two will be safe."

"And what about you?"

"Irrelevant."

Crystal doesn't move, doesn't flinch, but her eyes are suddenly wrapped in a fine mist of moisture, shining in the moonlight. The beginning of what might be tears. She blinks and the shine is gone. Just those blue-green tempered glass eyes. She brings her fist up to her face, sticks the edge of her thumb in her mouth and bites down hard.

I step forward, take her hand in mine. There's a thin rivulet of blood trickling down the side of her hand. She looks at the torn skin on my knuckles, the traces of blood that didn't come off on my jeans. I press my lips to the tip of her thumb, taste copper.

She puts her hand on my cheek, moves my face up, and kisses me. We linger like that, barely touching, trading breath, not wanting to pull back or get in too close. Hovering on the edge of each other. Pushing apart. Because no one actually touches. All you're really feeling is resistance.

When we step away she asks, "Why are you doing this? Don't give me some trite answer. Why would you do this for me?"

"Because it's the right thing to do."

Not the whole truth, but close enough.

There's nothing left to say. I take her hand in mine and squeeze it, and I look down and not into her eyes, because right now, I couldn't bear it. I drop her hand and walk back to the hatchback, look at the pool of Dirk's blood on the gray cloth seat in the back, illuminated in the yellow parking lot light. I take out my phone, dial the phone number that's registered to Ellen Kanervisto.

Wilson answers. "What?"

"I want to make a deal."

Pause. "I'm listening."

SiXtEeN

TODAY, OF COURSE, is the day the sun comes out.

I can't remember the last time the sun came out for more than a few minutes. It's been gray for so long. And I get that feeling, of the world being too big. The greens of the tree are too green, the browns and reds of the brick show too much contrast.

The world is so big I don't know if I can handle it.

I got to the warehouse a half-hour early. The empty parking lot where Wilson first put me on my knees, wearing that stupid fucking mask, and warned me to stay away. Someplace quiet, where he would think he had the upper hand. It's important for him to think he's got that.

I've dealt with people like Wilson before. He's smart. So smart he thinks he's smarter than everyone else around him. And that makes him do stupid things. Funny how that works.

I pace, exhaustion tugging at the edge of my brain. Hope he doesn't double-check his gun. Hope he shows up on time, and alone. Hope for things I have no business hoping for.

And I make a promise to myself.

I'm not going to hurt him.

That thing last night in the bar, that was a last resort. I've given in and given in and given in. Told myself I wouldn't pump myself full of poison anymore, and then mainlined nicotine and alcohol at the first sign of trouble. Told myself violence wasn't the answer and then wrecked a bar full of assholes. I fell into a life that mirrored the life I was trying to get away from.

No more giving in.

I'm going to solve this and we're both going to walk away.

He won't have any other choice.

At noon on the dot, the whole world devoid of shadows, Wilson's car creeps into the lot from around the corner of the building, sunlight screaming off the shiny paint. I adjust my hat to keep the glare out of my eyes. I can't see inside the car. It rolls to a stop twenty yards away and Wilson gets out. He's wearing the fancy gray sweat suit again. Dressed like he's got some heavy lifting to do. His face is a mess. His nose is taped up pretty good, and there's a massive bruise taking up the whole middle portion of his face, darkest underneath the eyes. He moves slowly, favoring his left side. I might have broken a couple of ribs, too.

And he's got the gun in his hand. That shiny silver revolver he pulled on me when we first met.

Good.

He holds it down at his side, ready to pull up, but he doesn't feel the need to kill me right away.

Also good.

"So," he says. "Here we are."

"You owe me for my cell phone, you know."

"What?"

"You broke my phone."

"Are you kidding?"

"They charged me thirty dollars to re-up my plan. I wouldn't have had to pay that if you didn't break my phone. I'll give you a pass on it, though, because I have a deal for you."

"Okay."

"You tell me where Rose is. Then you leave her and Crystal alone. We'll call the phone thing even."

He laughs a little, under his breath, which grows into a full-body fit. That drags on his ribs and he winces, pressing his hand to his side.

Even though the pain, he's smiling.

It's that fucking gun in his hand. Makes him think he owns the world.

He takes a few steps toward me, blond hair shining in the sunlight.

"I'm not a monster," he says. "The family I placed Rose with is good. They've been trying to adopt, but it's an expensive process. They were thrilled to get a kid, along with a pile of money to not say where they got her from."

"You're clever. I get it. Congratulations. Now tell me where to find her."

"So you know, I've been digging on you."

"Have you now?"

"Do you want to know what I found?"

I hold up my hand, beckon him to proceed.

"The cops liked you for a murder back in New York. They caught the killer, but seems they looked at you pretty hard. You've been skirting the edge of the law for a long time. Consorting with some very unsavory types, including a drug baron who dresses like a woman. I don't know what the fuck you think you are, or why you're getting wrapped up in this shit, but I was almost worried you'd try and get the drop on me here. Now I see you standing there like an asshole, empty-handed at a gun fight."

"I've never been very smart."

"Why get involved in this? Do you think you're a fucking cowboy or something? Ride into town and save the day? Or was it all about you wanting to fuck the stripper? Did you think she'd throw some pussy at you if you helped her out? Are you really willing to die over some slut?"

My teeth grate until they hurt. "Give me the address and this will all be over."

Wilson raises the gun and points it at me. My breath catches a little, even though I've got fair cause to believe this will work out.

"Why?" he asks. "Why the fuck would you get involved in this fight?"

I can't think of a better answer than the one I gave Crystal.

"Because it's the right thing to do," I tell him.

Wilson shakes his head. "You're a fucking idiot. The kid is with a very nice couple named Mike and Laurie Beck. Sorry that won't be of any help to you."

We stand there, the open space between us a vacuum.

The sunlight beating down on us.

He squeezes one eye, looks down the sight with the other, and fires.

I jump a little, because there's no way I wouldn't jump at something like that. The gunshot explodes, the sound of it bouncing off the walls of the warehouse, dissipating into the trees, and they're waving at us, as if they're trying to get our attention.

I place my hand to my chest, to be doubly sure that there's no gaping hole there. That Wilson didn't check his gun too closely.

Then I shrug at him and smile.

He tilts the gun, points it at me, really concentrating, thinking maybe he missed. He fires twice.

Again, I jump a little.

And, nothing.

He pops open the cylinder, peers inside. "What the fuck?"

I cross the space toward him. "Something I noticed at your apartment. Lots of whiskey bottles. I know your type. You move at high speed. You have a hard time sleeping, don't you?"

He closes the gun and fires three more times.

I'm still alive.

"So you drink yourself to sleep," I tell him. "Drinkers are heavy sleepers. I would know. Last night I snuck into your house and I found your gun and I replaced the bullets with blanks. Seems you're still not fucking smart enough to lock the back door."

His eyes go wide.

He fires again, but even the fake bullets are gone, so the gun clicks.

"And this week has been full of nothing but pain in the ass bullshit," I tell him. "But finally something worked in my favor, because the bullets fit. I was really worried about that. This wouldn't have been a very good plan if I was really going to let you shoot me."

I'm nearly on top of him now, and he reaches back to hit me with the gun. He swings it at me and I throw up my arm to block his, push him back against the car. He backs up a little, to put some distance between me and him, but he's on the balls of his feet, ready to lunge. I try to keep my voice calm and even.

"We don't need to do this," I tell him. "We can solve all of this right now."

He seems to think about it.

Then he throws the gun at me.

I put my arms up to protect my face and it smashes into my forearm, which hurts like fuck, and as I'm leaning forward to cradle it he comes at me. I throw a quick jab to stun him. He reels back and hits the hood of the car. Falls backward onto it, struggling to stay upright.

Now I'm annoyed.

When he gets to his feet I throw my fist into his stomach, hard. It's a preventative measure. I just need him to stop struggling. He doubles over and falls to the ground.

I pick up the gun, stuff it into my pocket, and head back over to Wilson, who's trying to get up. He launches himself at my legs. We tumble to the ground and he scrambles to get on top of me, but I'm stronger so I flip him around.

Instead of punching him in the face, I grab him by the collar and pull him close. "Where do the Becks live?"

He spits blood into my face so I jab him in the chin.

"Tell me where and this is over," I say.

He sputters. I hold onto his collar and slowly reach my fist back to hit him again.

"Tillamook."

"Good."

I jab one more time, because he deserves it.

That's not too much, right?

His head drops back against the pavement and I climb up, dust myself off. Wonder what to do next. Maybe it's finally time to call the cops. He'll have to explain the gun. I'm going to get in a shitload of trouble but it should keep the attention off Crystal, and she can get Rose and this whole thing will be over.

Fuck what happens to me. I don't care what happens to me.

I'm glad that I kept a promise.

To Crystal, and to myself.

There's a shuffling sound behind me. Wilson has gotten to his feet and he's charging at me. Arms flailing, face twisted and red.

"Motherfucker," I tell him.

The world slows down and I run through my options. Sidestep and throw my foot out to trip him. Move completely out of the way. But I am still angry at all the grief he's caused, so I throw an uppercut.

It's a perfect land, so hard that a jolt runs from my fist through the rest of my arm, and his head snaps back and his feet come off the ground.

He arcs through the air and his head cracks against the bumper of the car with a deep, wet snap.

His body goes limp.

I wait for a second. Look at him lying there out in the sun. The whole world quiet and laid bare.

He's not moving.

After a few moments, he keeps on not moving.

I drop to a knee next to him. His head twisted away from his shoulders at an inhuman angle. I reach for his neck to check for a pulse, but his eyes are wide globes of glass in his head.

It's the way my grandmother looked in her hospital bed moments after she died. The way the muscles in the face go lax and droop back. Everything drained out of it. Dead in movies never looks like dead in real life.

Dead in real life doesn't look like anything else. It's impossible to mistake.

Something in the middle of me drops out and crashes to the ground, shattering. So much broken there's no hope of putting it back together.

THERE'S A SHOVEL in the trunk. I find it when I shove Wilson's rag-doll body inside it. He must have had a clear idea about his endgame. I can see my hands loading his body into the trunk, his head rolling around on his neck, nearly untethered, but I can't feel the weight of him.

The sun is gone now, disappeared again behind clouds that stormed in from the horizon, bringing with them a light drizzle and the pleasant smell of petrichor. By the time I get behind the wheel of Wilson's car, it's pouring.

I drive. I don't know where I'm driving to, but I drive, making turns, on autopilot. Heading in the direction of Mount Hood, because it's the only thing I can think to do.

The city disappears, replaced by huge swaths of trees, the snow-peaked cap of Mount Hood poking its head out, disappearing, reemerging. I don't know why this is the guidepost I need. Maybe because it's there. Maybe because I know it's remote.

Maybe it's just a thing to focus on.

With the rain picking up I can't see much, but suddenly there's a turn-off for a hiking trail, and I pull into the small gravel lot, big enough to fit six or so cars around a small footpath that disappears into the trees. There's one other car, pulling out, the rain having ruined the few stray moments of sunshine, and with it the hopes of those who thought it might last.

I park as close as I can get to the trail, leave my cowboy hat on the seat, climb out of the car, and wait a few minutes to make sure no one is there. Within moments of standing in the rain, I'm soaked clean through, my hair plastered down into my eyes.

It's water. Things could be worse.

I try to light a cigarette but it very quickly becomes a waterlogged mess so I pitch it to the ground.

No one's pulled in. No one's coming down from the trail. I pop open the trunk and Wilson is still there, his neck kinked, his eyes still glass. I watch the raindrops smack and bloom on his shirt, turning the gray fabric black, and haul him onto my shoulder.

He's not heavy. I was going to come back for the shovel but I think I can manage it, so I pick that up, too.

I walk the trail for a couple of minutes, the rain lessened by the canopy of trees over us, and cut to the side when I find an area that I think might be level ground. Be careful where I step so I don't fall. This weight on my back, pushing me down into the wet earth.

The thick smell of feces cuts the air. I don't know if I stepped in something or if it was him. I hear dead bodies will often evacuate their bowels.

It helps to make some of this sound clinical.

After I've walked so long that my shoulders are burning and I can't see the trail anymore, I drop Wilson behind me but I don't turn around to look at him.

At the base of a massive tree, where the ground is soft but not saturated, I start digging. I lose myself in the work, in the feel of the wooden shovel handle and the way it rasps against my hand, throbbing where the beer bottle cut into it. In the rain patting down on the back of my head and cooling me.

These are the things I know: Wilson was a bad person. He split up a family. He was willing to kill me. Maybe kill Crystal, if it came to that. He tried to destroy Tommi's livelihood. And now those people are safe, will be safe, because he's gone.

Who knows what other sins he's committed? Probably more.

These are the things I repeat to myself. But they sound like knocking on an empty wall. There's nothing behind them.

HEY, CHELL.

Hey, Dad.

Here I am. This is me.

What do you think?

Dad, did you ever expect I would take your sterling example of heroism and twist it around until I turned myself into an agent of fucking doom?

Chell, all those times you warned me to calm down, be smart—how upset are you now that I've proven myself unable to take your advice?

I know you're both dead and gone but I'm afraid to turn around, for fear I'll find you both standing there in the rain, arms folded. Shoulder to shoulder, hair and clothes soaked. Looking down on me as I dig this hole. Disappointed beyond repair.

Is it weird that you're the ones I feel compelled to apologize to right now?

And Chell, remember that time we were walking through Washington Square Park, and some asshole sitting on the lip of the fountain catcalled you? He said something about your tits. I turned without thinking, totally on instinct, ready to smash the guy's face into pieces, because that's the way my body was primed to respond.

And this was the kind of guy who was clearly looking to throw down. He wanted to fight someone that day. He and his three friends were gearing up, and chances are I would have walked away from it, but it would have been bloody.

You grabbed my arm, stopped me cold. Got in front of me, said, *Ashley. Control your anger before it controls you. C'mon now. Deep breath. Inhale, exhale. It's not worth it.*

And I listened.

Those four idiots called after me, throwing out words like

"bitch" and "pussy" but that didn't bother me. They were nothing. Who gives a fuck what they think. What really made me feel small was that look of disappointment on your face.

You knew where it would get me.

And Dad, I don't even know where to start with you. Some son I turned out to be. You're this generation's definition of a hero. Here I am, digging a hole to hide a dead body.

You have to know I didn't want for this to happen. Both of you. You have to know that.

My regret is a mountain I can't see the top of anymore.

I DON'T KNOW HOW long it takes. The rain is still falling so hard I'm pretty sure we're in no danger of being found. I get down to where the hole comes up to the middle of my thigh and I figure that'll have to be deep enough. I climb out, my jeans and boots covered in mud, and I go to Wilson.

Look into those glass orbs, unblinking in the rain.

How can a person be sorry and not sorry at the same time?

I push the body into the hole and look at him lying there, water pooling in the crook created by where his arm presses against the muddy brown wall. His head almost twisted all the way around now. I take his gun out of my back pocket and toss it in there with him, then begin to fill it in.

And when the hole is filled, a soft mound of earth under that tree, I sit down, the shovel in my lap. Let the rain wash me clean, or at least make the attempt.

After a little while I get to my feet and walk back to the car, the rain finally letting up, and I get inside and sit there. Wonder if I should drive. Who knows. North, maybe? Remote as can be, where I can disappear. Go be a fisherman or a logger up in Alaska. Live in a cabin. Wait for the day someone comes crashing through my door with a warrant and a pair of handcuffs.

No. The job isn't done yet.

Wilson's BlackBerry is sitting in the center console. I pick it up and click through until I find a number for Fletcher.

A gruff voice answers. "What now?"

"I'm sorry to let you know that Wilson has tendered his resignation. You and I need to have a talk about your daughter."

There's a metallic pause on the other end.

Finally, Fletcher asks, "Where?"

AFTER STOPPING BY my apartment to grab a change of clothes and shove my meager belongings into a backpack, after leaving Wilson's car in a shitty neighborhood with the door open, the inside soaked in bleach, after calling a cab and riding it back to West Burnside, I sit along the window in the coffee room at Powell's, looking out at the street, at the normal, unblemished people walking by.

Set behind glass, like something pure that I can no longer be counted among.

Someone heaves into the chair next to mine. It's Fletcher. He's older and a little softer than his Wikipedia picture indicated. A little more gray around the temples. He hauls a briefcase onto the counter and slides it my way. Just like that.

This is the man behind all this bullshit.

He looks like such a sad little man.

He fidgets in the silence, not sure of where I plan to take this.

"How much were you able to get?" I ask.

"Fifty thousand. Best I could do on short notice. I hope it's enough to keep this all quiet."

I take the briefcase and move it away from him, to my left. Move my cup of coffee so it doesn't get knocked over.

"Where's Wilson?" he asks.

"Gone."

"Where?"

"Doesn't matter. How much did you know about what he was doing?"

Fletcher sighs. "Wilson kept light on the details. He called it plausible deniability."

"I'll start at the top. Your granddaughter is with a bunch of strangers out in Tillamook. Stolen from her mom. Your daughter is fucking bereft. The father of that little girl got shot, and even though he's a fucking idiot he probably didn't deserve the shit Wilson put him through. And the club where Crystal worked got severely damaged. Someone died, too. Got burnt up in a house fire that Wilson set." I take a sip of coffee. "And a bunch of cartel members went to jail, but that's actually probably a good thing. So, fuck your deniability."

Fletcher stares out the window, still refusing to look at me. The two of us watching the world walk by like we're talking about the weather.

"All this," I tell him, "to serve your ambition. Was it worth it?"

"I didn't mean for any of this to happen."

"Yes you did. You hired a man with no morals and told him to get the job done by any means necessary, didn't you?"

"I told him not to hurt the girls."

"When you trust someone with no morals you can't be too surprised when they go off script." I finish the last of my coffee. "Anyway. Figured you would want to know where things stood. Thanks for the cash."

I get up to leave and he grabs my arm. Finally he looks at me. And there they are. The thing that didn't come across enough to catchy my attention on that library computer screen. Those blue-green tempered glass eyes. Probably the one thing Crystal ever got from this man that's worthwhile.

I want to hurt him.

That's where my mind goes now.

Because it can.

He asks, "So this is enough, right? You're not going to say anything to anyone? All this just... goes away?" His voice is desperate, childlike.

I pull my arm back. "Seems we've had a miscommunication. This isn't hush money. This is reparations for your daughter and for the club. I've already called Molly Rivers and told her the entire story. She's going to confirm what she can and print whatever she can verify. So you're pretty much fucked."

Fletcher slumps into the chair.

"I'm ruined," he says, under his breath.

"Yes, you are." I take the briefcase, toss my empty coffee cup into a garbage bin, and leave him there.

SeVeNtEeN

THE BECKS WERE in the phone book. Wonder of wonders.

Before we hit the road I ask Crystal to stop at a Plaid Pantry, where I buy a small travel sewing kit. As Crystal drives I repair the gash that Thaddeus's shotgun left in Rose's pink teddy bear.

I don't know much about sewing, and I stab myself every time the car makes a sharp turn or hits a pothole. The cut is halfway across the bear's stomach, on the border of white and pink fur, so I do the white portion in white thread, and the pink portion in red because there's no pink thread.

When I'm done I hold it up to inspect it. Give it a tug and it stays together. It won't win any prizes, but it's better than giving a kid a torn up bear.

Finally, something I can point to and say that I fixed.

Working on the bear gave me a good excuse to not say

anything, mostly because I don't even know what to say. When I'm finished I twist around and put the bear on the car seat.

I turn to the window, crack it, take in the green, grand expanse of the Tillamook State Forest. This is what I'm going to miss. I love the way it smells out here. Home smells like piss and garbage. Car exhaust and street meat.

Here it smells like green.

And petrichor.

And citrus.

The forest falls away and we're in a small seaside town. Quaint is the first and last word you'd use to describe it. Nothing over four stories, houses not too close. Big stretches of sky. A nice place to put your feet up.

Crystal glances at the map on her phone and guides us through empty streets until we're in front of a big, red house with a pointy roof and a curved archway. Big hills off in the distance. The kind of house a kid should live in. Crystal turns to me, the gravity of the moment pressing down on both of us, and I tell her, "Go ahead. I'll wait here."

She hovers for a moment. Maybe she wants me with her, but this is something she needs to do. I'd feel like an intruder, standing there when she saw her little girl again. I wasn't even sure if I should come, but I wanted to see it through to the end. Make sure Wilson wasn't lying. Because if he was lying, there's not much else we can do.

Crystal crosses the lawn to the front door of the house and I sit down on the street, my back up against the car, and pull out my cigarettes. One left. This would be a good opportunity to quit again. Enjoy this last cigarette, go back to my monastic life. No more poisons. I light up, inhale deep, try to enjoy it. It tastes like ashes.

Crystal knocks on the door and shuffles, waiting, and a young woman in a black dress, with heavy tattoos and long black hair, answers the door. They trade tense words and someone from inside the house screams, "Mommy!"

The women disappear into the house and I stare up into the sky. It's blue out here, and there's so much of it. Big and empty, and I feel myself slipping away into it, like there's nothing to keep me tethered.

After the shock of what happened to Wilson wore off, I expected to feel something. Like when you take a painkiller and it slowly stops working and the pain creeps back up on you. That there'd be a tangible thing buried under the numbness.

Anger. Rage. Sadness. Something with a definition.

Instead, it's more numbness. I have to run my hand over the asphalt underneath me to remind myself that I'm real.

I'm a killer. I have killed someone with my own hands. A person who was breathing is now not breathing. This is the one thing in the world I didn't want. To cross over that line. Now I'm somewhere beyond the veil.

What does that make me?

Damned?

Before I can even think of how to answer that, there's a little girl standing in front of me.

Yellow dress with a white bow on the front, and yellow sneakers, and she's playing with her dark brown hair. The wind is blowing it into her face and she's trying to brush it away with her tiny little fingers but she's making it worse.

"Are you Ash?" she asks.

"Yes."

"My mommy said to come say thank you."

I look up at Crystal, who's standing beside me, smiling through tears. The woman with the black hair is standing at the door with a young man, the two of them holding each other up, sobbing.

I don't know if I could ever be a parent. Not after this. Whatever bullshit I'm going through pales to the maelstrom of emotion stirred up for these two families.

The girl shuffles her feet. I ask, "Your name is Rose, isn't it?"

She nods. "Uh-huh."

"Well, Rose, it is very nice to meet you. I have heard so much about you."

And I start to cry a little.

Because here's the name for that thing I feel, the thing hiding under all that numbness.

Shame.

Rose wraps her arms around my head and awkwardly pats it, like a kid who doesn't know how to be gentle with a pet, and she says, "Please don't cry."

She is so small.

And I cry a little harder.

ROSE KICKS OFF her yellow sneakers and runs to the surf. She splashes into the water and Crystal and I sit together in the sand, up where the water can't reach us, side by side, pressed into each other. Leaning into the resistance.

The clouds have burned off and the sunset is a brilliant watercolor explosion of purple and orange and blue. I've never seen the Pacific Ocean. When Rose jumps and comes back down she sends splashes of water into the air that sparkle like diamonds. She laughs a big awkward kid laugh.

This moment I will carry with me for the rest of my life.

Crystal kisses me on the cheek. I turn to her and she smiles. Those blue-green tempered glass eyes brilliant in the fading sunlight.

I'll carry this with me, too.

"She's a good kid," I say.

"I know."

"How bad was it, with the Becks?"

"Wilson told them I was dead and instructed them to ease Rose into that. At least they hadn't told her yet. It wasn't easy, but they understood. Anyway, they got paid a bunch of money, which they get to keep. It's not like it was a loss. I mean, it was, but…"

"Yeah."

Crystal pushes her fingers into the sand, takes them out and rubs them. "Are you going to tell me what you did?"

"Wilson is gone."

"How do I know we'll be safe?"

I shake my head. "Wilson is gone. And the truth about Fletcher will be out soon. He has much bigger things to worry about."

Crystal takes a breath. "Does that mean…"

Tears well up again. I push the feeling down. "In the car there's a briefcase. There's a lot of money in it. I'm going to take a little bit of it. Enough to survive. Give some of it to Tommi to put toward fixing Naturals and you tell her I'm sorry. Get Hood a new copy of the *Battlestar Galactica* box set. Then you take the rest of that money and get the fuck out of Portland."

"This is my home."

I nod toward Rose. "Home is wherever she is. I'm not too worried about Fletcher, but still, probably a good idea to be far away. At least for a little while."

Crystal nods. "And what about you?"

"I don't know. But I can't stay here. And I can't stay with you."

"Why not?"

"Because I can't."

Crystal huffs. "You know, I get that your life is hard. You've been hurt. But you're not going to get better by pushing people away. I don't care what happened to you or to Wilson or any of that. You found my little girl. You gave me my life back. I want you... to stay. With us. I want you to take us to New York. I don't want this to be the last time I see you."

"Crystal..."

"What? What excuse do you have? What sarcastic fucking bullshit are you going to feed me this time?"

"Do you know why I helped you?" I ask.

She shakes her head.

"Because I lost my dad when I was a kid and it broke me. It turned me into this horrible thing that I hate. And I couldn't let that happen to someone else."

"Ash..."

"I love you."

The word gets caught in her throat. "What?"

"Don't say anything. I don't want you to say it back. This isn't some magical happy story and I expect us to ride off into the sunset at the end. I want you to know that it was worth it. You said things I needed to hear and I do love you for that. This isn't love like we should get married love. It's just… I'm glad to have met you and everything that happened here mattered to me."

"Then why go, if it's good?"

"Because I'm a magnet for bad shit. I'm a target. You and Rose deserve better."

"I don't believe that."

"I don't need you to."

She puts her hand on my hand, holds it tight, pressing her fingers through mine, like she's trying to lock us together. Her skin gritty where there's sand stuck to it. "Where will you go?"

"Not sure yet. It's a big country."

Rose bends down to pick up something in the surf and gets splashed by a high wave, soaking the bottom half of her dress. She runs away from it, toward us.

"I'm glad to have met you too, Ash," she says.

"You can call me Ashley."

Rose comes running up to us holding a pile of sand, and she says, "Mommy, look what I found." She opens her hand and reveals a small white spiral shell.

And Crystal says, "That's beautiful, honey."

AS WE GET ready to load back into the car, brushing sand from our clothes and shoes, Rose mumbles something to Crystal, who leans down close to hear.

She straightens up and says, "Rose would like it if you read her new book to her."

I get into the back of the car and Crystal hands me the book from our visit to Powell's, which she had slipped between the seats.

Abby the Astronaut.

Rose climbs into her car seat, and I let Crystal buckle her up. Once she's strapped in, I get closer and open the book. I look up and see Crystal's face in the rearview mirror and she's smiling.

On the first spread, a little redheaded girl is sitting by her window, staring out at the night sky, which is lit up with stars. That image brings me back to a rooftop, a long time ago, where I learned what it means to take the things that are gone from us and still be able to hold them close.

I look over at Rose and she's already been rocked to sleep by the gentle hum of the car engine.

The sun is down now, the dark punctuated by the occasional pair of headlights that shoot past us like comets. Inside my chest there's a big black spot. I can live with that feeling, because at least I was able to do this one good thing.

That'll have to be enough for right now.

At a gas station off US 5 Crystal stops the car. I climb out and close the door carefully, making sure not to wake Rose. Crystal gets out of the car, too. She asks, "Are you sure?"

"Yes."

"Is there anything I can do?"

"One day tell her what I did. When she's old enough and you think it's okay. Tell her what someone was willing to do for her. And I hope it means something to her."

"I will," Crystal says, and she kisses me one last time, pressing her lips to mine slowly, like she wants to savor the moment, and for that, I am thankful.

The way she lingers, smelling of citrus, I wish I could live in that feeling forever.

We separate, and her face is a mix of anger and sadness and frustration and longing. Those blue-green tempered glass eyes practically glowing in the moonlight.

More things to carry.

She climbs back into the car and pulls away.

I watch it recede into the distance, until the red lights on the back of it disappear over a hill. The gas station is the only thing lit up in the darkness, so I go inside. It's shiny and clean, the light so blue and bright it feels clinical. I grab a bottle of water out of the refrigerator case and place that on the counter with a bag of peanuts.

The clerk, an old man in a blue vest with a snub nose, his greasy gray hair pulled back into a sloppy ponytail, asks, "Anything else?"

I nod toward a display of my brand of cigarettes. "Pack of those."

He grabs one and places it down with my items. "These things will kill you."

"Yes, they will."

He furrows his brow but doesn't say anything to that. I stick the water in my bag, the peanuts in my pocket, and step out front.

Adjust my cowboy hat, spark a smoke, and get ready to stick out my thumb toward the next car that passes, hoping that I don't blend too much into the darkness.

ABOuT tHE AUTHOR

Rob Hart is the associate publisher at MysteriousPress.com and the class director at LitReactor. Previously, he has been a political reporter, the communications director for a politician, and a commissioner for the city of New York. He is the author of *New Yorked* and *The Last Safe Place: A Zombie Novella*. His short stories have appeared in publications like *Thuglit*, *Needle*, *Shotgun Honey*, *All Due Respect*, *Joyland*, and *Helix Literary Magazine*. He's received both a Derringer Award nomination and honorable mention in *Best American Mystery Stories 2015*, edited by James Patterson.

He lives in New York City.

Find more on the web at
www.robwhart.com
and on Twitter at
@robwhart.

AcKnOwLeDgEmEnTs

Thanks to the folks I left out of the first book's acknowledgments, or who have been kind or helpful since then: Hilary Davidson, Alex Segura, Leah Rhyne, Steph Post, Angel Colon, Ron Earl Phillips, Lyndsay Faye, J. David Osborne, Bracken MacLeod, Gabino Iglesias, Steve Coulter, Pam Stack, Jon and Ruth Jordan, Dan and Kate Malmon, Dave White, Brian Panowich, Chelsea Cain, and Terrence McCauley. To anyone I missed (and I'm sure I missed a few)—I am so very sorry. Please don't be mad. Also, I would like to rescind the thanks I gave to Bryon Quertermous in my last book.

Thanks to Robert Fullum. My model for the cranky New Yorker transplanted to Portland. Special thanks to Kirsten Larson and Michelle Stevenson, who helped with some additional Portland intel. (Extra credit to Kirsten, who actually went to Portland Union Station and took pictures.)

Much thanks to Jacqui Kennelly and Renee Pickup, for early reads and invaluable editorial insight. Special thanks to Lark, for giving me a glimpse of the Portland stripping scene, as well as Viva Las Vegas, for her excellent memoir, *Magic Gardens*.

Tremendous thanks to my agent, Bree Ogden, and my publisher, Jason Pinter, for their tireless work on my behalf.

Thanks to my mom, who worked her ass off to promote my

first book.

Huge thanks to my wife, Amanda, who is the smartest, prettiest, most supportive wife in recorded human history. I could not do this without her.

Finally, thank you, Abby. I finished this book the week after you were born. I'm probably not going to let you read this until you're much, much older—but I really appreciate that you took enough naps so I had time to finish it.